W9-CBP-091

Also by David Rosenfelt

Sudden Death
Bury the Lead
First Degree
Open and Shut

DEAD CENTER

DAVID ROSENFELT

NEW YORK   BOSTON

Copyright © 2006 by David Rosenfelt
All rights reserved.

Mysterious Press
Warner Books

Time Warner Book Group
1271 Avenue of the Americas, New York, NY 10020
Visit our Web site at www.twbookmark.com.

The Mysterious Press name and logo are registered trademarks of Warner Books.

Printed in the United States of America
First Edition: May 2006

Library of Congress Cataloging-in-Publication Data

Rosenfelt, David.
    Dead center / David Rosenfelt.
        p. cm.
    ISBN-13: 978-0-89296-002-6
    ISBN-10: 0-89296-002-7
    1. Carpenter, Andy (Fictitious character)—Fiction. 2. Attorney and client—Fiction. 3. Trials (Murder)—Fiction. 4. Cults—Fiction. 5. New Jersey—Fiction. 6. Wisconsin—Fiction. I. Title
        PS3618.O838D43 2006
        813'.6—dc22
                                                                              2005034335

To Debbie

Acknowledgments

This is the page on which I usually thank the people who helped me with the book, but this time I'm not going to do it. Why should I? Do you think that if the positions were reversed they would thank me? Trust me . . . no way.

In fact, on any of my previous books, have they ever thanked me for thanking them? Have they ever said, "Hey, thanks for thanking me. I'm really thankful for that?" No.

That's the thanks I get.

They spend their time thinking, not thanking. They're thinking . . . "How come I wasn't thanked first? How come so-and-so was thanked before me?" They don't come out and say it, but that's what they're thinking . . . I'm just thankful I can see through it.

Thanking people is a thankless job.

I've just figured out a way to get back at them. I'll thank them in alphabetical order—and in that way I'll teach them a lesson on the evils of elitist thank-ism. Here goes: Stacy Alesi, Stephanie Allen, John and Carol Antonaccio, Nancy Argent, Susan Brace, Bob Castillo, David Divine, Betsy Frank, George Kentris, Emily Kim, Debbie Myers, Martha Otis, June Peralta, Les Pockell, Jamie Raab, Susan Richman, Robin Rue, Nancy and Al Sarnoff, Norman Trell, Kristen Weber, Sandy Weinberg, and Susan Wenger.

Maybe this page will accomplish something: Perhaps they'll see the error of their ways. But do I want them to apologize? Thanks, but no thanks.

On a more serious note, I would like to sincerely thank those readers who e-mailed me with feedback on the previous books. Please continue to do so at dr27712@aol.com.

Thank you.

DEAD CENTER

• • • • •

DO YOU GET SPIRITUAL credit for celibacy if it's involuntary?

This is the type of profound question I've asked myself a number of times during the last four and a half months. This is the first time I've asked it out loud, which may say something about my timing, since the person hearing it is my first date in all that time.

Actually, "date" may be overstating it. The quite beautiful woman that I am with is Rita Gordon, who when she's not dressed in a black silk dress with an exceptional cleavage staring straight at me, spends her days as the chief court clerk in Paterson, New Jersey. Rita and I have become fairly good friends over the last few years. No small accomplishment, since her daily job is basically to ward off demanding and obnoxious lawyers like me.

We're in one of North Jersey's classier restaurants, which was her choice entirely. I have absolutely no understanding why certain restaurants succeed and others don't. This one is ridiculously expensive, the menu is totally in French and impossible to understand, the portions are so small that parakeets would be asking for seconds, and the service is mediocre.

With all that, we had to wait two weeks to get a reservation on a Thursday night.

The extent of my relationship with Rita until now has basically been to engage in sexual banter, an area in which her talents far exceed mine. She has always presented herself as an expert in dating, sex, and everything else that might take place between a man and a woman, and has volunteered to go with me on this "practice date" as a way to impart some of that knowledge to me.

I can use it, as evidenced by my celibacy question.

"There's an example of something you might want to avoid asking a date," says Rita. "Celibacy can be a bit of a sexual turnoff."

I nod. "Makes sense."

"On the other hand, swearing off sex increases your dating possibilities, since you could also go out with guys."

I shake my head. "Finding dates is not my problem; there are plenty of women that seem to be available. The problem is my lack of interest. It's the ironic opposite of high school."

Rita looks me straight in the eye, though that doesn't represent a change. She's been looking me straight in the eye since we sat down. She takes eye contact to a new level; it's like she's got X-ray vision and is looking through to my brain. I've never been an eye-contacter myself, and I almost want to create a diversion so she'll look away. Something small, like a fire in the kitchen or another patron fainting headfirst into his asparagus bisque.

"How long has Laurie been gone?" she asks.

I must be healing emotionally, since it's only recently that a question like that doesn't hit me like a knife in the chest. Laurie Collins was my private investigator and love of my life. She left to return to her hometown of Findlay, Wisconsin, where she will probably fulfill her dream and become chief of police. I had always wanted her dream to be a lifetime spent with me, Andy Carpenter.

"Four and a half months."

She nods wisely. "That explains why women are coming after you. They figure you've had enough time to get back into circulation, to get your transition woman behind you."

"Transition woman?"

She nods. "The first woman a guy has a relationship with after a serious relationship ends. It never works out; the guy's not ready. So women wait until they figure the guy's had his transition and he's ready to get serious again. The timing is tricky, because if she waits too long, the guy could be gone."

I give this some thought, but the concept doesn't seem to fit my situation, so I shake my head. "Laurie was the first woman I went out with after my marriage broke up. And she transitioned me; I didn't transition her."

"Have you spoken to her since she left?"

Another head shake from me. "She sent me a letter, but I didn't open it." This is not a subject I want to be discussing, so I try to change it. "So give me some advice."

"Okay," she says, leaning forward so that her chin hovers over her crème brûlée. "Call Laurie."

"I meant dating advice."

She nods. "Okay. Don't do it until you're ready. And when you do, just relax and be yourself."

I shift around in my chair; the subject and the eye contact are combining to make me very uncomfortable. "That's what I did with Laurie. I was relaxed and myself . . . right up until the day she dumped my relaxed self."

For some reason, on the rare occasions when I talk about my breakup with Laurie, I emphasize the "dumping" without getting into the reasons. The truth is that Laurie had an opportunity to fulfill a lifetime ambition and at the same time go back to the hometown to which she has always felt connected. She swore that she loved me and pretty much begged me to go with her, but I wanted to be here, and she wanted to be there.

"You've got to move on, Andy. It's time . . ." Then the realization hits her, and she puts down her wineglass. "My God, you haven't had sex in four and a half months?"

It's painful for me to listen to this, partially because it's true, but mostly because the waitress has just come over and heard it as well.

I turn to the waitress. "She meant *days* . . . I haven't had sex in four and a half days. Which for me is a really long time."

The waitress just shrugs her disinterest. "I'm afraid I can't help you with that. More coffee?"

She pours our coffee for us and departs. "Sorry about that, Andy," Rita says. "But four and a half months?"

I nod. "And I have no interest. The other day I found myself in the supermarket looking at the cover of *Good Housekeeping* instead of *Cosmo.*"

"Pardon the expression," she asks, "but you want me to straighten you out?"

The question stuns me. She seems to be suggesting that we have sex, but I'm not sure, since I can count the number of times women have propositioned me in this manner on no fingers. "You mean . . . you and me?"

She looks at her watch and shrugs. "Why not? It's still early."

"I appreciate the offer, Rita, but I'm just not ready. I guess I need sex to be more meaningful. Sex without love is just not what I'm looking for anymore; those days are behind me." These are the words that form in my mind but don't actually come out through my mouth.

What my mouth winds up saying is, "Absolutely." And then, "Check, please."

• • • • •

RITA LEAVES MY house at three in the morning. She had agreed to come here instead of her place because I would never leave Tara, my golden retriever and best friend, alone for an entire night. But she had shaken her head disapprovingly and said, "Andy, for future reference, you might want to avoid telling the woman that you prefer the dog."

I don't walk Rita to the door, because I don't have the strength to. Even after summoning all the energy I have left, all I'm able to do is gasp my thanks. She smiles and leaves, apparently pleased at a job well done.

"Well done" doesn't come close to describing it. There are certain times in one's life where one can tell that one is in the presence of greatness. Sex with Rita would be akin to sharing a stage with Olivier or having a catch with Willie Mays or singing a duet with Pavarotti. It is all I can do to avoid saying, "Good-bye, maestro," when she leaves.

As soon as she's gone, Tara jumps up on the bed, assuming the spot she so graciously gave up during Rita's stay. She stares at me disdainfully, as if disgusted by my craven weakness.

"Don't look at me like that," I say, but she pays no attention. We both know what the payoff to buy her respect will be, but the biscuits are in the kitchen, and it's going to take an act of Congress to get me out of bed. So instead I just lie there awhile, and she just stares for a while, both of us aware how this will end. I won't be able to fall asleep knowing she did not get her nighttime biscuit, and right now sleep is my dominant need.

I get up. "Why must it always be about *you?*" I ask, but Tara seems to shrug off the question. I stagger into the kitchen, grab a biscuit, and bring it back into the bedroom. I toss it onto the bed, not wanting to give her the satisfaction of putting it in her mouth for her.

Determined to remain undefeated in our psychological battles, Tara lets the biscuit lie there, not even acknowledging its presence. It will be gone in the morning when I wake up, but she won't give me the satisfaction of chowing down while I'm awake.

Tara and I have some issues.

When I wake up in the morning, I use a long shower to relax and reflect on my triumph with Rita last night. "Triumph" may be too strong a word; it was more a case of me accepting a sexual favor. But it seems to have the effect of improving my outlook. I know this was a one-night stand, but in some way it helps me to see a life after Laurie.

I take Tara for our usual walk through Eastside Park. The park is about ten walking minutes from my home on Forty-second Street in Paterson, New Jersey. The look of the park has not changed in the almost forty years I have lived here. It's a green oasis in what has become a run-down city, and I appreciate it as much as Manhattanites appreciate Central Park.

The park is on two levels, with the lower level consisting basically of three baseball fields, two of which are used for Little League. The two levels are connected by a winding, sloping road that we used to refer to as Dead Man's Curve, though I'm quite sure it did nothing to earn the name. Looking at it from an adult perspective, it's not even scary enough to be called Barely Injured Man's Curve.

The upper area is where Tara likes to hang out, because there are four tennis courts, which means there are lots of discarded tennis balls. I don't even bring our own anymore; Tara likes to find new ones for herself.

We throw one of the tennis balls for a few minutes, then stop off on the way home for a snack. I have a cinnamon raisin bagel and black coffee. Tara opts for two plain bagels and a dish of water.

I love spending time with Tara; we can just sit together with neither of us feeling the need to talk. I've had a lot of good friends trying to "be there" for me since Laurie left, but Tara has been the best of all, mainly because she's the only one that hasn't tried to fix me up.

I've become something of a celebrity lawyer in the last few years because of a succession of high-profile cases that I've won. The excitement and intensity of those cases, coupled with a twenty-two-million-dollar inheritance I got from my father, have left me spoiled about work and incredibly choosy about the cases I accept.

In fact, in the four and a half months of life without Laurie, I've only had two cases. In one I represented a friend's brother, Chris Gammons, on a DUI, which we won by challenging the accuracy of the arresting officer's testimony. I took the case only after getting Chris to agree to enter an alcohol rehab program, win or lose.

Chris was also my client in the other case, which was a divorce action brought by his wife. She was apparently not impressed by my cross-examination of the arresting officer and was a tad tired of living with a "loser drunk," which is the quaint way she described Chris in her testimony.

I've filled in the rather enormous gaps in my workday by becoming one of the more prominent legal talking heads on cable television. I've somehow managed to get on the lists that cable news producers refer to when they need someone to comment on the legal issues of the day. Generally, the topic is a current trial, either a celebrity crime or a notorious murder. I go on as a defense attorney, and my views are usually counterbalanced in the same segments by a "former prosecutor." There seems to be an endless supply of former prosecutors.

I'm to be on CNN this morning at eleven-fourteen. They're incredibly precise when informing me of the starting times, but then I can sit around for hours waiting for the interview to actually begin. I've finally gotten wise to this, and I show up as late as possible. Today I'm planning to arrive at eleven-twelve for my eleven-fourteen segment.

That gives me plenty of time to stop off at the Tara Foundation, a dog rescue operation that Willie Miller and I run. We finance it ourselves, the costs evenly provided for by my huge inheritance and the ten million dollars Willie received in a successful civil suit. Willie spent seven years on death row for a murder he didn't commit, and after I got him a new trial and a subsequent acquittal, we sued the real bad guys for the money.

Willie and his wife, Sondra, do most of the work at the foundation, though lately I've been able to help a lot more than I could when I was working more regularly. Together we've rescued more than seven hundred dogs in less than a year and placed them in good homes.

Willie has taken two dog training classes in the past month, which in his mind qualifies him to change the act to Siegfried, Roy, and Willie. As far as I can tell, the only command he gets the dogs to obey is the "eat biscuit" command, but in Willie's mind he's turning his "students" into canine geniuses.

When I arrive at the foundation, Willie is working with Rudy, the dog he describes as the most difficult case in his entire training career. Rudy is a German shepherd, generally considered one of the smarter breeds, and he's living up to that reputation by being smart enough to ignore Willie.

Willie has decided that the only possible reason for his lack of success in training Rudy is that Rudy has only learned to speak German. Unfortunately, Willie, who butchers English on a regular basis, hasn't had occasion to learn much German, so he's somehow latched onto *schnell*.

"Schnell," Willie says as Rudy just sits and stares at him. "Schnell . . . schnell," Willie presses, but Rudy doesn't move. Willie is about six two, a hundred and eighty pounds, and he seems to athletically glide as he moves. As he gives commands to the oblivious Rudy, he steps around him as if he's a fashion photographer doing a photo shoot, trying to find just the right angles.

"He doesn't seem to want to schnell," I say, and Willie looks up, surprised that I am there.

"He schnelled a few minutes ago," Willie says. "He probably saw you come in and didn't want to do it with you here."

I'm aware that Willie speaks only the one German word, has no idea what it means, but uses it all the time. "What exactly does he do when he schnells?" I ask.

"It depends on how I say it." He turns back to Rudy and says, "Schnell. Schnell, boy." His tone is more conciliatory, but Rudy doesn't seem any more impressed. In fact, he just seems bored and finally lies down and closes his eyes.

"Good boy . . . good boy," Willie says, rushing over to pet Rudy, though failing to wake him in the process.

"So 'schnell' means sleep? Very impressive," I say. "There's not another trainer in the state that could have gotten that dog to schnell."

I only stay for about ten minutes, discussing with Willie which of the local shelters we will go to this weekend to rescue more dogs. We've placed eleven this week, so we have openings. Every dog we rescue would otherwise be killed in the county shelters, so we are always anxious to fill whatever openings we have.

I arrive at the CNN studios in Midtown Manhattan at ten-forty-five, which gives me some time to hang out in the city and decide how I'd like to get ripped off. I could play three-card monte with the shady guys huddled against buildings, leaning over their makeshift tables, or I could spend four times retail for something in the thirty-five electronics stores on each block, or I could take a tourist bus ride stuck in Manhattan traffic. Instead I choose to pay forty-eight dollars to park my car, a price that would be reasonable if I were parking it in a suite at the Waldorf.

I get into the studio five minutes before my segment is to begin. The host, a genial man named Spencer Williams, is just finishing a segment on the expected automobile traffic during the Labor Day weekend. According to the experts, there is going to be a lot of traffic, a major piece of breaking news if ever I've heard one.

The topic I'm here to discuss is the ongoing trial of Bruce Timmerman, the CEO of a technology company who is accused of murdering his wife as she slept in their bed. Timmerman claims that he came home late from a meeting and found her dead, the victim of a robbery gone violent.

The case doesn't interest me in the slightest, and all I know about its current status is the brief report I heard on the radio while driving to the studio. Fortunately, lack of knowledge is not a handicap to pundits like me, and I start the segment by pointing out that the prosecutor has not been presenting an effective case. I say this even though I wouldn't know the prosecutor if he walked into the studio, pulling his case in a wagon.

My former-prosecutor panelmate starts vehemently disagreeing with me, and I'm about to counter his counter when the host of the show cuts in. "Sorry to interrupt, gentlemen, but we have to go out to Findlay, Wisconsin, for a breaking story. Please stay with us."

Hearing him say "Findlay, Wisconsin" is jolting, since that's where Laurie now lives. But that jolt doesn't compare to the one I receive when there, on the monitor in a police uniform, is Laurie herself.

This is not going to be fun.

• • • • •

THROWING UP ON national television would be rather embarrassing, but at this point it's a real concern. The sight of Laurie on the five monitors that I can see from my studio vantage point is so jarring that there is a definite chance I will unload my morning bagel on the table.

Laurie is at a makeshift podium in front of what appears to be a government building. When I first started coming on TV, they told me that the camera adds ten pounds to a person. If that's the case, they must use different-type cameras in Wisconsin, because Laurie hasn't gained an ounce.

Since she's behind a podium, it would be hard for the viewer to know that she is five foot ten. I'm five ten too, but I always used to claim that I was five ten and a quarter. That seemed a little obvious, so I changed my height to five ten and a half, which I've since rounded up to five eleven. It's the first growth spurt I've had since high school.

Standing behind Laurie are five men, four wearing dark suits and the fifth in an officer's uniform. She is talking to an assembled group of perhaps twenty members of the press, though it is hard to see from the camera's vantage point. The graphic along the bottom of the screen identifies her as the Findlay, Wisconsin, Acting Chief of Police.

"I just have a brief announcement to make, and then I'll answer a few questions," Laurie says. "A little more than an hour ago, officers placed Jeremy Alan Davidson under arrest for the murders of Elizabeth Barlow and Sheryl Hendricks. The bodies of the victims were recovered pursuant to a search warrant on Mr. Davidson's home."

She starts taking questions, though provides very little in the way of answers, claiming that she cannot discuss evidence in an ongoing investigation. She does say that the cause of death in both cases is believed to be multiple stab wounds, but that autopsies are being conducted. Being on national television, especially to announce an arrest, should be a big moment in any small-town police officer's career, yet Laurie looks as if she would rather be anywhere else than where she is.

I'm fascinated by what I'm watching, while at the same time wishing I could turn it off. The fact that I'm in a studio surrounded by monitors makes turning it off impossible and quite frustrating: I'm used to ruling my television with an iron remote control.

My mind keeps flashing to good times that we had together, times I have tried these last months to forget. Denial is a difficult state to remain in, but intentional, conscious denial is that much tougher. Until now I was doing pretty well at it.

Laurie ends the press conference rather abruptly, turning and walking back toward the building. The men that were standing behind her follow her as she goes; at least some of them might be the town's political leaders, yet Laurie seems very much in charge. I feel a flash of pride in her, which subsides when I force myself to remember how much I hate her.

Within moments the red light is on and we're back on the air. Spencer reminds the TV viewers that we're in the middle of a discussion of legal issues, and he directs his first question at me.

"Andy, before we get back to the Timmerman case, didn't

you once work with Laurie Collins, the police chief conducting that press conference?"

I nod weakly. "I did. She was my investigator before she moved back to Findlay."

"And you represented her when she was herself accused of murder, did you not?"

"I did. She was wrongly accused and completely exonerated by a jury."

"And just so our audience will know the full picture, is it true that Laurie Collins, the love of your life, dumped you? And is it also true that you didn't have sex until Rita Gordon took pity on you last night?" Spencer doesn't ask me these questions; they only reside in the pathetic recesses of my mind.

We go back to discussing the Timmerman case, though for the moment I forget who Timmerman is and what his case might be. We're on for another five minutes, which seem like five hours, and as soon as the light goes off, I head for my car. I know one thing: If the murder in Findlay becomes a subject of these cable discussions, my career as a pundit has come to an end.

It's only just past noon when I leave, which seems too early to get drunk or commit suicide, so I head back to the office. It hasn't been a beehive of activity in recent months, but I usually hang out there for a couple of hours a day. It gives me the illusion that I actually have a job.

Waiting for me there is Edna, my longtime secretary. Work has never been Edna's passion, and she would be quite content if I never took on another client. She spends her six-hour day working on her crossword puzzle skills, which are world-class.

Edna just about jumps out of her chair and rushes toward me when I come in. Fast movements by Edna, rare that they may be, always worry me. That is because she carries her crossword pencils everywhere . . . in every pocket, in her ear, sometimes in her mouth. I'm always afraid that she is going to slip and impale herself.

"Andy, I'm glad you're here," she says. "We need to talk about my microwave."

"Your microwave."

"Right. Remember I left it to my Aunt Helen?"

It's all I can do to stifle a moan. Two months ago I agreed to Edna's request that I help her draw up a will. It was a prudent move on her part, since her estate is fairly considerable. A while back I divided the million-dollar commission that I earned in the Willie Miller lawsuit among Edna, Laurie, and Kevin Randall, my associate in the firm.

Willie and the other beneficiaries of my largesse have since almost doubled their money with successful, albeit bizarre, investment decisions, while I have been decidedly less fortunate. Edna's share is now worth almost four hundred thousand dollars, and if that were the reason for her sudden urge to have a legal will, I would be more tolerant of the process. But it is not.

Edna has the largest extended family in America. There is simply no one that is not related to Edna on some level, either by family or by friendship, and she feels obligated to leave something to every single person she has ever encountered.

At this point the will is a seventy-one-page document, and until moments ago I thought it was a seventy-one-page finished and approved document. But now Edna tells me that she visited her Aunt Helen over the weekend and discovered that Helen possesses a state-of-the-art microwave, far nicer than the one Edna was planning to leave her.

She has it all figured out. "I want to take the ficus plant that I left to cousin Sylvia and give it to my Aunt Helen. Helen's microwave can go to Uncle Luther, who loves popcorn, and Luther's poker chips can go to Amy, my hairdresser, who has a regular game. I'll give Sylvia the scented candles I bought in Vermont last year."

"That's amazing," I say. "It's exactly what I was going to suggest."

She nods in satisfaction. "I'll type it up."

She heads off to do just that, and I proofread it when she's finished. After that, I hang around until it's time to head to Charlie's, the best sports bar/restaurant on the planet.

I often talk about how great it is to live just a half hour from New York City, which provides me access to the finest theaters, museums, and restaurants in the world. The way I take advantage of this access is to hang out every night at Charlie's, which is about eight minutes from my house.

Charlie's has forty or fifty tables, and never has a room been designed more perfectly. Each table is within twenty-five feet of the bar and forty feet of a restroom and has a direct line of sight to at least a half dozen televisions showing sporting events.

Waiting for me at our regular table are my friends Pete Stanton and Vince Sanders. Pete is a lieutenant in the Paterson Police Department, and Vince is the editor of the local newspaper. Both distinguished citizens, except for the fact that when they're not working, they have the combined maturity age of eleven.

Pete is six three and slim, while Vince is five eight and round. They remind me of Abbott and Costello, but with less dignity.

Before I join them, I make a quick phone call to place a bet on the Mets game that we will be watching. When I go to the table, everything looks normal: Every square inch of it is covered with burgers, french fries, and beer. However, I soon sense that something is amiss, as ten minutes go by without either of them insulting me.

I decide to confront them. "Okay, what's going on?"

They spend the next few minutes denying that anything at all is going on when suddenly Vince asks, "What did you do today? Work . . . watch television . . . what?"

"I saw Laurie, if that's what you want to know."

Vince feigns surprise. "Oh, was she on?"

"Yeah."

Pete chimes in. "She ain't looking so great, I'll tell you that."

Even if I hadn't seen her, I would know this is nonsense. Pete and I are both aware that Laurie would look good if she were wearing a storage bin. "Thanks, Pete, that's really helpful."

"You should take out Karen Sampson."

Karen Sampson is a friend of Pete's wife's who is completely unappealing to me in both looks and personality. "I don't think so," I say. "I think she's more Vince's type."

Vince considers this for a moment and shrugs. "Sure, I'll take her out. Why not?"

"Why not?" Pete asks. " 'Cause I like her, and 'cause she's a normal human being, that's why not."

The conversation continues like this for a few hours, with the intellectual content inversely proportional to the number of beers consumed. By the time I've lost my bet on the Mets, I'm ready to go home, though Vince and Pete seem glued to their chairs.

When I arrive home, I have one of those moments that come from out of nowhere and, while seemingly insignificant, can prove to be life-altering. I walk into the kitchen, and there is an empty pizza box on top of the sink. It's been there for two days, and the dishes under it established squatter's rights well before that.

I guess it's been precipitated by my seeing Laurie today, but whatever the reason, it suddenly hits me. I don't want to live like this. I've always felt anger toward Laurie since she left, but now it comes to the fore and is directed at myself as well. She's gone, that's over, and it's time for me to take control of myself and my life.

It's time for me to get a grip.

• • • • •

T HE VOICE ON the phone says, "Hello, Andy."
Since it's my phone I've picked up, this is not a particularly
shocking statement. What sends a jolt of electricity through
my body is the fact that the voice belongs to Laurie.

It's rare that I'm rendered speechless, but this seems to be
one of those times. Though I don't say anything, my mind
and eyes are still working, and I pick up on the fact that the
clock says five-fifteen, and the call has woken me from a
deep sleep. In fact, there's probably an eighty percent chance
that I'm dreaming.

I sit up and turn on the light on the night table, as if that
will help me understand what is happening here. I glance at
Tara, lying on the end of the bed, but she looks as confused
as me.

"Andy, it's Laurie." These new words provide just as big
a jolt and cut the dream likelihood down below fifty percent.
I also feel a flash of worry: It's got to be four-fifteen in Wisconsin. Why is she calling me in the middle of the night?

"Hello, Laurie," I say, displaying my keen conversational
touch and rapier wit. This is not fair. The suddenness of the
call and the time of day have left me without a strategy.
Should I sound angry? Concerned? Aloof?

Maybe I should pretend there's a woman lying next to me. I could giggle a couple of times and say, "Bambi, stop that. I'm on the phone."

Or maybe I should be honest. But if I adopted such an uncharacteristic strategy, what would that honesty consist of? Maybe I should fake honesty . . . I think I can pull that off.

"I'm sorry I called you at this hour, Andy. But I need help."

"I'm listening."

"Actually, it's not me that needs help. It's someone else."

My mind is not processing this too well. What the hell is she talking about? "What the hell are you talking about?"

"I arrested somebody today . . . for two brutal murders. It's a young man. I've known his family since I was a child."

"I saw you on television."

"The thing is, I'm not sure he did it, Andy."

"Then why did you arrest him?"

"Because the evidence is there; I had no choice. A jury will convict him without question. But I know this kid . . . and I just don't buy it."

"So what do you want me to do?"

"Talk to his father. You're better at this than anyone I know, and I know I have no right to be calling you, but I felt I had to."

"Laurie, I know nothing about this case. What am I going to tell his father: to keep a stiff upper lip?"

"Forget it, Andy," she says. "I shouldn't have asked." Then, after a few moments of uncomfortable silence, she asks, "How are you?"

"Fine . . . really good. I'm married with two kids. Right now we're working on their college applications."

Laurie laughs her pure, uninhibited laugh. It's a sound that brings back such pleasant memories that I wish I could bottle it. "Thanks, Andy. I haven't laughed in a while."

"I'm here to serve."

There is another protracted silence, less uncomfortable this time. Then, "I've got to go, Andy. It was good talking to you . . . good to hear your voice."

"Same here." This couldn't be more true; just the sound of her voice rekindles long-dormant feelings, feelings that were so good I've devoted all my energies to trying to forget that I don't experience them anymore.

"Bye," she says.

"Laurie?"

"Yes?"

"Have the guy call me."

"Thank you, Andy. Thank you so much."

Click.

Thus concludes my first conversation with Laurie in four and a half months. Simultaneously concluding is my "get a grip" vow from the night before. What I'm reduced to now is replaying the conversation in my mind, judging my performance, and trying to decipher if she had other motivations for calling besides helping the guy she arrested.

I take Tara for a quick walk and then head for the office. It's Saturday, so Edna is not there to bombard me with questions about the status of her estate. I'm not exactly a champion Internet surfer, but I know how to find out-of-town newspapers online, and I read as much as I can about the murders in Findlay.

Most of the papers have picked up the AP story, which reports the basic fact that Jeremy Alan Davidson, twenty-one, a resident of Findlay, Wisconsin, was arrested for the stabbing murders of Elizabeth Barlow and Sheryl Hendricks, residents of Center City, about ten miles from Findlay.

Davidson and Barlow were students at the Findlay campus of the University of Wisconsin and were said to be planning to marry. Speculation is that Barlow broke off the relationship and went home to Center City, where she and her friend Hendricks commiserated over the situation. Davidson, unable to handle the rejection, is said to have gone crazy and murdered both Barlow and Hendricks, who had the misfortune to be with her friend at the time. The bodies were buried in a hurried, makeshift grave in Davidson's backyard.

The *Milwaukee Journal,* the home-state paper of record, goes one step further and alludes to a religious conflict between Barlow and Davidson, speculating that perhaps she chose "her faith" over him and that he could not tolerate that. The reporter does not have many specifics, but the religion speculation presents an interesting aspect to the case. Conflicts about religion have broken up many young couples over the years, although to my knowledge it's quite rare that they lead to murder.

I'm about to head home to watch some college football when the phone rings. It's unusual for it to ring in the office on a Saturday; in fact, lately, it doesn't ring much at all. I have a quick flash of hope that it might be Laurie, which is supported by the caller ID showing an area code I don't recognize.

"Hello," I say, figuring just in case it's Laurie, I might as well be at the top of my conversational game.

"Mr. Carpenter?" It's a male voice that I don't recognize, and definitely not Laurie.

"Speaking."

"My name is Richard Davidson. Laurie Collins said that you would speak to me."

"Right."

"Would now be a good time?" he asks.

"As good as any."

"I can be at your office in less than an hour. If that's okay."

This is not computing. Wisconsin is not an hour away. If it were, Laurie and I would still be living together. "Where are you?"

"In a cab leaving Newark Airport."

I agree to wait for him, masking my annoyance. Laurie obviously told him that I would speak with him even before she spoke to me. She just as obviously has confidence that she can manipulate me and get me to do what she wants. I'm pissed off because she's been proven right.

Richard Davidson arrives within forty-five minutes. He's probably six foot two, a hundred and sixty pounds, the kind of annoying guy who can suck in a freezerful of Häagen-Dazs without gaining an ounce.

I instantly feel sorry for him for two reasons. First, he has the look of a man who is totally exhausted, his face already bearing deep lines of concern, be it from lack of sleep or intense stress. Considering that his son has been arrested for a brutal double murder, it's probably both, and I expect his black hair should be gray within the hour. Second, he's wearing a suit, meaning he figured that to do so would impress me. This is a desperate man.

My office is about as unimpressive as one is likely to find, situated above a fruit stand in downtown Paterson. It looks as if it was decorated in early Holiday Inn, during a chambermaid strike. Yet Davidson does not seem to notice any of this; his total focus is to try to get me to help his son.

I offer him water or a cup of coffee, and I'm relieved when he chooses the former, since I have no idea how to make the latter. "I've planned what I was going to say on the way here, but right now I have no idea where to start," he says.

"I've read up as best I can on your son's case," I say. "Just the newspaper stories."

He nods. "It's horrible . . . just horrible. Those two poor girls."

"Did you know them?" I ask.

"Just Elizabeth . . . not Sheryl Hendricks. Elizabeth and Jeremy were talking about getting married. They were so terrific together."

"Until she broke it off?" I ask.

"Yes, until she broke it off. She told Jeremy that she still loved him but that it just couldn't work."

"Why not?"

"Pressures from her parents, her town, her religion . . . the place she's from is a very closed society. I had warned him about that; those people have always kept to themselves. But even though she ended it, he would never hurt her, not ever. Mr. Carpenter, I know my son is innocent."

"You believe he is." It's an important distinction to make; I'm pointing out that he has no real evidence.

"It's the same thing. There is simply no way he could have done this. Laurie knows that as well as I do." He's exaggerating this for effect; Laurie has not professed a strong belief in his son's innocence, she has simply expressed doubts about his guilt. There's a difference.

"How do you know Laurie?"

"We lived next door to each other growing up. She and my little sister were best friends. She's gotten to know Jeremy some since she moved back."

Laurie's doubt about Jeremy's guilt is compelling. She has spent her adult life in law enforcement, and in the face of powerful evidence is not inclined to take the side of the accused. It's the main reason I don't think she ever felt fully comfortable working for a defense attorney like me. She was always concerned she might contribute toward letting a guilty person go free.

Also adding to the significance of Laurie helping Jeremy

is her position as acting chief of police. She has taken a real chance of alienating her constituency by facilitating the conversation between Davidson and me.

My sympathy for Davidson is starting to be challenged by my desire to get home and watch football. "What is it you want from me?" I ask. "I don't know nearly enough about the facts of the case to make any coherent recommendations."

He's obviously surprised by the question. "I want you to represent Jeremy."

I guess Laurie forgot to mention that part. "Mr. Davidson, that is not going to happen. I'm sorry."

"Please," he says, in such a childlike, desperate way that I expect his next words to be "pretty please."

"I just can't pick up and go to Wisconsin to try a murder case. It's really out of the question."

"Can't you at least look into it before you make your decision?"

"It's too late for that; I've already made my decision. And I'm sorry, but looking into the case wouldn't change anything."

"I can pay whatever your fee is."

I nod. "Good. Then you can afford any lawyer you want . . . except me." I can see the disappointment in his face, so I soften it a little. "I can do this for you: I can make some phone calls and help you find a first-class lawyer closer to the trial venue."

He's not satisfied by this or anything else I say, and I soon give up trying. I have no desire whatsoever to go to Wisconsin and represent someone who is probably a brutal murderer. At this point I haven't even factored in the close proximity I would have to Laurie, but were I to, it would no doubt be a negative rather than a positive. I'm not going to get on with my life by spending an upcoming chunk of it in her hometown.

As Davidson is leaving, Kevin Randall is coming in, and they mumble a quick hello to each other. Kevin has been my associate for almost two years now, after his disenchantment with the justice system prompted him to take a three-year hiatus from practicing law. During that time he opened the Law-dromat, an establishment that offers free legal advice to customers while their clothes are washing and drying. Kevin still spends much of his spare time away from the office at the Law-dromat, and since we have no clients, that spare time is in no short supply.

It is quite unusual for Kevin to be in on Saturdays; in recent months it's been unusual for him to come in Monday through Friday. The odds against our both being here today are off the charts.

"Andy, what are you doing here?" he asks.

"I came in to research something on the computer."

He is instantly alert. "We've got a case?"

I shake my head. "No, nothing as drastic as that."

His reaction is one of relief. "That's good."

"Why is that good?" I ask. "And what are you doing here on Saturday?"

He can't conceal a small grin. "Carol and I are getting married."

"Today?" Kevin and Carol met on one of those computer-matching services about three months ago. She's a personal trainer at a fitness center in Glen Rock; every time I see her I'm afraid she's going to demand I do twenty push-ups. I know that things are going well between her and Kevin, but I didn't know they were going well enough that marriage was under consideration.

He laughs. "No . . . but I hope soon. I haven't actually asked her yet; I'm just getting things in order before I do."

"What kind of things?"

"Like the honeymoon, for one."

"Where are you going?"

"That's what I'm trying to figure out now; I came in to do some research on the computer as well."

Kevin proceeds to tell me the places that he's thought about but has been forced to reject, due mainly to the fact that he is the absolute biggest hypochondriac on the planet. Tropical resorts are no good because of his sun allergy . . . big cities have too much smog and aggravate his asthma . . . places with spicy cuisine are likely to inflame his heartburn . . . and on and on.

"Maybe you can get a time-share on a plastic bubble," I offer, but it doesn't so much as raise a chuckle. Apparently, Carol isn't totally enamored of Kevin's hypochondria; my guess is that Kevin neglected to mention it on the computer-matching questionnaire.

In fact, Kevin might be annoyed at my joke, because he quickly turns the conversation in an unwelcome direction. "Did you see Laurie on television yesterday?"

"Yes."

"That's quite an arrest for her to make. I mean, to get national attention like that . . ."

"That guy you just saw walking out of here is the father of the accused."

Kevin is shocked to hear this, and I recount to him my conversation with Laurie, as well as Davidson's attempt to hire me to represent his son.

"Are you going to do it?"

"Absolutely not."

"Because of Laurie?"

The question is jolting to me, mainly because I should have asked it of myself. "No," I say too quickly. "I do not want to spend the winter in Wisconsin. My life is here."

"Which life would that be?" he asks. Kevin is one of the

long list of people who have been counseling me to start dating.

I ignore the dig, and he lets the subject drop. I head home, leaving him alone to do his honeymoon planning on WebMD. When I get there, I place a couple of calls to lawyers I know and trust in Chicago, asking for recommendations in the Findlay area, though it's a good distance away. I get a couple of names, and I will give them to Davidson when I call him tomorrow.

I take Tara to the park and pick up a pizza on the way home. My normal style is to open the pizza in the kitchen and eat the whole thing while standing against the counter. Since I've resolved to start my post-Laurie life fresh, this time I sit at the table, using a paper towel for a napkin and eating the pizza off a plate. I know it's more civilized, but pizza just doesn't taste as good off a plate.

I get into bed and turn on a *Seinfeld* rerun. I watch the whole show, but I don't have to. I've seen them so many times that just hearing one sentence is sufficient to trigger the entire thirty minutes in my memory bank.

When the show ends, my thoughts go back to Wisconsin, much as I might resist. I try to analyze major decisions logically, absent emotion. One of my techniques is to break a situation down to its various key aspects and then remove those aspects one at a time, seeing how that impacts on the decision I am making.

This time I try to imagine what I would have done if the murders had taken place in some state besides Wisconsin, with Laurie not involved. In this new scenario another person whose opinion I respect calls and tells me about the murder and their view that the accused is innocent. The father then comes to me with an impassioned plea to represent his son, or at least to look into his case.

There is no escaping the obvious truth that in such a situation I would at least look into the particulars of the case. At first glance a young man who might be innocent yet faces a potentially life-destroying murder trial makes my legal adrenaline start to flow. Yet this time I rejected the offer out of hand.

The reason is Laurie, which really pisses me off. There is no longer anything I should do, or not do, because of Laurie.

She is yesterday's news.

• • • • •

I'VE DECIDED TO come to Wisconsin."

"That's wonderful," Richard Davidson says when he hears this. "I can't thank you enough."

"You need to understand that I'm not agreeing to take the case. I'm going to come up there, look into things, talk to your son, and then make up my mind."

"I understand completely, and I respect whatever decision you make," he lies. "When are you coming?"

"I should be there in a few days," I say.

"Just let me know when your flight is. I'll pick you up at the airport."

"I'll be driving. I'm bringing my dog, and I won't put her in a crate under the plane."

"Okay. Can I get you a hotel room? Or you're certainly welcome to stay with us."

I let him reserve me a hotel room in town, and then I ask him if his son has current representation. "Yes," he says. "A local lawyer. Calvin Marshall."

"Please tell Mr. Marshall about our conversations," I say.

He promises to do so, and I end the call.

I spend the next twenty-four hours getting ready for the trip. This consists of packing and filling the car up with gas, and I put a similar amount of care into both. I pump as much gas in as the tank will hold, and I throw in as many clothes as my two suitcases will hold.

I call Edna and Kevin and tell them about my decision. Kevin mercifully agrees to handle Edna's estate requirements, should further changes be necessary on the will. Edna seems fine with the fact that my not being around means there is absolutely no possibility she will have any work to do.

I meet Pete and Vince at Charlie's and shock them with the news of my departure tomorrow morning.

"Wisconsin?" Pete asks. "You got any idea how cold that is? You ever see a Packers game?"

They both assume I'm chasing after Laurie, and even though I deny it, it may be the truth. This causes them to spend most of the night sneaking looks at each other, saddened at how pathetic it is that I can't let her go. It's not until the sixth or seventh beer that they can put it behind them and get back to watching sports and leering at female customers.

Tara and I are out of the house and in the car by nine o'clock, for what is supposed to be a sixteen-hour trip. I've decided to go at a leisurely pace and make it in two days, stopping at a Holiday Inn in Indiana that allows pets. I plan to spend the time in the car thinking about the Davidson case, and not thinking about how I will deal with being in the same town as Laurie.

Tara sits up in the front seat the entire time, head out the window, soaking up the wind and the local culture. One of the many great things about her is that she doesn't seem to mind that I dominate the radio.

I listen to mostly sports talk radio along the way, and I soon discover that "Larry from Queens," who always calls to complain about the Knicks and Rangers, has a counterpart in every other city. But I'm nothing if not an intellectual, so I listen to all of it.

I'm also a gourmet, so I take full advantage of the fact that every city along the way seems to have a Taco Bell. Even better, many of them are in combination with Pizza Hut, so I can get a grilled stuffed burrito while making sure Tara gets her beloved pizza crusts. America is a wonderful place.

About ten minutes before the Findlay exit on the highway is an exit for Center City. I know from the newspaper articles that this is where the two young murder victims were from, so I decide to get off and check out the town. I probably won't learn anything, but it will delay my arrival in Findlay. I would stop off for a rectal exam if it would delay my arrival in Findlay.

Center City turns out to be a good fifteen minutes in from the highway, tucked away in the middle of nowhere, surrounded by farmland. There is a small airport set in the fields on the northeast side of town, which makes it about ten minutes from Lake Superior. The airport amounts to little more than a landing strip, a hangar, and a small shack. If there are planes there, I don't see them, but there could be one or two in the hangar.

The town center is no more than two blocks long. Calling this a city is a total misnomer; "town" is a stretch. Outside this two-block center are small houses, mostly identical in size and style, that spread out for perhaps a mile, nudging up against the farmland. Just north of the town is a large factory that processes the dairy products of the local farmers. I would guess that Center City has a population of maybe five thousand, except for the fact that almost none of those people are visible.

Even in the center of town, where the stores are, the streets are eerily empty . . . almost *Twilight Zone* empty. It's only six o'clock in the evening; could everybody be asleep?

Looming over the entire town is a building, perhaps seven stories high, with the designation "Town Hall" on the front. There is a large grassy area in front of it, and on that area is what looks to be a makeshift memorial to the murder victims. Townspeople have brought flowers and written notes in tribute to the deceased young women, and they have been arranged in a circular manner, almost as if they are spokes on a wheel.

I walk over with Tara to get a closer look. The fact that there are no people around is more than vaguely unsettling; something seems either wrong or unnatural. The notes, as I start to read them, are heartfelt and mostly religious in nature; the town is clearly mourning these two lives that were cut way too short.

"Have you got business here, sir?"

The sound of the voice is jolting and causes me to jump. I look over and see a man, no more than twenty-five years old, wearing a tan shirt and pants, which seems like a uniform. I have to look up to see his face; he's probably six foot four, two hundred and thirty pounds. "Man, you scared me," I say. "Where did you come from?"

"Have you got business here, sir?" he repeats, in exactly the same tone. He may be young, but he's already developed into quite a conversationalist.

"No, just driving through." I look around. "Where is everybody?"

"There is a town meeting," he says, and at that very moment the doors to the town hall open, and the good citizens of Center City come flooding out en masse.

"I guess attendance is mandatory," I say, but the officer doesn't react.

Instead he says, "Where are you staying, sir?"

I don't answer right away, since I'm somewhat distracted by the fact that most of the people leaving the town hall are staring at me as if I'm an alien. I also notice that everybody seems to be paired up and holding hands, including children no more than seven years old. I never had a sister, but I know for a fact I wouldn't have held hands with the little brat.

"Sir, where are you staying?" he repeats.

"Not here. Why do you ask?"

"We just don't get many strangers, so we like to keep track of them. We're a friendly community."

"Good, 'cause I'm a friendly guy," I say, and Tara and I start to walk back to the car. I see a large group of people walking in the same direction and staring at me, so I wave.

"Hi," I say, a big fake smile on my face. It does not attract a return "Hi" from any of them, nor does it stop them from staring. Maybe Wisconsin friendly communities are different from friendly communities back on earth.

We get back on the road and head to Findlay, stopping for dinner along the way. I've been to Findlay before; last year I checked out a lead on a case and the possible future home of Laurie at the same time. I've developed something of a jealous hatred for the place, since Laurie chose it over me, and I can sense that hatred returning as I get closer.

Coming here is feeling like a major mistake.

Fortunately, I come in under cover of darkness, since it's almost nine o'clock when we finally arrive. Findlay is a conventional small town, larger than Center City, with about an eight-square-block town center. The largest building is the Hotel Winters, a stately, six-floor establishment that Richard Davidson mentioned was a prewar building. Based on the look of it, I think he was talking about the Revolutionary War. Tara and I enter, secure in the knowledge that we're not going to find a casino adjacent to the lobby.

In fact, we also don't find many people in the lobby, just a bellman and two guests sitting on high-backed chairs, reading. The front desk is unmanned, and I'm reduced to ringing the small bell on the desk repeatedly to attract attention. Finally, a sleepy man of about seventy comes out from the office, trying to comprehend through the grogginess that there is actually someone up at this hour. Worse yet, that person is seeking his attention.

Fortunately, Davidson has made the reservation and has me in what the clerk describes as the presidential suite on the top floor. My sense is that it isn't often occupied, and perhaps has been empty since President Jefferson himself used it.

I have my key in my hand when the clerk finally realizes that Tara is standing next to me.

"We don't usually allow dogs in here," he says.

I nod and hand him the key. "That's fine. Why don't you just direct me to a hotel that does?"

He hesitates but doesn't take the key, not wanting to blow the suite sale. "I suppose it will be all right."

"We'll let Tara be the judge of that," I say, and we head upstairs to sample the accommodations.

The room is the kind you'd expect if you drove up to a New England bed-and-breakfast and planned to spend the next day antique shopping. The only problem with that is that it's on a high floor, and if I were going to spend an entire day antique shopping, I'd be looking to jump out the window.

Everything is so old that the lobby seems modern by comparison. There's a canopy bed with a mattress so soft that it's going to take a crane to get me up in the morning. The bathroom fixtures, when initially manufactured, must have ushered in the era of indoor plumbing, and it was probably fifty years after that before someone figured out that the hot and cold water can come out of the same sink faucet.

A note has been left in the room by Davidson, informing

me that he has set up a meeting at nine tomorrow morning with Calvin Marshall, Jeremy's current lawyer. Davidson will be there as well, but he will understand if I don't want him to sit in.

I'm too exhausted right now to know what I want. I give Tara a biscuit and start to climb into bed. I briefly debate whether I should bring a cell phone with me, since there's a possibility I'll sink so far into the mattress that I'll have to call 911 to get out.

"Tara," I say, "why the hell did we decide to come here?"

Tara's look tells me in no uncertain terms that she did not participate in this particular decision, but she's too diplomatic to come right out and say it.

I wake up at seven after a fairly decent sleep, and start to get dressed to take Tara out for a quick walk before showering. While getting dressed, I attempt to turn on the *Today* show, an act made much more difficult by the fact that there is no television in the room.

No television! It's possible I'm in still another *Twilight Zone* episode, and this time I've woken up in a prison camp or maybe back in colonial times. Either way, I can do without food, sleep, or sex (I've proven that), but not without television.

On the way out with Tara, I stop at the front desk and report that someone has stolen the television from my room. "Oh, no, sir," he says, "not all of the rooms have televisions. Some of our guests prefer it that way."

"What planet are those guests from?"

"Sir?" he asks.

I need to stop being so obnoxious; it's my own fault that I'm here. "Look, I'm going to need a television. Can you take one from another room? Or if you want, you can move me into a room that already has one. Maybe the vice president's suite . . . or even the secretary of state's."

He promises to take care of the problem, and Tara and I go out for a brisk walk. The temperature is in the low forties, and it actually feels invigorating. We find a small place for coffee; I would get Tara a bagel, but there's as much chance that they sell aardvark smoothies as bagels. She settles for a couple of rolls, and I have a terrific blueberry muffin.

I take Tara back to the hotel, shower, and dress. I feel guilty about leaving her in this room all day, and if I stay here long, I'm going to have to make other arrangements for her. For now I give her a couple of extra biscuits as a peace offering, and she seems content to crawl onto a pillow and go to sleep.

It's a three-block walk to Calvin Marshall's office, which in Findlay means it's on the other side of town. I walk at a brisk pace, and even in this small town it's amazing I'm not hit by a car, since I focus all my attention on watching for any sign of Laurie. My hope is that I see her, or don't see her, I'm not sure which.

There is a small sign indicating that the office of Calvin Marshall, Attorney-at-Law, is above a travel agency. Waiting for me at the entrance is Richard Davidson, and the look of relief on his face when he sees me is palpable. Obviously, he was afraid that I would change my mind and not come to Findlay.

"Mr. Carpenter . . . thanks so much for coming."

"Andy," I correct him.

He shakes my hand. "Andy. I can't tell you how much I appreciate what you're doing."

I take a few moments to remind him that all I'm doing is checking things out, that I haven't agreed to become involved in the case. He nods vigorously that he understands that, but I'm not sure that he does. Then he asks me if I want him in the meeting with Calvin Marshall.

"Actually, I don't," I say. "I think it's better just the two of us for now."

Again he nods vigorously, showing his full understanding. I could tell him the Vancouver Canucks were going to play the Yankees in the World Series, and his nod would be just as vigorous. He wants me on his side.

I head up the stairs to Calvin Marshall's office. It's two flights, and I notice with some annoyance that I'm breathing heavily when I get to the top. Apparently, working the remote control is not putting me in the kind of shape I'd like to be in.

The door is open, but I don't see anyone in the cubbyhole that qualifies as a reception area, so I knock.

"Come on in, hotshot!" says the voice in more of a drawl than a yell.

Since I'm the only hotshot in the doorway, I enter and walk into the office. I turn a corner and see a person I presume to be Calvin sitting on a chair, feet up on another chair, scaling baseball cards into a wastebasket. This could well be my kind of guy.

"Help yourself to some coffee," he says without looking up.

I look to the side and see a pot of coffee, about a third full. I pour a cup, which takes a while because it's so thick. "You sure this isn't kerosene?" I say.

"It ain't Starbucks fancy, but it drinks good going down," he says. "I'd have my secretary make a fresh pot, but she quit in July."

I walk over to him, coffee in my left hand, my right extended in an offered shake. "Andy Carpenter, visiting hotshot."

"Calvin Marshall, grizzled, cantankerous small-town attorney" is his response as we shake hands. He's probably in his late fifties, gray-haired but not particularly grizzled. At least that's not what I notice; what I notice is that he's missing his left leg.

Unfortunately, I do more than notice the missing leg; I stare at where it would be if it weren't missing. He catches me on it. "I used to climb mountains for fun," he says. "I got trapped in a landslide . . . a boulder pinned me down. Had to cut my own leg off to get free." He shakes his head at the memory. "Sort of took the fun out of mountain climbing."

"What an awful story," I say.

He nods. "And it's also bullshit. I had bone cancer when I was twelve years old."

I can't help but laugh out loud at the blatant lie.

"You think bone cancer is funny?" he asks.

"I think it's funny that for no reason you told me a totally bullshit story thirty seconds after we met," I say. "Why exactly did you do that?"

"It's the way I test new people," he says.

"And did I pass?"

"I don't know . . . I haven't graded it yet."

I tell him that I'm here to talk about the Jeremy Davidson case, but Richard has already briefed him fully about my purpose. He doesn't quite understand it. "You live in civilization, you like to win cases, yet you travel to the middle of nowhere to get involved in a sure loser. Now, why is that?"

"Richard and his wife adopted Jeremy when he was an infant. I knew his real parents very well. They died in a plane crash. I was . . . I am . . . Jeremy's godfather."

He looks at me strangely. "Bullshit story?" he asks.

I smile. "One hundred percent. Not bad, huh?"

He laughs. "Not bad at all."

Having established a relationship supported by a sea of bullshit, we get down to business. Calvin really does see the case as an almost sure loser. "I'm not saying he did it, but the evidence is sure saying it."

"What's your gut?" I ask.

"My gut doesn't trust anything that comes out of Center City," he says. "Not even two murder victims."

"I stopped there on my way in."

"Friendly place, huh?" he asks.

"Everybody was in some kind of meeting, except a cop. He questioned me like I was Osama bin Laden."

He nods; what I am saying is no surprise. "It wasn't a meeting; it was a religious service."

I can't conceal my surprise. "What religion is that?"

"They call themselves Centurions."

"And the town is named Center City?" I'm seeing a pattern here. "Is the town named after the religion, or the religion named after the town?"

He shrugs. "Sort of one and the same. They have some kind of longitude/latitude formula which shows that the piece of ground the town is on is the spiritual center of the universe, and everything else comes off it like spokes on the wheel. That wheel runs their lives, and has been for over a hundred years."

I don't know what he's talking about when he says that the wheel runs their lives, but now is not the time to analyze their religion. "How does all this relate to the murders?" I ask.

He shrugs again. "Probably doesn't. But the pressure on that girl not to marry outside the religion would have been overwhelming. People born in that town stay in that town, and nobody from outside moves in. That's just the way it is."

We talk some more about the case, but the local prosecutor has not yet handed over much material in discovery, so Calvin doesn't know that much about it yet. He does know Jeremy Davidson, though, and has known his family for years, and he doesn't believe him to be a brutal murderer. "It doesn't compute," he says. "These girls got stabbed maybe ten times each. I just don't think this kid is capable of that, no matter how pissed off he might have been."

His feelings pretty much mirror Laurie's, but if there's one thing I've learned, it's that people are not always what they seem and that you find murderers in the strangest places, shapes, and sizes.

The arraignment is going to be today at eleven-thirty, and Calvin invites me to sit in on it. Afterward I'll be able to meet Jeremy and hear his side of it. "You think you're going to jump in?" Calvin asks, referring to my taking on the defense.

"I honestly don't know."

"You're going to have to decide soon. This thing is going to move quickly."

I nod. "I know. If I do come in, will you stay on as second chair? I'm obviously going to need local help."

"Whoever handles this is going to need all kinds of help," he says. "Yeah . . . why not? Count me in."

● ● ● ● ●

COURTROOMS ARE THE nation's common denominator. They have the same feel wherever you go. North or South, rural or urban, it doesn't matter. When you walk into a courtroom, you feel like something important is going to happen. It's the one place where society seems to have a right to take itself seriously.

Not that they all look alike. This particular courtroom could be Findlay's tribute to *To Kill a Mockingbird*. My guess is that it looks exactly the same as it did fifty years ago, with the notable exception being the laptop computer sitting atop the judge's bench.

Calvin is sitting at the defense table when I arrive, but he is not the focus of my attention. George Bush, Angelina Jolie, and Shaquille O'Neal could be dancing a naked hoedown on the table and I would barely notice, since in the far corner of the room, talking with three other people, is Laurie. She looks the same as always, which is disappointing. I had hoped she would have gained thirty pounds and had her face break out in pimples since I saw her on TV.

She doesn't see me, so I pretend I don't see her. I walk down toward Calvin, shake his hand, and try to get myself under control. He can tell something is going on. "You nervous?" he asks with some surprise.

I fake a laugh. "Yeah. I've never been in a courtroom before."

He points toward the prosecution table. "That's where the bad guys sit."

I don't want to look in Laurie's direction, so I might as well make conversation. "Which one is the prosecutor?"

"Lester Chapman. He's not here yet, the prick."

"Let me guess . . . you don't like him," I say.

"He's an okay lawyer, but he's covered with about ten layers of bullcrap. He's maybe five feet tall . . . without the bullcrap he'd be four foot three." Calvin says this loud enough so that a woman at the prosecution table can clearly hear him, though she pretends not to.

He notices this as well, which prompts him to up the ante and the volume. He points to the woman. "That's his assistant, Lila Mayberry. Word is that Lester and Lila are making sticky sheets. Course, I myself don't believe it. I mean, look at her. Lila's tall . . . she could eat watermelons off Lester's head."

At that moment a man who could only be Lester enters and walks to the prosecution table. Calvin was right: Lester is no more than five feet tall. "See what I mean?" Calvin says. "He spends his life looking up at the world."

Lila takes Lester's arm and talks softly to him, occasionally glancing at Calvin as she does so. My guess is, she is updating him on Calvin's insulting monologue.

"Hello, Andy."

I look up knowing exactly who I am going to see: Laurie. She has a smile on her face and her hand extended. "I didn't know you were here."

"Hi," I say, my crackling wit coming to the fore. I shake

her hand, wishing mine weren't already shaking on its own. "I just arrived last night."

"Hello, Calvin," she says, and he returns the hello.

"All rise," says the bailiff, and Laurie quickly retreats from the table, lightly touching my arm as she does so. Calvin watches her go and then whispers to me, "I got a feeling there's more going on here than meets the eye. You want to let me in on it?"

"No."

Calvin is not the type to take "no" for an answer. "You're here two days and you got something going on?" he asks. "I've been here since the Eisenhower administration and I can't get arrested."

"Calvin . . ." is my feeble attempt to get him to drop it.

He shakes his head in probably mock disgust. "You two-legged people really have it made."

The bailiff, not privy to Calvin's monologue, continues. "Findlay County Court is now in session, the Honorable Matthew Morrison presiding."

Judge Morrison comes striding into the room and takes his seat at the bench. He is maybe sixty years old, a large imposing man who packs a good two hundred thirty pounds onto his six-foot-two- or three-inch frame. He could stand to lose ten or fifteen pounds, but not much more than that.

He instructs the bailiff to bring in the defendant, and moments later Jeremy Davidson is brought into the room and sits on Calvin's left, while I'm on Calvin's right. Jeremy is slightly shorter and thinner than his father, hardly the fearsome presence that one would think everyone is here to deal with. Calvin whispers an introduction, and Jeremy and I shake hands. His handshake is weak, and he is clearly petrified. It's an appropriate feeling whether he is guilty or innocent; life as he knows it is over.

My initial reaction to Jeremy's demeanor is to want to

help him, though that reaction is more emotional than logical. Fear and worry in a defendant are not a sign of innocence; if he were guilty, he'd have just as much or even more reason to be afraid.

Judge Morrison then peers down at the assembled lawyers. When he looks at our table, he says, "I do believe there's a face I don't recognize."

Calvin stands. "Andrew Carpenter, Your Honor. At this point he is a consultant to the defense."

The judge nods, unimpressed. He must not watch a lot of cable TV. He then turns to Lester. "Talk to me," he says, and Lester launches into a summation of the dire situation in which Jeremy Davidson finds himself.

Like courtrooms, arraignments are consistent everywhere. Nothing of real consequence ever happens, and no real news is made. Calvin does all the proper things: He has Jeremy plead not guilty and then asks for bail. The judge denies the request without a second thought, or even a first one. Bail in cases like this simply does not happen.

Judge Morrison asks Calvin if he plans to waive Jeremy's right to a preliminary hearing, and Calvin says that he does not. That hearing will be to determine if the state has probable cause to try Jeremy for the murders. It is a very low threshold of proof for the prosecutor, and he will prevail, but it is still a smart move for Calvin to demand it. In the process he, or we if I take the case, will be able to get prosecution witnesses on the record, which will be helpful in cross-examination at the actual trial.

The preliminary hearing is set for ten days from now, and this session is adjourned. The courtroom quickly empties out, Laurie included. Calvin, Jeremy, and I move to an anteroom, with a guard planted outside the door in case the handcuffed Jeremy attempts an escape.

Jeremy looks shaken but comes right to the point. "My father says you're the best."

"He's only repeating what he's been told."

"So you're not the best?"

"Jeremy, I'm not here to talk about me. I'm here to talk about you."

He sits back. "Okay . . . I'm sorry. What do you want to know?"

"When did you see Elizabeth and Sheryl last?"

He takes a deep breath. "I saw Liz the night she died. We met at the Crows Nest . . . it's a bar out on Highway 57."

"So it was a date?" I ask.

He shakes his head. "No, she had already broken up with me. I got her to come out there just to . . . to ask her to come back."

"But she said no?"

He nods. "She said no. She was only there maybe ten minutes. And I think her ex-boyfriend was waiting for her in the car."

"Why do you say that?"

"I saw somebody in the driver's seat, but it was pretty far away, and it was dark, so I couldn't make out his face."

"Could it have been Sheryl Hendricks?"

He shakes his head. "I don't think so. I asked Liz straight out if this was about her old boyfriend. She said that in a way it was, but that there was more to it than that. Then she said they were running away; she seemed really upset."

"What was the boyfriend's name?"

"I don't know. She never mentioned his name. She always told me that she was going to make decisions for herself and that their relationship was a thing of the past." He shakes his head sadly. "And then I guess all of a sudden it wasn't."

"So she told you again that it was over between you. Then what happened?"

"I got mad, and I started yelling at her, saying she was being unfair, making a big mistake, that kind of thing. But she didn't want to listen to me anymore. She said I just couldn't understand, and then she just left. I . . . never saw her again."

"After she left, what did you do?" I ask.

"I was going to go into the bar and get a drink. I felt like getting drunk, you know? But I had the truck with me, and no other way to get home, so I didn't. I just went home and went to sleep."

"Truck?"

He nods. "A pickup truck; that's what I drive."

"Were your parents at home when you arrived?"

He shakes his head. "No, they were out of town, visiting my aunt and uncle in Milwaukee."

"Did you know Sheryl?"

"No, I actually never met her, but she was Liz's best friend from Center City," he says. "Liz talked about her a lot."

Calvin asks, "Why did Liz break up with you?" He's obviously been over this ground with Jeremy, so if he's asking this question, it's an answer he wants me to hear.

"It was because of her religion," Jeremy says with more than a trace of bitterness.

"You were of different religions?" I ask, though I already know the answer.

He nods. "She's a Centurion. To be one, you have to be born in that town."

"People can't convert to it and move there?"

"Nope. Not according to Liz."

This is something of a surprise; it's rare that a religion would turn down members.

"Any idea who might have killed her?"

"No."

"Was there anybody else she ever mentioned she had a problem with? Something or someone she was afraid of?"

"No . . . I've been racking my brain."

Jeremy has little more to offer, and the session evolves into an effort by him to get me to take on the case. I don't commit, and Calvin doesn't seem fazed by the implied insult that Jeremy and his father don't seem to think they're in sufficiently good hands with Calvin.

I leave after telling Jeremy I'll likely have a decision within twenty-four hours, but that either way he'll be well represented. I owe that to him and Calvin as well, though in truth I've done nothing toward advancing my decision-making process. Calvin gives me some papers relating to the case to go over; he's prepared a brief summary of the events, or at least his knowledge of them. It's a professional gesture that I appreciate, and I tell him so. He also invites me to come to his house later for a drink so that we can discuss the case further. He even says I can bring Tara, so I agree to come.

I feel vaguely out of sorts here in Findlay, and I certainly don't have a feel for the case. It's disconcerting, though on the positive side I haven't thought about Laurie for almost an hour, which represents a record for me.

Right now I just want to go home, and the closest thing to that is Tara, waiting at the hotel. The man behind the desk in the lobby tells me that they have the TV ready to install, but they were afraid to do so with "that dog" in the room. Little do they know that "that dog" is probably smart enough to have installed it herself.

Tara is beyond thrilled to see me and just about drags me to the elevator. We go for a long walk, maybe an hour, which pretty much covers all of Findlay. I mentally guess which houses could be Laurie's, but it's not that challenging a game, and my thoughts switch to the case.

Jeremy doesn't seem like a young man capable of slashing two coeds to death, but I certainly can't be anywhere near sure of that. I've never seen him enraged or rejected or distraught, and I have no idea what those powerful emotions might do to him. Or cause him to do.

The bottom line is that this is probably a case I would take if the murder were committed in North Jersey. It has the elements that can make what's left of my legal juices flow. But I have to look at this on a personal, perhaps selfish level. A murder case takes an enormous amount of time and energy, and I really don't want to turn my life upside down for the duration. It's a good case, but it's in little danger of being referred to as the trial of the century.

My level of guilt at the selfishness of my approach is pretty low. Calvin is probably competent to give Jeremy a good defense, but that will be a decision Jeremy and his father can make. If they have the money to hire me, they have the money to hire pretty much anybody they want, so my departure will not mean he will have poor representation.

Basically, it comes down to this: I want to stay in my own house, I don't want Tara stuck in a hotel, I want to go to Charlie's with Vince and Pete when I feel like it, and I don't want to worry that every time I go somewhere I could run into Laurie. Or worse yet, Laurie and some boyfriend.

As my mother would have said, "Why do I need the aggravation?"

● ● ● ● ●

OUR WALK ENDS at Calvin's house, and he's waiting on the porch for us. He spends some time petting Tara which immediately wins her over. In Tara's mind petters are good people, nonpetters are not. I pretty much look at life the same way.

We sit on the porch for a while, with Calvin and me literally in rocking chairs. I keep waiting for Aunt Bea to appear with homemade apple pie and ice cream. But it feels comfortable, and I briefly wonder if I could stay here long-term. There's no doubt that I couldn't; I'd go absolutely nuts. But for this moment it's okay.

"This is actually a pretty nice town," I say. It comes out more condescending than I intended.

"Depends on who you are," he says with a trace of bitterness.

"What do you mean?"

He looks at me with a mixture of disdain and surprise. "You have any idea what it's like to be the only openly gay person in a town like this?"

Now it's my turn to be surprised. "You're gay?"

"Nope," he says, and then laughs at his nailing me with another lie. "Come on in."

We go inside, and Calvin takes Tara and me into what he calls his sports room. It's a small guest bedroom that has been converted into a shrine to the long-departed Milwaukee Braves baseball franchise.

There is baseball memorabilia everywhere, all relating to the Braves. Calvin was only eight years old when the Braves won the 1957 World Series, but he remembers virtually every pitch.

His prized possessions are a foul ball that Warren Spahn hit into the stands and Calvin's father caught one-handed, and a piece of gum that Eddie Matthews spit onto the ground on the way into the stadium. "It's one of the few pieces of baseball memorabilia that could be authenticated with a DNA test," he says.

Tara and I spend an hour at Calvin's, but he and I talk very little about the case. This is more my choice than his; my decision is clearly going to be more personal, more about me than about Jeremy Davidson's legal situation.

As I'm getting ready to leave, Calvin asks me, "You think you're gonna do this?"

"I don't think so," I say. "I'm not saying I'm a traveling superhero, but for me to inject myself into this situation, to transfer my life here, I sort of need to think an injustice has been committed. I'm just not sure it has."

"I know the kid may have done it," he says, "but I just don't think he did. To tell you the truth, I'd defend him either way."

"And that's another point," I say. "He's already got you."

"You know, I don't spend all my time scaling cards into wastebaskets," he says. "I checked you out, read some transcripts of your cases . . ."

"Why?"

"Because I'm a good attorney . . . competent. I cover all the bases," he says.

"And?"

"And Jeremy Davidson needs more than that. He needs you."

"More bullshit?" I ask, ever wary.

He shakes his head. "Not this time."

I tell him that it's flattering but not necessarily convincing, and he doesn't make any further effort to recruit me. Another effort he doesn't make is to feed me and Tara, and by the time we head back to the hotel, we are famished. As evidence that there is indeed a merciful God, He has placed a pizzeria just a block from the hotel. I order a large pie with a thin crust, but "thin" must be a relative term. This crust is almost an inch thick and is stuffed with cheese. I'm starting to discover that in Wisconsin, even the cheese is stuffed with cheese.

Tara and I sit at a little table outside the pizzeria and chow down. It's not an East Coast pizza, but it's not bad. I get Tara some bread, which she seems to find to her liking. Pigs that we are, we order a second pie and some more bread, and by the time we're finished, we look and feel like the Pillsbury Dough Boy and the Pillsbury Dough Dog.

We go for another hour walk to get rid of the bloated feeling, which again takes us through the entire town. By the time we approach the hotel, it's almost seven o'clock and we've gotten enough exercise that it's soon going to be time to think about an evening snack. Perhaps a couple of pizzas . . .

To my surprise and delight, the hotel gets cable TV, including the ESPNs and CNN. Between the pizza and a Knicks-Spurs game, for the first time I feel like Findlay is providing the intellectual and cultural stimulation I require. I settle down on the bed and start reading through the case notes that Calvin gave me, with the basketball game on as background music.

There is a knock on the door, and when I open it, I see the bellman, who is bringing me a small coffeemaker that I had requested. He gives it to me, and I hand him a five-dollar bill, the smallest that I have. For a moment I'm afraid he's going to have a stroke.

"You gave me a five-dollar bill."

"I know that."

He's clearly unsettled by this. "I don't have change."

"I didn't ask for any."

It finally dawns on him that this is for real, and he goes through an endless vow that if there's anything I need, ever, all I have to do is ask. I promise that I will, and he finally leaves.

Tara and I are no sooner settled back on the bed to watch basketball than there is another knock on the door. It's probably the bellman offering to brush my teeth for me. As I get up to answer the door, I make a silent vow to undertip the rest of my stay here. "Just a second," I call out.

I reach the door and open it, but the bellman is not standing there. Laurie is standing there. I'm positive of this; there is absolutely no similarity between them.

"Hello, Andy," she says, but before I can answer, a missile comes flying past me. This particular missile is named Tara, and she has literally leaped across the room and up into Laurie's arms. Tara always loved Laurie, but I thought I had talked her out of that during these past few months.

Laurie lands on the floor under Tara's weight, and she struggles to get up, laughing and petting all the while. I stand there watching in a state of semi-shock, which is actually my home state, but finally, I reach a hand down and help Laurie get to her feet.

She comes inside the room and closes the door behind her. We look at each other for probably five seconds, though it feels like an hour and a half. Then she moves toward me and kisses me, and the anger I have been feeling for the last four and a half months is overwhelmed by something that feels nothing like anger.

Our clothes are off and we're in bed so fast that it's as if we're in a movie and the scene has been edited . . . as if the director has mandated they do a quick cut from the clothed scene at the door to the naked scene in bed. In all the times I pictured meeting Laurie, never once did it wind up like this. I need to work on my picturing skills.

It is the most intense experience I have ever had; I even think that for a moment I lose mental control. I have always, and until now I really mean always, had the ability, or curse, to be able to remain somewhat detached from whatever might be going on. I can view anything with some semblance of reason, and it gives me a feeling of control.

That control is lost in the excitement, fun, and incredible intensity of these moments. When we are finished, when Laurie is lying back and laughing her joyous laugh, I have to consciously bring myself back into the world of reason. I'm not sure why I do, since not to have to reason gave me a feeling of exhilarating freedom, but back I come.

She looks over at me and smiles. "Hi, Andy."

I act surprised to see her. "Laurie, how are you? I hadn't recognized you."

"I was just coming over to see you, that's all, I swear. I wanted us to be able to talk without a bunch of people around."

I nod. "You did the right thing. This would have created something of a stir at the diner."

We both get dressed, maybe a tad self-consciously, and we start some small talk. Laurie wants to know how some of our common friends are doing, and I'm surprised to hear that she's been in occasional contact with them. I had thought, apparently incorrectly, that they had taken my side in the Andy-Laurie war.

I ask her how she came to be acting chief of the Findlay Police Department, since she had taken a job as captain, the number two person in the department. She tells me that Chief Helling has been quite ill and has been on a leave of absence. Laurie likes him very much and is rooting for his quick return, but it's becoming increasingly unlikely. She doesn't say what the illness is, and I don't ask.

A town council vote installed her as acting chief, and the deciding vote in swinging things her way was Richard Davidson. It's a major reason that she is so sensitive about how it would look if her role in luring me to Wisconsin ever got out; it could seem like she is repaying a political favor.

Laurie doesn't think we should even talk about the Davidson case, even after I tell her that I am not likely to take it on. There's an awkwardness here, and even though it's slight, it's not something I was ever used to having with Laurie.

She prepares to leave. I know this because she takes out her car keys, although she will have to go down the elevator, leave the hotel, and walk across the street to her car before she'll need them.

Taking out car keys is a nonverbal way that people say, "I've gotta get out of here." I do it all the time; sometimes I'll take them out even if I haven't driven to the meeting. A friend of mine has a Mercedes that doesn't use keys; it will start for him just because it is able to identify his fingerprint. I would never get a car like that. How would I get out of meetings? By giving people the finger?

So Laurie makes her postcoital getaway, much as Rita Gordon did. I'm starting to feel like a piece of meat. There are worse feelings.

I put those humiliating thoughts aside for the time being,

and Tara and I once again settle down to watch some television.

I've been sleeping for almost two hours, based on the clock, when there is another knock on the door. In my groggy state I figure it could be either the bellman or Laurie, and I'm so tired I'm not sure which one I'm rooting for.

I force myself out of bed and go to the door. When I open it, Laurie is standing there. The look on her face is not one of passion.

"Andy, something's happened that you should know about."

Her tone makes me instantly clearheaded. "What is it? What's the matter?"

"The Davidson house was firebombed."

"Oh, shit. Who did it?"

"We don't know yet," she says. "Come on, I'll tell you on the way."

"On the way where?"

"To what's left of the house."

• • • • •

WHAT DO PEOPLE around here think about Jeremy? Do they think he did it?" I ask this because it's quite likely that someone was getting revenge against Jeremy for his alleged crime by trying to destroy his house.

Laurie thinks for a few moments before answering. "I haven't talked to many people about it, but I think it's probably split down the middle. The ones who know him best can't imagine him murdering anyone, but others . . . well, you know how it is. I've heard from a lot of angry people these last few days; when someone is charged with a crime, a lot of people assume that person is guilty."

"Yes, I certainly know how that is."

"And they usually are guilty," she says.

We're talking about an issue on which Laurie and I have always taken opposite sides. She's an officer of the law, and I'm a defense attorney, so we have a naturally different point of view as to the guilt or innocence of the average accused. She says *toh-may-toh* and I say *toh-mah-toh*.

"But in this case he's not."

"Probably not," she grudgingly admits. The ironic thing is that Laurie's more convinced of Jeremy's innocence than I am. "Andy, this is not a town full of vigilantes. I just can't see people firebombing a house out of anger or frustration. People here are inclined to let the justice system run its course."

"Of course, it just takes one who isn't so inclined," I point out.

She nods. "That's true."

"What about the Centurions?" I ask. "Are they the vigilante types?"

She looks quickly at me, surprised by the question. "Well, haven't you been the busy boy." Then, "I don't know . . . they certainly do not have a history of violence. At least not one that I'm aware of."

"What can you tell me about them?"

"Not too much . . . although there were some newspaper articles written about them maybe five years ago. You might want to read them. But I do know that their town couldn't be any more closed off from the world if they put up barbed wire. But they don't really have to, because nobody wants to get in, and it sure seems like nobody wants to get out."

"But Elizabeth Barlow was out," I say. "She was out and going to college."

She nods. "That's true; I should have mentioned that. Some of them, mostly Elizabeth's age, leave the community for training that they can only get in the outside world. That's how they get their doctors, lawyers . . . Elizabeth was going to be a lawyer."

"But they always go back?" I ask.

"As far as I know. It's the way the community remains totally self-sufficient."

"I met one of the members of their police force."

She seems surprised by this but doesn't probe. "It's not really a police force; they're not accredited by the state. But it doesn't matter, because I don't know of any crime ever being committed there. We technically have jurisdiction over them, and they have access to the state police, as we do. But to my knowledge they've never called them or us. Not once."

We arrive at the Davidson house, and it is still a busy place. The fire seems to have been extinguished, but I count four fire trucks, two state police cars, one Findlay police car besides Laurie's, and an ambulance.

We get out, and Laurie leads me toward the house. It's a one-story, ranch-style farmhouse, with a small building attached to it that looks like a barn but is apparently a guesthouse. That is where the firebomb landed, destroying about thirty percent of the place. Firemen are still applying water to the damaged area, but they have already won the battle.

Laurie introduces me to Lieutenant Cliff Parsons, who responded to the first emergency call and has been supervising what is a crime scene. I recognize his name because Calvin's case file shows that he was the officer who arrested Jeremy. It's not exactly a massive coincidence; there aren't that many ranking officers in the Findlay Police Department.

Parsons is about my age, tall, well built, and good-looking, exactly the kind of guy I don't want Laurie working with. To make matters worse, Calvin mentioned that he was once an Army Airborne Ranger. The closest I can come to that is that I used to watch *The Lone Ranger*, and I was sitting in the third row behind the goal when the Rangers won the Stanley Cup. Actually, when it comes to raw, physical courage, I'd like to have seen him try to fight through the crowds on the way out of Madison Square Garden that night.

Laurie asks Parsons to bring her up-to-date, but he hesitates, glancing at me. "Don't worry," she says. "He's not a problem."

"Stop," I say, trying to control my blushing. "I'm no better than any of you."

Parsons describes what they know so far, which is not a hell of a lot. An unknown person drove up and threw what amounts to a sophisticated Molotov cocktail at the house. It went through a window of the attached guesthouse, and the attacker apparently drove off immediately afterward.

Richard was home alone in the main house at the time. He called 911, and firemen were on the scene in just a few minutes. The damage is not nearly as great as it could have been, in both physical and human terms.

Parsons, it turns out, is the person in the department assigned to any trouble that may happen concerning Center City. It's not exactly time-consuming for him, since no trouble is ever reported in Center City. But Laurie asks him my question concerning whether it's likely that the Centurions are behind this.

Parsons's response is to shrug. "Somebody did it. No reason it couldn't have been them. It was their girls that got killed, so they certainly have the most reason to be pissed off."

I see Richard Davidson standing with a woman at the end of the driveway, and I walk over to them. He introduces me to his wife, Allie.

I express my regrets at what happened and ask if they have any idea who might have done it.

"It has to be someone from Center City," Richard says. "They blame Jeremy for the murders."

"Might there be people in Findlay who do so as well?" I ask.

"No, people here know better," is his quick response.

Allie shakes her head. "We don't know that, Richard. We only know what people tell us; we don't know what they are thinking."

Richard turns to me. "You've got to help our son, Mr. Carpenter. Please . . . I'd like to say we can handle this on our own, but there's no way."

I deflect the request as best I can, and I'm relieved when

Laurie and Parsons come over to question the Davidsons. I fade off into the background, and it gives me time to reflect on the situation.

Six hours ago I had decided not to take on the case. Since then, the Davidsons' house has been firebombed, I've had sex with Laurie, and I've discovered that the hotel has ESPN. To say the least, these are new factors to consider.

The truth is, the most important new factor is what happened at this house. I simultaneously possess a lack of physical courage and a refusal to back down from bullies. It's amazing I've lived as long as I have. But it's becoming obvious that powerful forces, both inside and outside the justice system, are lining up against Jeremy and his family. It makes me want to stand with them.

Laurie finishes what she's doing and leaves Parsons behind to secure the scene. She drives me back to the hotel, not having learned much more than she knew before.

"Parsons says whoever did it knew what they were doing," she informs me. "He knows much more than I do about these things, and he says the firebomb was well constructed. The fire chief said the same."

"The world seems to be lining up against Jeremy Davidson," I say as we are reaching the hotel.

She pulls over in front and turns to look at me.

"This is going to make you stay and take the case," she says. It's a statement, not a question.

"Yup," I say.

"And my being here complicates things."

"Yup."

"We need to talk at some point . . . you know, about how things will be between us while you're here."

"Yup."

"I'm the arresting officer, you're the defense attorney. It's a rather unusual situation."

"Yup."

"I don't want to behave in a way that could . . . you know . . . hurt you again."

"Yup."

"Do you remember how much I used to hate when you went into your 'yup' mode?"

"Yup."

"Yet I seem to want to kiss you good night."

"Go for it," I say, and she does, after looking around first to make sure no one can see us. She breaks it off quickly and drives away.

Do I think I'm in for an interesting few months?

Yup.

● ● ● ● ●

AS SOON AS Tara and I are back from our morning walk, I call Richard Davidson. Ironically, the call is forwarded to the hotel that I'm already in; Richard and Allie spent the night here, since they couldn't stay at home. We agree to meet for breakfast at the local diner, but before I leave I call Calvin to tell him that I'm going to take the case.

"Because they set fire to his house?" he asks.

"Partially," I say. "Things like that bug me."

"You multilegged people can be mighty strange. But whatever works for you, partner," he says.

Richard Davidson is already at a booth in the back when I arrive. On the way toward the booth it feels like every eye in the place is staring at me. That may be because when I check it out, it turns out that in fact every eye in the place *is* staring at me. News is both rare and quick to travel in a town like this, and arriving as an outsider to take on a double murder case has made me a person of significant interest.

Richard greets me with a warm handshake and tells me that they are going to start rebuilding the damaged area of their house immediately. He seems quite upbeat about it, which is rather amazing. If my son was charged with murder and my house firebombed, I'd be up on a roof somewhere with a high-powered rifle.

I offer to help in any way I can, but if he needs me to so much as drive in a nail, he's in big trouble. Fortunately, I can help him in another way. "I'm willing to defend your son," I say.

His relief is palpable. "I can't tell you how much I appreciate that."

"I'll need to talk to Jeremy, to make sure he wants me to represent him."

"He does. He definitely does."

"That's fine," I say. "But I'll need him to personally confirm that."

He nods. "No problem. But I'll be paying your fee."

"That's fine," I repeat, and proceed to tell him that my fee is two hundred thousand dollars, which can move up or down depending on the length of the trial and the number of expert witnesses we will need to call and pay. I add that I will pay Calvin from the money Richard pays me.

I think I see him flinch when I tell him my fee, but it could just be a tic. "No problem," he says. Then there is a rather uncomfortable silence, which he breaks with, "Here's how I'd like to work this, if it's okay with you. I'd like to give you twenty-five hundred now, and the remainder as soon as I get a mortgage on the farm."

It's all I can do not to moan. I've got almost twenty-five million dollars in the bank, and this guy is mortgaging his farm to pay me to help his son? "You're mortgaging the farm?" I ask, just in case I heard wrong. I'm hoping what he really said was, "And the remainder as soon as I can have the money wired from my Swiss bank account."

He nods. "Right. But don't worry. Even with the damage from the fire, it's worth at least that."

"Why don't you give me the twenty-five hundred and

hold off on selling the farm until we get a better idea of how things are going to proceed?"

"Are you sure?" he asks.

"Positive."

He comes with me to the jail, and within a few minutes we're in to see Jeremy. Jeremy shares his father's relief that I'm going to represent him. I tell Jeremy that he will have to sign a document appointing me as his counsel, and he vows to sign it the moment he gets it.

My next stop is the courthouse, where I fill out an application for *pro hac vice,* which will be presented to the judge. It's to allow me to practice on this occasion in Wisconsin, even though I've never taken or passed the bar here. It's a mere formality, and the clerk assures me it will be acted on quickly. This case is going to be a high priority in the Findlay judicial system.

I've got to rent a house; there is no way I can spend any length of time in that hotel. I stop off at the only real estate agent in town, Janice Taylor, who tells me that I am one lucky guy. It turns out, and I want to pinch myself to make sure that it's true, that ninety-five-year-old Betty Camden recently died, and her family decided just this week to put her place up for rent.

Janice takes me over to see it, and it further turns out that Betty, bless her dear heart, had a yard that Tara will like to play in. She also has a houseful of furniture, which may be antiques or just old stuff. I can never tell the difference. If antiques are things from another time period that are highly valued in their old age, wouldn't my sweatpants qualify?

Sealing the deal is the fact that the late, great Betty also had cable television, so I take the place even before I hear what the rent is. Besides, what am I worried about? I've got a twenty-five-hundred-dollar retainer.

I'm going to need to go back to Paterson to get some

more things, close up the house, etc., but I want to do it quickly. Therefore, I don't want to drive, and since I still won't put Tara in the bottom of a plane, I call Laurie at her office. I bring her up-to-date on what's going on and ask her if I can leave Tara with her for a few days. She makes no effort to conceal her delight at the prospect, especially since tomorrow is Saturday and she'll have a couple of days off to play with her. Tara will be thrilled.

Tara and I spend a quiet evening by the television set and get to sleep early. Laurie comes by at seven in the morning to pick Tara up; I briefly wonder why she didn't want me to drop her off. Is there some reason she doesn't want me to see where she lives or who she's living with? Doesn't she know I'll just pump Tara for the information when I get back?

"By the way," I say as they get into the car, "that Lieutenant Parsons guy I met the other night . . . not much in the looks department, huh?"

"You don't think so?" she asks with fake surprise.

"You and he good friends?"

She nods. "I've known him since grammar school."

"So you know his wife also?" I ask, growing more pathetic by the moment.

"He's not married," she says. Then, "Andy, do you think in a million years I would stoop to having a relationship with someone who works for me?"

"You worked for me," I point out.

She nods. "I never said *you* wouldn't stoop that low." She and Tara then pull away, leaving me with still another conversational defeat.

I fly from the nearby Carwell Airport to Milwaukee, from where I'll fly to Newark. It's not until I'm on the plane that the full impact of what has transpired hits me. I'm going to be spending months in Findlay, Wisconsin, working a prob-

ably unwinnable case. And in the background, or the fore-
ground, or who knows where, will be Laurie.

After landing I head straight for my office, where I've
arranged for Edna to be waiting for me. I had called ahead
and asked her to find me temporary legal secretarial help that
can freelance for me in Findlay.

She surprises me by being on top of things; she has located a firm in Milwaukee that will provide whatever secretarial help I need. She also promises to check in on my house
every few days to make sure it hasn't burned down.

I had also asked Kevin to do some research on Center
City and the Centurion religion, and he's characteristically
prepared a complete report on it, which is waiting on my
desk.

I go through some paperwork, trying to clear things away,
since I'll be spending so much time in Findlay. The clearing
process is made easier by the fact that I have no current
cases, so it barely takes me a half hour.

I head down to the Tara Foundation to tell Willie Miller
the news. I dread doing this, since I'm essentially abandon-
ing him and leaving him with the total responsibility of car-
ing for the rescue dogs. First I tell him about the situation in
Findlay and then the fact that I'm planning to spend quite a
while there.

"Don't worry about it, man," he says. "Sondra and I got it
covered."

"You can hire some help, you know. I'll pay for it."

"Not necessary. I'm telling ya, Sondra and I got it covered." He can see I'm feeling guilty, and he tries to head it
off. "Andy, we like doing this, you know?"

I nod. "I know, but I still appreciate how easy you're
making it for me."

"I'm more worried about what you're running into up
there," he says.

"How's that?"

"Firebombing houses ain't something you'd be real good at dealing with, you know?"

Until this moment I haven't thought about myself being in any kind of personal danger, but Willie might be right. People who hate someone so much that they'll firebomb his house might not take too kindly to the lawyer trying to get him off. "I can take care of myself," I say, even though we both know I can't.

"Oh, yeah," he mocks, "I forgot." Then, "Why don't you bring Marcus with you?"

Willie is talking about Marcus Clark, who I've employed as a freelance private investigator on recent cases. Marcus has a number of unusual attributes, but the one that most stands out is that he is the scariest, toughest person on the face of the planet. Bringing Marcus to Findlay would be like bringing a bazooka to a Tupperware party.

"I think I'll wait and see how things go." While Marcus and Findlay would not be a great fit, Willie's question causes me to focus on the fact that I will need an investigator up there. My not thinking about that until now is a sign of how poorly prepared I am at this point. When I get to Findlay, I'll ask Calvin for a recommendation. I can also ask Laurie; she'll be familiar with the local talent, and she knows what I look for in an investigator.

I spend my last evening in civilization at Charlie's with Pete and Vince, watching sports and overdosing on crisp french fries and beer. Their attitude about my going is similar to what it would be if I were being sent to Afghanistan to chase after the Taliban; they've decided that I must be miserable, and they take it upon themselves to make me feel better.

Pete says, "I had a cousin who lived in Indiana, which is

like around the block from Wisconsin, and he said it's not even that cold in the winter."

Vince nods vigorously. "Right. You don't really feel it. It's a dry cold."

"And they practically invented beer up there," Pete says. "You can drink a different beer every day for the rest of your life, and not try them all."

Again Vince couldn't agree more. "People got beer trees growing in their front yards."

"Listen, morons," I say, "I wasn't drafted. I'm going up there because I want to. It's an important case . . . a kid's life is on the line."

"Right," Pete says.

"Sure," Vince agrees.

They think I'm going up there to win Laurie back, and the case is my excuse.

They're wrong.

Probably.

• • • • •

I USE THE RETURN flight to read the report Kevin has prepared. He went online to learn whatever is available about the Centurion religion and the town of Center City. He could not find the five-year-old articles to which Laurie referred, but he found references to them.

Kevin learned some striking things about the religion. Apparently, they don't just believe that they are on a blessed piece of land. They also believe that God speaks to them, through their leader, and thus directs their lives. The device through which God communicates is some kind of wheel, which sits in the town hall. That town hall is in the center of the town, which in their mind makes it the absolute center of the spiritual universe.

The Centurion version of a priest or rabbi, the leader of the flock, is called the Keeper, short for "Keeper of the wheel." The current Keeper is Clayton Wallace, who has held the title for almost four years, since the death of the previous Keeper. Keepers are apparently elected by the other leaders of the church, like popes.

Very surprising, to both Kevin and me, is the total lack of effort the Centurions make to recruit outsiders. They have no desire to convert, or even interact with, the outside world.

The town and the people in it are subject to the laws of the state and the country, and they offer no resistance to those laws, but they very strictly maintain as much separation as possible.

Kevin relates the Centurions' belief that the land they occupy will be the only land left intact when Armageddon comes. The extent of my knowledge of Armageddon is that Ben Affleck and Bruce Willis were in it, so I'm not all that interested.

I land at the airport and go straight to my rented house, having called Laurie and told her of my impending arrival. She is there waiting for me with Tara.

I invite her in, and she seems to hesitate and look around for a moment before accepting. "Something wrong?" I ask.

"No . . . it's just that we're on opposite sides of this, Andy, at least in terms of our jobs."

I nod my understanding. "I won't ask you to compromise that, and I won't intentionally put you in an uncomfortable position."

"I know that," she says, and comes inside the house.

We enter the kitchen, which represents the first time I've been in it; I had previously neglected to check the house further once I discovered the cable TV. "I'm sorry I have nothing to offer you," I say as I open a cabinet, "but I haven't had time to . . ."

I stop talking because I see that the cabinets are filled with groceries of all kinds. I look at Laurie, who smiles. "It's my 'welcome to Findlay' present," she says.

"I thought you gave me that the other night."

She shakes her head. "That was my present to myself."

"You were amazing," I say. "Almost like you've been practicing."

"Andy . . ." is how she admonishes me for prying. Then, "I've been doing some thinking. I'm the one who left . . . and

now you're here to do me a favor. I've got to be careful not
to take advantage of the situation."

"So . . . ," I prompt.

"So I want you to take the lead, okay? You decide where
this goes and how long it goes there."

I understand what she's saying, but taking the lead in a
romantic relationship runs counter to my normal style.
"That's fair, but I don't know yet which way I want it to go,"
I say in a rare burst of honesty. "I'm not going to be here
forever, and I found out that I wasn't crazy about being
dumped."

She nods her understanding. "I know that. I wasn't wild
about doing it. It was the hardest thing I've ever had to do."

I notice something in the cabinet. "Pistachio nuts. You got
me pistachio nuts." Pistachios are among my favorite things
in life, and if there were a professional pistachio speed-
eating league, I'd be an even richer man today.

She smiles. "And tangerines. And cut-up honeydew melon.
And potato chips. And"—she does a little drumroll on the table
with her hands—"Raisinets."

We kiss again, more romantically this time, but it doesn't
lead to sex. I guess since I've just been appointed the leader,
it's my fault that it doesn't. That's something I'll have to get
used to.

Instead we talk about the case, and I ask her if she has
any recommendations for private investigators I can call on.
She says that this area is not exactly a hotbed of investigative
talent but that she'll come up with some names.

"By the way," I ask, "do you think the Davidson farm is
worth a quarter of a million dollars?"

She laughs. "Only if they found oil on it."

This confirms my worst financial fears. Richard Davidson
barely has enough money to hire a public defender, but he
was not about to let that stand in the way of doing the best

he can for his son. He probably decided he'd just have to figure it out as he goes along.

"Anything new in the investigation?" I ask. "You find out
who firebombed my client's house?"

She hesitates. "That's really something I can't share with
you. You need to go through channels."

I understand what she's saying and regret forcing her to
say it. I'm going to be seeking a great deal of information in
the normal course of pretrial discovery, and I will have to get
it from the prosecution, not the police.

"Sorry. I guess I'll just have to start torturing Lester Chapman."

She smiles. "I'm sure he's expecting nothing less. By the
way, Andy, don't underestimate him. He's actually very good."

I return the smile. "So am I, babe. So am I."

• • • • •

CALVIN WANTS TO use my house as our base of operations. It's fine with me, since this way I'll spend more time with Tara, but I had just assumed we'd use his office. "Why?" I ask him.

"Because you've got a refrigerator, and I'll shame you into keeping it stocked with beer."

"What kind do you like?"

"The kind that says 'beer' on the label."

I go out to fulfill Calvin's request, a rather easy task in this area. In addition to the national beers, there is an entire wall of beers I've never heard of, which are brewed locally. I let the clerk advise me on three of the best, and I buy enough to stock the entire upper shelf of the refrigerator.

A few minutes after I get home, Calvin arrives. He opens the refrigerator and nods approvingly at my efforts. He takes a beer out, opens it, and then finds a comfortable spot on the couch in the den on which to enjoy it. "Okay, let's talk about our case," he says.

"First we need to talk about your fee," I say.

He holds up the bottle. "I'm drinking it."

"Richard Davidson wants to mortgage his farm," I say.

He laughs. "Yeah, right." Then, "I thought you were already rich."

"I am."

He smiles and holds up the bottle again, showing it to me. "Me too. So let's talk about the case."

Since we're only starting to receive discovery material, we don't have many facts to go on, yet some potential investigative tracks are quite clear. First of all, we need to look into the lives of the victims, Elizabeth Barlow and Sheryl Hendricks. They were murdered by someone, that much we know, and we have to operate on the assumption that the killer is not our client. Therefore, by knowing who these young women were, and who they knew, we could hit upon the real killer. Or at least some potential killers that we can point to.

At this point we can't even be sure that Elizabeth, Jeremy's girlfriend, was the primary, intended victim. The prevailing view is that she was, and that Sheryl was an unfortunate bystander, caught in the carnage. That view is held because Jeremy is the presumed killer, but if he is not, then it could be that Elizabeth was the person in the wrong place at the wrong time. Working against this hypothesis, but not destroying it, is that the bodies turned up on the Davidson property.

We also need to learn much more about the Centurion religion and its possible role in this case. These people appear to be at the very least zealous, and possibly fanatical, in their beliefs. Such strongly held passions can often fit neatly into murder cases, and we must find out if they do in this case as well. Unfortunately, the very eccentricities that have sealed them in their own world will make penetrating that world very, very difficult.

The two most logical places to start are the university that Jeremy and the victims attended, and their hometown, Center City. Calvin volunteers to check out the school, leaving me with Center City. Of the two, it would have been my second choice, but I don't argue the point.

I tell Calvin that I'm annoyed with the lack of speed at which the prosecutor is providing us discovery material.

"I told you," he says, "Lester is an asshole."

We talk for a while longer, mostly to divvy up the assignments so we don't duplicate each other's work. We have little manpower and less time, so it's important we operate efficiently.

Once we convince ourselves we have our act together, Calvin suggests we go over to the diner to get something to eat. Just before we leave, we get a phone call from the court clerk, informing us that Judge Morrison has scheduled a nine o'clock hearing tomorrow to discuss pretrial matters. It will be conducted informally, in his chambers.

On the way to the diner Calvin says, "Since we're buddies now, you want to tell me how Laurie fits into all this?"

I nod. "Back in New Jersey we were a couple. We talked about getting married, but then she moved back here."

"And now?"

"And now I don't have the slightest idea where it's going."

"You can do a hell of a lot worse," he says. "Hell, I've spent my whole life doing a hell of a lot worse."

"You ever been married?" I ask.

He nods. "Three times. Each one a bigger disaster than the one before it." Then, "How do you want to handle things with Laurie when it comes to the case?"

I shrug. "She's a cop. She's the investigating officer . . . the arresting officer. That's how she deals with us; that's how we deal with her."

"That'll work for you?" he asks, his skepticism evident.

I nod. "So far, so good."

As we walk, I keep having to force myself to slow down. Missing a leg, Calvin can't walk as fast as I can, and I apologize for my pace.

"You need to get the small-town shuffle down," he says. "You walk like a big-city guy."

"How do big-city guys walk?"

"Fast and stupid. Like they're in this big hurry to get somewhere, but when they get there, they'll just stand around with their thumb up their ass, wondering what to do next."

"So big-city people are stupid?" I ask.

"No, they just look stupid to small-town people. And you don't want to look stupid to these particular small-town people, because they're going to be on the jury."

Once we're seated in a booth at the diner, the waitress comes over with two menus. I wave the menus off. "That's okay," I say. "We'll have two specials and two soda pops."

She nods and leaves, and I say to Calvin, "See? I've even got the lingo down. I used to watch *The Andy Griffith Show*, so I know more about places like this than you think."

He nods. "Let me ask you this. Do you want us to starve?"

The waitress brings the sodas, and Calvin asks her, "Donna, tell Gomer Pyle here what the special is today."

"Scrapple potpie."

"On second thought," I say, "we'll look at the menus."

She nods and goes to get them, winking at Calvin as she does.

Calvin's point about my not knowing the local ways and customs, while humorous in nature, is actually an important one. I am out of my element here, yet these are the people that I am going to have to convince that Jeremy is innocent.

I let Calvin order for me; I can't hear what he says, but I know he orders two of them, so I assume we're having the same thing.

Once the waitress has taken the order, I ask, "What do you think about a change of venue?"

When a murder like this takes place in a small town, there is a strong possibility that the people in that town will be very aware of the case and very predisposed against the accused. The firebombing makes my concern about this even more acute. We need to determine whether it is possible for Jeremy to get a fair trial in Findlay, and if not, we've got to move to have the trial somewhere else. It's one of the first decisions we have to make.

Calvin nods. "Been thinkin' about that; I think we should try the sucker right here."

"You think the locals are on Jeremy's side?"

He shrugs. "Maybe half and half. But all we need is one."

He is advancing a theory that most defense attorneys agree with: A hung jury is good for the defense, and it only takes one vote for acquittal to hang a jury. It's not a theory I subscribe to; I prefer to go after outright victories.

"I prefer twelve," I say.

"And I preferred Raquel Welch, but I married Celia Bagwell."

Our food arrives; it looks like it's some kind of sausage. Back home I would order tinted broken glass before I would order sausage, but I figure, when in Findlay, do as the Findlayans do. So I take a bite, albeit with my eyes closed, and it tastes okay. Maybe a little better than okay.

"Andy, I heard you were in town." The voice comes from the back of the room, and it causes me to open my eyes. When I do, I see Sandy Walsh, a prominent local businessman who I met last year when I was in Findlay. He is a really terrific guy who made the suggestion to Laurie that she move back here, so I would like to rip his eyes out of their sockets and put them in the scrapple potpie.

"Sandy, how are you?" I say, shaking his offered hand. He says hello to Calvin as well; they obviously know each other.

I invite Sandy to sit down, and unfortunately, he does, launching into a few minutes of how much the town loves having Laurie back. I'm about to commence strangling him when he switches and refers to the Davidson case. "So you guys are representing him together, huh?" he asks.

"We are," I confirm. "Let me ask you a question. If we polled the people in this room about whether or not they believe he's guilty, what do you think they would say?"

"Tough question," he says, and then thinks for about thirty seconds, confirming what a tough question it is. "There's a lot of angry people, more than I would have thought. Everybody's always liked Jeremy and his family, but most people think if somebody's arrested, he's probably guilty. And with all the evidence they supposedly have . . ."

I attempt to make eye contact with Calvin, but I've never been that good an eye-contacter, and no connection is made.

Sandy continues: "But on the other hand, I think most people would want to believe he's innocent."

"Why do you say that?" I ask.

Sandy thinks for a few more moments and then says, "Because these murders . . . things like that don't happen around here. And now that it has . . . well . . . people would want to deny it, blame it on the outside world. But if the killer was from our town and just a boy . . . well, then somehow we're all to blame. I know that doesn't make much sense, but I think that's how a lot of people will feel. On some level I think it's how I feel."

It's a thoughtful point of view, and helpful because I hadn't expected it. Obviously, Calvin finds it moving, because he gets up to go to the bathroom. Since Sandy's on a roll, I decide to try him on something else. "We're going to want to talk to the families of the victims and some other people in Center City. Any suggestions how we go about that?"

"Boy, that's a tough one," he says. "Those people really keep to themselves and talk to outsiders as little as possible."

"What about if we go through Clayton Wallace?" I ask.

"He's the Keeper, right? That's what they call their leader."

I nod. "So I'm told."

"Yeah, I guess you should go through him. But you'll probably wind up with Stephen Drummond."

"Who's he?" I ask.

"Sort of like the town's general counsel. Handles all their legal affairs, which basically means doing whatever he can to keep the outside world outside."

I thank him, and after offering to help in whatever way he can, he goes back to join his friends for dinner. Calvin comes back a few moments later.

"Where's your friend?" asks Calvin in a tone that indicates he's not a big fan of Sandy.

"You don't like him?" I ask.

"Not particularly."

"Why not?"

"He's part of a group, mostly guys, who sort of make the decisions for the town. Kind of like influential citizens that the mayor basically listens to because he wants to stay the mayor."

I nod my understanding. "He's the guy who got Laurie the job back here."

"My point exactly. He butts in where he shouldn't, and because of him you're not in a fancy New York restaurant eating pheasant and pâté and caviar and shit. Instead you're sitting here sucking up a face full of sausage."

We finish our meal, and I pay the check, eight dollars and ninety-five cents. At this rate the twenty-five-hundred-dollar retainer will go a lot further than I thought.

On the way to the door I see Laurie at a table at the other end of the diner. She is with three women, all maybe ten or fifteen years her senior, and they are roaring with laughter.

I briefly debate whether to go over there, but Laurie sees us and stands up. "Andy . . . over here."

I go over, but Calvin chooses to wait out front. By the time I get to the table, the laughter has pretty much subsided. Laurie does the introductions. "Andy Carpenter, this is my Aunt Linda and my Aunt Shirley and my cousin Andrea. My family."

The way she says "my family" drives home more clearly than ever why Laurie needed to come back to Findlay. The job opportunity was important, as were the old friends, but this cemented the deal. Her family is here.

We banter for a few minutes, and they all tell me how much they've heard about me from Laurie. And how wonderful it is to have Laurie home.

And that's where Laurie is.

Home.

• • • • •

JUDGE MORRISON has scheduled a nine A.M. meeting in his chambers, the invited guests being defense and prosecution counsel. He wants to go over the ground rules for the upcoming preliminary hearing. It's a typical move for a judge who does not like surprises in his courtroom, which is just the way Calvin described him.

The judge asks me to arrive fifteen minutes before the meeting is to start, never a good sign. I get the same feeling I have every time a judge summons me without opposing counsel; it's as if I'm being called to the principal's office. Actually, it's worse: The principal's power never extended to declaring me "in contempt of homeroom" and sending me to jail.

I call Calvin and suggest he arrive for this advance meeting with me.

"Did he say he wanted me to be there early?" Calvin asks.

"No, but he didn't say he didn't either."

"Then I'd rather have my eyebrows plucked," he says.

There's a definite possibility I'm going to have to teach Calvin the subservience etiquette involved with his being my second-in-command, but this is not the time. So I head down to the court, and the clerk takes me directly into Judge Morrison's chambers.

"Mr. Carpenter, thanks for coming in early."

"My pleasure, Judge."

"I had a conversation yesterday with a mutual friend of ours," he says.

Uh-oh, I think, and gird for the worst.

"Judge Henderson," he says, and I realize that even though I thought I had girded for the worst, I hadn't. *This* is the worst, and I stand here ungirded. He is referring to Judge Henry "Hatchet" Henderson of Passaic County, New Jersey, who I have appeared before on numerous occasions. We have had our share of run-ins; he's not fond of some of my more unconventional trial techniques. "He and I have met at a number of legal conferences," the judge continues. "Good man."

I nod. "Very good man. Outstanding man."

Judge Morrison starts looking through some papers on his desk. "Let's see . . . ah, here it is," he says as he finds the paper. "He said you were a fine attorney."

"He did? Well, he's a fine judge. Very fine," I say.

"And he also said you were"—he starts to read from his paper—"a disrespectful wiseass who considers proper court procedure something to trample on and make fun of."

"Maybe 'fine' was too strong. He's a decent judge. Somewhat decent."

Judge Morrison takes off his glasses and stares at me. "I trust I will not have a similar problem with you?"

I nod. "I don't anticipate any problems at all."

He nods. "Excellent."

He calls in Calvin and Lester, both of whom reveal their dislike for each other in their body language. Calvin introduces me to Lester. "Lester's the DA," he says, then smiles slightly and adds, "He ran unopposed...and still almost lost."

The court stenographer comes in as well, since this little chat will be on the record. In a case of this importance it's prudent to do it that way, and Judge Morrison strikes me as the prudent type.

Judge Morrison opens the proceedings by formally accepting me to practice in the state of Wisconsin. I thank him, telling him that it is my honor to do so. I smile when I'm finished, showing him that I'm on my best behavior. He doesn't smile back.

The judge lays out the parameters of the preliminary hearing, which are pretty much the same as in New Jersey. The prosecutor will present some witnesses, though certainly not his whole case. He doesn't have to prove guilt beyond a reasonable doubt in the hearing, simply probable cause that Jeremy should be tried for the murder. It's a low burden, and one Lester will have no trouble meeting.

"How long will you need?" the judge asks. He seems very concerned with time; his docket must be filled with upcoming jaywalking trials.

"Less than a day," Lester says. "We'll be calling only two or three witnesses."

I tell the judge that we will likely not be calling any witnesses of our own, though we reserve the right to change that according to circumstances. Our advantage in the hearing is that Lester will have to reveal some of his cards, while we do not. That would be a more significant help if we had any cards not to reveal, but at this point we don't.

Judge Morrison goes over a few more points, mostly housekeeping in nature, and closes with, "Anything either of you want to bring up?"

"Yes, Your Honor," I say. "To date we have received less

than one hundred pages of discovery. No witness reports, no forensics . . . only some basic police reports."

Lester jumps in. "The materials are being prepared even as we speak, Your Honor."

I shake my head. "The defense was entitled to them even before 'we speak.' Your Honor, Mr. Chapman has had access to all this information and we have not. That is a distinct disadvantage for us and prevents us from being adequately prepared for the preliminary hearing. Therefore, we request a continuance, the length of which to depend on how much longer the prosecution continues its improper delaying tactics."

Lester shakes his head in annoyance. "Your Honor, these things—"

Judge Morrison cuts him off. "Mr. Chapman, where are these reports?"

"In my office, Your Honor."

"Then make certain that copies of them are in their office by three o'clock today." He points to Calvin and me. "If they are not, I will be obliged to grant a continuance, and that is something I do not want to do."

Lester is smart enough to know when to keep quiet, and the meeting concludes with his promise to comply with the court's directive.

Calvin and I drive over to the school that Jeremy and Elizabeth Barlow attended until her murder. It's the Findlay campus of the University of Wisconsin, located about seven miles northwest of Findlay itself.

I visited a friend at the main University of Wisconsin campus back when I was in college, but this has a decidedly different feel. This is a cozy, rather sleepy campus, the main feature of which is a central mall where the students can congregate and freeze to death in the winter. There's certainly none of the Big Ten environment here; the closest this place will come to the Rose Bowl is the rounded greenhouse next to the botany building.

Jeremy had not lived on campus, though Elizabeth had. Jeremy has said that it was a bone of contention between Elizabeth and her mother, but that Elizabeth's desire to experience life away from home prevailed. The deciding factor was the amount of snow that they get here in the winter, and the long drive through that snow that Elizabeth would have to make to get to class.

Calvin, who seems to know everyone in Wisconsin, called ahead to a friend, the dean of something, and we have been given permission to talk to students on campus, providing we do so with courtesy and discretion. Courtesy and discretion are not traits for which I have ever been known, and I expect Calvin is not particularly well trained in them either, but we'll do our best.

Our first stop is Silver Hall, the dormitory in which Elizabeth resided. It's a girls' dorm, but you could never tell that from the people in the lobby. There are as many boys as girls there, and both sexes stare at Calvin and me as if prehistoric creatures have arrived.

We go to the desk in front and speak to a young woman whose sign identifies her as Renee Carney, Resident Adviser. She can't be more than twenty-one herself and is dressed in a "Rage Against the Machine" sweatshirt. I think that if she were my adviser, I would take her advice under advisement.

"We'd like to speak to some friends of Elizabeth Barlow," I say.

"She's dead," says Renee.

"Yes, we're aware of that," I say. I'm also aware that there are students behind us, drawing closer so as to hear our conversation.

"So why do you want to talk to her friends?"

"Because we're lawyers involved in the case and because

Dean Oliva has given us permission to do so." I point to the phone on her desk. "You might want to call him to confirm that."

She looks at the phone as if considering the possibility, then shrugs. "Pretty much everyone here was Liz's friend, so talk all you want."

That's as close as we're going to get to a ringing endorsement from the resident adviser, so we turn toward the assembled students, who have no doubt heard the entire exchange.

We walk up to a young woman standing off to the side and seeming less interested in us than the others. Calvin starts out as our spokesman, probably as a result of my less-than-inspiring success with the resident adviser.

"Hi," Calvin says, turning on the charm. "My name is Calvin Marshall, and my double-legged friend is Andy Carpenter. What's your name?"

"Emily Harrington."

"Emily, can we talk to you about Elizabeth Barlow?"

Emily eyes us warily. "Are you on Davidson's side?"

"We're just here to gather information . . . try and get to the truth," is Calvin's evasive reply.

She's having none of it. "But you're on Davidson's side?"

Calvin nods. "We're representing him, yes."

Emily casts a glance at the other students, hanging on every word. "I'm sorry, but I've got nothing to say to you."

This starts something of a trend, as every other student in the place also refuses to answer any of our questions. Most of them seem less conflicted about it than Emily, but clearly, no one is going to do anything to help the person they believe killed their friend Elizabeth Barlow.

Calvin and I head to our car, in the parking lot just outside the main gate. "Didn't Jeremy have any friends here?" I ask.

He shrugs. "I guess we should find that out."

As we approach our car, we see that three young men, probably students, are sitting on the hood. They are all rather large, at least compared to Calvin and me, and they watch us as we near. My guess is that they didn't choose our car at random.

We reach the car, and I decide to try the conciliatory approach. I generally find that this fits in neatly with my basic cowardice. "Hey, guys, you mind getting off the car? We've got to be going."

One of them, wearing a Wisconsin football jersey, smiles an annoying, smug smile. "Is that right?" he asks.

I think the question was probably rhetorical, but I answer it anyway. "Yes, that's right." I figure a snappy comeback like that is likely to cow them into departing.

"You in a hurry to get back to Davidson? Maybe help him get out so he can kill a few more girls?"

My patience is wearing a tad thin. "Time to go, boys," I say.

He smiles again, still reclining comfortably on the hood. "Is that right?"

"YOU'D BETTER GODDAMN BELIEVE THAT'S RIGHT!" screams Calvin, exploding in anger. He holds up his fist. "You want some of this, you little shit?"

The three of them sit up straight, as stunned as I am by the explosive outburst from this short, old, one-legged lunatic. My concern is that their surprise will not prevent them from realizing the obvious, that unless Calvin has a bazooka in his jacket, they can handle us with absolutely no problem.

I decide to intervene, albeit verbally. "Guys, you don't want to deal with him. And even if you're able to, it's just going to get you thrown into jail and out of school. I'm a lawyer, and I'll see to it. Now, please get off the car."

They look at me, then at the still-fuming Calvin, and apparently decide that it makes more sense to deal with me. Pretending to maintain their dignity, they slowly but surely get off the car. The leader says to me, "We don't want to see you around here again."

"Good for you," I say as I hold open Calvin's door for him. I want to make sure he is in the car, so he can't change his mind and kill these three guys that combined aren't as old as he is and outweigh him by about four hundred and fifty pounds.

As we pull away, I look at Calvin, who offers a small smile. "Boy, that was a close one," he says.

● ● ● ● ●

JUST THE NAME "preliminary hearing" says all you need to know about our chance for success. By definition, "preliminary" means there's something else to follow, something bigger and more important. It's like a preliminary boxing match: You know that the main event is coming up a little later. In this case the main event will be Jeremy's trial for murder.

In theory we are trying to defeat the prosecution in this hearing, to sway the judge into the belief that there is not enough evidence to hold Jeremy over for trial. In real life this never happens; the prosecution meets their burden of probable cause every single time.

This is not to say that the exercise doesn't hold its rewards for our side. Lester will not call all of his witnesses, nor will he present all of his evidence, but it will still be helpful to assess the witnesses that do come in. We will also get to question them under oath, which gives us the ability to use this testimony to impeach them at trial.

A major negative in the process, and the reason Lester is going this route rather than a grand jury indictment, is that the unchallenged prosecution case will get into the media, and their victory will assume an importance in the eyes of the public that it does not deserve. If we were involved in an obscure, run-of-the-mill case in an inner city somewhere, this would not be a problem, since the media coverage would not be there. And the reason the media would not be there is that it seems they've all decided to come to Findlay.

Waiting for Calvin and me on the courthouse steps when we arrive is a ridiculously large group of media types, including a number from the national cable networks. I should have expected this, since the original arrest caused them to cover Laurie's press conference.

I am at a loss to explain why the national media cover certain crime stories and not others. Thousands of murders are committed every year, and thousands of people disappear, so why did the media choose to saturate America with Elizabeth Smart, Jon Benét Ramsey, and Laci Peterson?

Maybe they're latching onto this one because pretty young coeds have been murdered, or maybe it's because there's apparently a religious aspect to it. All I know is that I've had enough media attention on my recent cases, and I don't relish it on this one.

The problem is really one of timing and focus. Preparing a murder trial requires a full-time commitment, mentally and even physically, and any energy devoted to spinning the media is inevitably a distraction. However, the media will be fed, and will fill their airtime with information, accurate or not, and I can't cede that territory to the prosecution. In other words, if the media are going to broadcast bullshit to potential jurors, I want it to be our bullshit.

I stop to answer some questions, mostly to get the point across about how the preliminary hearing process disproportionately favors the prosecution and that viewers should not attach any importance to it. The media people, of course, do not want a lecture on our legal system, they want juicy details about the case. This exchange, therefore, is not at all satisfying to either side.

As it's wrapping up, a reporter from MSNBC who I know from my panelist days, which seem like a hundred years ago, throws me a softball. "So, Andy, how do you see the case shaping up?"

"Well, the prosecution has more resources and obviously has the home field advantage, so it won't be easy. The only thing we have going for us is an innocent client."

"Any chance of a plea bargain?"

"Zero." I say this even though I have no idea if it's true. New facts can come out, trials can go south in a hurry, and our determination to fight to the end can change to a desperate attempt to avert the death penalty.

When we're out of earshot of the media, Calvin whispers to me, "I never thought I'd say this to anyone, but it's possible you're even more full of shit than I am."

"Calvin, no one is more full of shit than you are."

"You're just saying that to make me feel good," he says.

Once we're inside, I see that Lester has already arrived with his mini-entourage. I nod to him, but he doesn't return the nod. This is hardball, Findlay-style.

We sit down at the defense table, after which Jeremy is brought out. He takes his seat next to Calvin and within about two seconds asks if there is anything new with his case. If he is like my previous defendants, this is the first of five thousand times he will ask that question. What he's really asking is if there has been a stunning development that will immediately cause his release, and he's disappointed when he finds out there isn't.

Laurie is sitting near the front of the room, though she will not be testifying. She was not on duty the night of the murders, and Cliff Parsons handled the investigation. I assume he will testify, since he's on Lester's list, and I plan to rough him up some.

Judge Morrison starts the hearing at precisely nine o'clock and begins by informing the packed gallery that if they are the cause of any disruptions, they will rue the day. I have a feeling there's not going to be any ruing this particular day; I think the judge's warnings will have the desired effect. To the nonmedia people in this room, this is the World Series, the biggest public event that Findlay is likely to experience. At least until the trial.

Lester calls as his first witness Dr. Clement Peters, the county medical examiner, who Laurie and everybody else refers to as Clem. He is here to discuss the results of his autopsy to determine the cause of death, as well as to report on the results of tests taken to identify the bloodstains on the front seat of Jeremy's truck.

If left to his own devices, Dr. Peters could say in about thirty seconds that the deaths were due to multiple stab wounds and that the blood on the front passenger seat belonged to both victims. In Lester's publicity-hungry hands it takes just under an hour; he's never played to a media-packed house before, and he does not want to step back out of the spotlight.

Finally, reluctantly, he turns the witness over to me. "Dr. Peters, about how much blood was there in the front of the car?" I ask.

"In layman's terms, maybe ten or twelve specks."

"But it could be seen with the naked eye?" I ask.

"Yes."

"How did it get there?"

He seems surprised by the question and takes a moment before saying, "I really don't know."

"Do you think it's likely that the victims were both in that front seat bleeding?"

He considers this. "Well, it's a small area . . . I doubt if both of them were there, but it's possible."

"If they were cramped into the seat like that, bleeding from the stab wounds, would you expect to see more blood?"

"Absolutely."

As prosecution witnesses go, this is an outstanding one for the defense, mainly because he seems to be open and not partial to either side. He doesn't bring an agenda to this hearing, as Lester and I both do.

"But if they hadn't been stabbed yet, and were cramped into that same seat, they wouldn't each have left blood specks, would they?"

"Not unless they both had other wounds of some sort."

I accept that and move on to a discussion of the bodies, which Dr. Peters had said had at least ten stab wounds each and had bled profusely. "In your considered opinion is it possible that the person who committed these murders was able to avoid getting blood on himself or herself?"

"I'm not an expert in blood spatter, but I would say no. In the case of Elizabeth Barlow the carotid artery was cut, and that would have created a spurt of blood. And other wounds on both women would have done the same."

I let him off the stand; he's not the guy whose credibility I need to damage. Lester, seemingly pleased with how well this has started, quickly calls Dwayne O'Neal, a patron at the Crows Nest bar on the night of the murder.

O'Neal, in his mid-twenties himself, seems relaxed and delighted to be here as the center of attention. He testifies that he saw Jeremy and Elizabeth arguing in the parking lot that night and that Jeremy was yelling at her. He was a good fifty feet away but had no trouble hearing them.

"What could you hear them saying?" Lester asks.

"He was yelling, 'How can you say that? How can you say

that?' And she said that she was leaving, and he said, 'You're not going anywhere.'"

This is damaging testimony, and Lester takes another half hour to milk it, before turning the witness over to me.

"Now, Mr. O'Neal," I say, "you've testified that you saw the defendant in the parking lot. Were you arriving at the bar or leaving at the time?"

"I was leaving. It was past twelve o'clock."

"Did you have friends with you that heard the argument as well?"

He shakes his head. "No, I was there alone."

"So your friends were inside?"

Another shake of the head. "No, I knew a couple of people there, but I was by myself. I like to go there sometimes to relax, you know, unwind."

"Does drinking help you unwind?"

"Sure, a little bit."

"How much unwinding did you do that night?" I ask.

"What do you mean?" he asks, now a little wary.

"How much did you drink?"

"I don't know . . . not much. A drink or two."

I introduce as evidence a credit card receipt from that night, showing that O'Neal spent fifty-two dollars for eight drinks. I then get him to admit that the receipt is in fact his.

"So since you didn't have any friends in the bar, can we assume you weren't buying rounds of drinks for everyone? Can we assume that you were doing a lot of unwinding that night?"

O'Neal's attitude switches to sullen and worried. "I don't remember . . . but I wasn't drunk."

I nod as if that makes perfect sense. "Fine. So you spent fifty-two dollars on drinks, after which you and your blood alcohol level head to your car for a pleasant ride home. By the way, do you find that driving drunk helps you unwind as well?"

Lester objects and the judge sustains, but my point is made: This is not a model citizen. I continue. "So when you got near your car, you heard the defendant and Elizabeth Barlow arguing?"

"Right."

"Was it violent?"

"No."

"Did you intervene?" Dwayne doesn't seem to understand what I'm asking, so I spell it out. "Did you walk over, break up the argument, because you were afraid someone would get hurt?"

"No, but I thought about it. I guess I should have, seeing as how she died and all."

"Did the defendant and Ms. Barlow leave together?" I ask.

"I don't know for sure; I left before them."

"Even though you were so worried," I say, concluding the cross-examination. I can't decide who's happier that he's getting off the stand, Lester or Dwayne.

For myself, I have mixed emotions with the way things are going. The good news is that I've made points with this witness, at least partially discredited his testimony, and made him look bad. The bad news is that I've done this now, rather than at trial, which is when it will be important.

Judge Morrison is not going to throw out the case today; he is going to schedule it for trial. Lester will be able to use this experience to better prepare Dwayne for his trial testimony, and in that sense what I accomplished will have been counterproductive. The reason I did it is the media coverage; it is crucial I get the public to understand that this case is not a slam dunk and that there is another side to the story, our side.

Lester calls Cliff Parsons, the officer who investigated the case, discovered the bodies, and arrested Jeremy. Lester slowly takes him through his life story, literally beginning with his time as an all-state football player at good old Findlay High. By the time he's halfway through his heroics as an Army Ranger, I can't take any more.

"I object, Your Honor. The witness's life story, while thrilling and the stuff of which TV movies are made, is not relevant here."

"Your Honor, Lieutenant Parsons's exemplary record is important towards supporting his credibility," Lester says.

"How about if we wait until cross-examination to see just how credible he is?" I say, throwing down the gauntlet. I want this witness worried about what I'm going to do to him.

Judge Morrison asks Lester to speed things up, and after a few more questions they move into testimony having to do with the case at hand. Lester takes him through his story step by step, beginning with the missing persons report called in by both Liz's mother and Sheryl's father. Parsons took twenty-four hours to determine that they were in fact missing under suspicious circumstances, and then started an investigation to learn their whereabouts.

Parsons comes off as an experienced witness. He speaks slowly and carefully, answering the questions completely but not volunteering more than is necessary. He and Lester have obviously spent some time together preparing, since the story comes out easily and coherently.

Once Parsons determined that the young women's disappearance was indeed suspicious, he learned from Dwayne O'Neal of the argument between Liz and Jeremy outside the bar. He further learned that Liz had recently broken up with Jeremy and that Jeremy was unhappy about it.

As Parsons relates it, he went out to Jeremy's the next night to discuss all this with him. Jeremy's truck was parked in front of the house, and Parsons looked in the window as he walked by. He saw what seemed to be bloodstains on the front seat and called for backup help.

Before the help arrived, Parsons rang the bell, and there was no answer. Jeremy was in the guesthouse, asleep, but Parsons said he had no way of knowing that. Parsons then pried open the door and commenced a search. Backup arrived, and one of the other officers found the bodies, the fresh dirt and leaves having caused him to notice the shallow grave. Jeremy heard noises, came into the main house, and was read his rights, arrested, and taken into custody.

Calvin and I have discussed the dilemma of how hard to hit these witnesses in the preliminary hearing, and as I get up to cross-examine Parsons, Calvin whispers to me, "You gonna leave any bullets in the gun?"

"What do you think?" I ask, although I've already made my decision.

"Rat-tat-tat-tat-tat-tat" is the machine-gun sound he makes, a sentiment I fully agree with.

I steal a quick glance at Laurie as I walk toward Parsons. He works for her, and she will not be happy if I damage his credibility. But it's something I have to do; it's why they're paying me the little bucks.

The only issue that holds any real promise for our defense is that Parsons failed to get a search warrant before checking out the truck and house. If it could be determined that he acted improperly, then all evidence discovered in those searches would be thrown out. It won't happen, but it's all we have to shoot for.

Lester has already had Parsons explain why he did not get a search warrant, but I plan to take him through it again. "Lieutenant, you testified that when you arrived at Mr. Davidson's house, the truck parked in front attracted your attention."

"Yes, it was parked at a strange angle, as if it had been left quickly."

"I'm not from around here, but is 'quick parking' a felony in Wisconsin?"

Lester objects and Judge Morrison sustains, casting a warning stare in my direction.

"So you thought this was suspicious enough to look into the truck?"

He nods. "I did. Two young women were missing."

"And had been missing for twenty-four hours." I point this out in an effort to show that if Jeremy had indeed been worried about how he quickly parked, or about bloodstains on the seat, he would have had plenty of time to remedy the situation. The truth is, I questioned Jeremy on this, and he said he had not used the vehicle in those previous twenty-four hours.

Parsons has a ready answer. "That doesn't mean the truck was there that long. For all I knew, it could have just gotten back to the house."

"Which window did you look through?" I ask. "The driver's side or passenger side?"

"Passenger side."

I show him a picture of the car parked in front of the house. The driver's side is toward the driveway entrance, and the passenger side is facing the house.

"So you pulled up, saw this suspiciously parked truck, but didn't look in the window closest to you. Instead you walked around to the other side? Is that correct?"

"Yes."

"What were you looking for?"

"Anything relevant to my investigation," he says.

"You mean like a clue or something? Do quickly parked trucks usually contain clues?"

"I was looking for anything relevant to my investigation," he repeats.

"And you saw what looked like blood to you," I say.

"It was blood," he says with the confidence of twenty-twenty hindsight.

"Dr. Peters characterized the blood on the seat as 'specks.' Would you agree with that?"

He shrugs. "It was enough for me to know what it was."

"You know blood when you see it?"

"I do. I unfortunately see a lot of it in my line of work."

I nod and walk over to the defense table. Calvin hands me a sixteen-by-twenty-four-inch manila envelope. I ask if we can approach the bench, and when Lester and I are out of earshot of the witness and everyone else, I take out a small poster board and tell the judge what it represents. I further state that Dr. Peters prepared this for us yesterday and gave us a document swearing that it is as represented.

Lester objects to my using the exhibit, but the judge correctly overrules him and allows me to show it to the jury and then Parsons. "Lieutenant Parsons, as you can see, there are four red stains, identified as A through D, on this board. I'm sure you'll agree that they are all larger than specks."

Parsons doesn't say anything, which is fine, since I haven't asked a question. "As an expert in blood identification, perhaps you can tell us which of these are bloodstains."

Lester objects again, but the judge again overrules him. Parsons seems disconcerted by the exercise and looks upward, complaining that "this isn't the best lighting."

I nod. "You mean compared to a dark driveway at ten o'clock at night, looking through a quickly parked car window? Those are better conditions?"

Finally, reluctantly, he points to C. "That appears to be a bloodstain."

I nod and hand a document to Parsons. "You've chosen

the stain labeled 'C.' Please read from Dr. Peters's sworn statement and tell the jury what C actually is."

Parsons looks at the document and says softly, "It's melted red licorice scraped on the surface." There are a few snickers in the gallery, and Judge Morrison gavels them away, but they heighten the effect.

I wasn't worried that Parsons would correctly identify a bloodstain, because none of them were blood. To Parsons I say, "I take it you're not also an expert on licorice identification? You haven't unfortunately seen a lot of licorice in your line of work?"

Lester objects and Judge Morrison strongly admonishes me. He's coming to the unhappy realization that Hatchet's characterization of me as a wiseass was all too accurate.

I continue. "So you make the decision that because of these specks that looked like blood in the truck, and because the truck was 'quickly' parked at an angle, you couldn't wait for a search warrant. You had to rush in."

He nods. "Right. I thought someone inside could be bleeding or otherwise in danger."

"Yes. You testified that a dangerous criminal could conceivably have been inside, holding the young women, or even Mr. Davidson, hostage."

"That's correct."

"Doesn't proper procedure call for you to wait for backup in such a situation? Unless there is obvious and imminent grave danger to someone?"

"Yes, but—"

I interrupt. "But you couldn't wait. Not with all that blood or licorice in the car."

Again Lester objects, and this time Judge Morrison issues what he says will be his final warning. Parsons is handling this ridicule pretty well, remaining calm and relatively impassive.

"It was a decision I made in the moment," he says. "Under the same circumstances I would make it again."

"And you would be violating the law again, Lieutenant. Because this was clearly a case in which you should have first obtained a search warrant. You knew this, and yet you chose not to do so."

Lester stands. "Your Honor, counsel is making an argument under the guise of direct examination."

He's right about that, so I turn instead to the judge and move that all evidence found after the unlawful search of the truck be stricken. The judge says that we should continue this hearing and that a separate hearing will be necessary to decide the search warrant issue, which is an unpleasant surprise for Lester.

I let Parsons off the stand, having badly embarrassed him, and in the process I've made an impact on the media. But little has really been accomplished legally, and the search warrant hearing will go nowhere.

Lester wraps up his case, and Judge Morrison correctly rules that the prosecution has met its burden and that Jeremy will be held over for trial. A trial in which Lester will hold all the cards.

● ● ● ● ●

I AM FINDING it simply impossible to avoid bratwurst. It is everywhere, prepared in all different styles. Not only do I not want to eat it, I don't want to see it or hear about it. But there it is . . . everywhere.

What marketing genius came up with the name "bratwurst"? Did they think they could make a food sound more appealing and appetizing by including "wurst" in the name? I'm sure there must have been a reason they did it; maybe "bratshit" was already taken.

And what exactly is a brat? Where are they found? All everybody talks about around here is hunting; maybe I could get in good with the local citizens by grabbing a gun and going out and shooting me a bagful of brats.

Calvin inhales a plate of it at the diner, while I have a tuna salad sandwich. We take the opportunity to discuss the best way to divvy up our responsibilities. Calvin suggests that he continue to interview classmates of Jeremy and Elizabeth at the university, a logical plan considering my performance in the dormitory. He will also do additional research into the Centurion religion, something he and everyone else in Findlay know amazingly little about, considering how close by it is.

My short-term efforts will be directed toward learning what I can about Elizabeth's and Sheryl's lives within Center City and what effect their religion had on events as they unfolded.

When I get back to the house, I start by placing a call to Elizabeth's mother, Jane Barlow, and the phone is answered by a female who sounds like a teenager.

"Jane Barlow, please."

"Who's calling?"

"My name is Andy Carpenter."

I hear some muffled whispering, as if the person has her hand over the receiver while she talks to someone. After a short while she comes back on the line. "What's this about?"

"I'm the attorney representing Jeremy Davidson."

"Hold on," she says, after which there is another long pause, with muffled talking.

Finally, an adult woman's voice comes on. "This is Jane Barlow."

"Mrs. Barlow, my name is Andy Carpenter. I'd like to come out there and speak to you about your daughter, if I may."

There is a pause of maybe fifteen seconds. If you don't think that's a long time, look at your watch and hold your breath. "Oh," she finally says, a comment not necessarily worth waiting for.

"Would that be all right?" I ask.

Another pause, just as long. In the background I can hear the teenager urging, "Talk to him, Mom." But when Jane finally speaks to me, she says, "I don't think so."

"I won't take much of your time, and it might help us find out who killed Elizabeth and Sheryl Hendricks. I think that is something everyone wants."

Another lengthy pause; if I were charging by the hour,

Richard Davidson would be getting a mortgage right now. "I'm sorry, I have nothing to say to you, Mr. Carpenter."

Click.

This isn't going as well as I had hoped.

My next call is to the First Centurion Church, and the receptionist answers and wishes me a "fine and healthful day." I ask for Keeper Clayton Wallace and tell her "Andy Carpenter" when she asks who is calling.

Within moments a man's voice comes on the line. "Stephen Drummond."

"I'd like to speak to Clayton Wallace, please."

"I'm sure you would, Mr. Carpenter, but that's not likely any time soon. So how can I help you?"

"That depends on who you are," I say.

"I'm a resident of Center City, as well as legal counsel and vice president of the First Centurion Church. So, again, how can I help you?"

"Well, I'm representing Jeremy—"

He interrupts. "I'm aware of that."

"Then I'm sure you're also aware that I'm attempting to learn everything I can about the victims, including information about the town they lived in and the religion that was apparently so important to them."

"Fair enough. I'm your guy."

I'm pleasantly surprised by this open invitation, and we make arrangements to meet tomorrow in his office. Right now I feel like I should be doing something, but there's nothing else I can think of to do, so I take Tara for a walk.

I'm starting to like these walks; I may even be starting to like Findlay. The air is crisp, fresh . . . for some reason every time I go outside I feel like tailgating and throwing a football around. I'd better be careful, or in a few weeks I'll be wearing a plastic piece of cheese on my head and rooting for Brett Favre.

There seems to be more of a spring in Tara's step as well. She's been showing some signs of age, although that is not terribly significant, since Tara will live forever. But she seems more cheerful since she's been here; it's possible she might be a small-town dog at heart.

When we get back to the house, I am pleasantly surprised to find Laurie waiting for us in the living room. "You left the door open," she says. "I figured you wouldn't mind if I waited inside."

"Make my home your home," I say.

She looks at the pictures on the walls of various people doing various things, like having picnics, going to amusement parks, and mugging for the camera. "Who are these people?" she asks.

"I would guess they're friends and relatives of the dead woman who used to live here," I say.

She smiles. "I love how you've given the place your personal touch."

"I even watered one of the plants the other day."

"You missing home?" she asks.

I think about that for a moment and am surprised by what I come up with. "No . . . not really. Not yet. I'm becoming very involved with the case, so I haven't had much time."

"Everybody's talking about how you beat up on Lester in court today."

I shrug. "No big deal . . . I had the facts on my side. When I don't, he'll beat up on me."

She shakes her head and smiles. "I've seen you in action, so I know better."

I'm not real big on compliments; they're the one thing that can effectively shut me up. So I don't respond.

"You made Parsons look pretty bad up there," she says. She can't be happy about this; he works for her, and his performance reflects negatively on her department.

I nod. "He deserved it. He should have gotten a search warrant; he knew there was no reason to rush into that house."

She doesn't agree. "There were two dead young women at that house, Andy. They could have still been alive, and that would have been plenty reason to rush."

I'm not about to back down on this one. "He did what he did, and then he made up reasons for doing it after the fact. That's called lying, and he did it under oath. That's called perjury. So I'm not going to feel bad that I embarrassed him."

"He's a good cop, Andy."

"Look, I'm not saying he wasn't trying to serve the cause of justice. I'm saying he didn't follow the rules."

This is not the first time that Laurie and I have disagreed in this manner. She is a law enforcement officer, and I'm a defense attorney. Not exactly two peas in a pod. "You want to go out to get a bite to eat?" I ask. It's my version of being conciliatory.

"I can make dinner," she says, a little tentatively.

Then it hits me. "You let yourself in here because you didn't want people to see you waiting outside. And that's why you don't want to go out to eat. You're worried about being seen as being on my side, because of our previous relationship."

"This is a small town, Andy, and people depend on me . . . on my doing my job."

"Hey, it's okay, Laurie. You're in a bad spot."

"Worse than you think. Lester has gone to the mayor and told him about our relationship. He doesn't trust me."

"What did the mayor say?" I ask.

"That Lester should worry about his own job and let me do mine. But that could change, Andy. If I give him half a reason . . ."

"Laurie, you called me, I didn't call you. I'm here because

of you." After I say it, I realize that she could take that last sentence one of two ways: that I'm here because she told me about the case, or that I'm here because I wanted to be near her. I don't know which is true, so I don't clarify it.

"I know," she says, "and I'm glad you are, really I am. Jeremy will get the best defense possible, and I won't have to miss you the way I have. I just don't know how to behave, Andy."

"You mean in your job?"

"In my job, but out of my job as well. If we want to go out to dinner, I don't want to have to worry about how it will look. I want people to trust me enough to know that I'll live up to my responsibilities as a police officer, no matter what is going on in my personal life."

"Anybody who doesn't trust you is an idiot."

She's not about to just accept that. "And it's not just trust, Andy. I want people to respect me. I want my fellow officers to respect me. Some of them got passed over for a promotion because I was brought in. I want them to respect that decision. I need them to."

I walk over to her and hug her. Hugging is not an act that comes naturally to me, but this time I do it without even thinking. She looks at me, and for a moment I'm afraid she is going to cry. "I don't want to screw this up, Andy. Not any of it."

I hold her tighter. "When you're young and so alone as we, and bewildered by the world we see, how can we keep love alive, how can anything survive, what a town without pity can do."

She looks at me strangely. "What?"

As further evidence that I am unable to control my mouth, I've just been inappropriately song-talking, a game that my friend Sam Willis and I play back home. The object is to work song lyrics smoothly into a conversation. "That's 'Town Without Pity.' Gene Pitney."

"My life is going up in flames, and you're song-talking?" she asks incredulously.

I nod. "Not bad, huh?"

She laughs. "Not bad at all." Then she kisses me, perhaps unaware that she is providing positive reinforcement to my childish behavior.

"You know, I've got an idea," I say. "We behave professionally out there in the world, but we meet back here maybe ten or twelve times a day to have secret sex."

She smiles. "You're the boss. But you might want to be careful. At the pace you're suggesting, you wouldn't last until tomorrow."

"We'll see about that. You want to have a sleepover date tonight?"

"I think that can be arranged," she says.

"Then arrange it," I say, trying not to drool as I talk. It may not be the smartest thing to do, but the idea of spending the night lying next to Laurie, something I thought I'd never experience again, is just too good to pass up.

• • • • •

LAURIE LEANS OVER at five-thirty in the morning. "I have to leave for work," she says.

"What are you, a night watchwoman?"

"No, I like to get in early and make sure organized crime doesn't take over Findlay."

"I was hoping you could stay a little longer," I say.

She leans over and kisses me. "Like until when?"

"Next August."

I obviously overreached, because she's out of bed within three minutes. After her shower, while she's getting dressed, she asks, "So what's on tap today in the legal world?"

"Well, I can't speak for the whole day, but this morning I'm meeting with a guy named Stephen Drummond."

She does a mini–double take in surprise. "Really?"

"Yup. By the way," I say, "did you talk to Elizabeth Barlow's ex-boyfriend?"

She shakes her head. "Jeremy tried to implicate him, without knowing his name. But nobody in that town will even confirm there is such a person."

Laurie leaves, and I shower and take Tara for our walk. I'm not big on introspection, and I really need to focus on the case, but I still can't help thinking about the situation with Laurie. Things are good now, and we still love each other, but this case is going to come to an end. I'm going to go back home, and she's going to stay here.

If I were smart, I'd stop seeing her right now and focus only on the case. Maybe that way it would hurt less when we separate again. But I'm not smart, and I can feel myself heading toward the edge of the cliff. Unfortunately, I've been over that cliff, so I know what a long drop it is to the bottom.

When Tara and I get back to the house, Calvin is there waiting for us, an envelope in hand. "I got something for you to read, city boy," he says, holding up the envelope.

The pages inside turn out to be copies of the newspaper articles written by a man named Henry Gerard, identified as a former resident of the town of Center City. Mr. Gerard's job was "servant of the Keeper," which put him in the employ of the church. Based on the uniform he wears in a picture accompanying one of the articles, the uniformed man who questioned me when I was in Center City was also a servant of the Keeper.

Gerard became disenchanted with the Centurion religion, for reasons left unexplained by the articles. His writing them seems almost an act of revenge, trying to hurt his former church by exposing its secrets.

Those secrets, if these articles are to be believed, are bizarre. The Centurions believe that God speaks to them through an enormous wheel housed in the town hall, with symbols on it that the Keeper deciphers and interprets. The wheel is literally spun, once a week, and where it lands determines what the Keeper ultimately says.

All major decisions in Center City are made through the spinning of this wheel. People's occupations, their mates, all of their significant life choices, are determined by the Keeper's interpretations of the wheel. It has been this way for almost a hundred and fifty years, as generation after generation in Center City has willingly made the choice to give up its right to make choices.

If Liz Barlow had an ex-boyfriend, as Jeremy claims, then he was likely matched up with her by their religion, by the spinning of the wheel. For her to have broken off their relationship and pursued Jeremy instead would have been a blasphemy, according to the world Gerard describes. The pressure to go back to him would have been overwhelming, which no doubt explains Liz's ultimate rejection of Jeremy.

I have no time to discuss the implications of the articles with Calvin, since I'm in danger of being late for my meeting with Stephen Drummond. I manage to arrive at his office just at ten o'clock. He is in the two-story building next to the town hall, and I pull into the small parking lot behind the building. Two men, each one at least six two, two hundred and twenty pounds, are standing in front of me by the time I get out of the car. Their uniforms identify them to me as servants of the Keeper. The Keeper must have more servants than Thomas Jefferson.

"You're here to see Mr. Drummond," one of them says.

"Right."

"Follow us, please."

They proceed to lead me, in a weird procession, into the building and to the receptionist's desk. "Thanks," I say, "I shudder to think what could have happened if I tried to make it here on my own."

If there was a joke there, they don't get it, and they melt away, leaving me with the receptionist. "Mr. Drummond will see you now. Down that hall and to the right."

I follow her directions, passing an office that the sign says contains the town clerk, and another woman is at the end of the hall waiting for me. It seems like the entire town has mobilized to get me to this meeting. "Right in here," she says.

I enter the office, and a man I presume to be Stephen

Drummond rises from his desk to greet me. He is in his early sixties and wears a conservative three-piece suit. Compared to the mode of dress I've seen so far in these small towns, he would look less out of place if he were wearing a space suit.

He extends his hand, and I shake it. "Mr. Carpenter, it's a pleasure to meet you."

"The pleasure is mine," I say, charming as always. The line between me and Cary Grant gets thinner every day.

"Please sit down. Would you like some coffee?"

"No thank you," I say, but I sit in the offered chair. On his desk is a family photo of him, a woman I assume to be his wife, and a man in his early twenties. The young man is dressed in the garb of a servant of the Keeper, and since the resemblance is apparent, I assume he is Drummond's son. They are all standing in front of a small airplane, the kind with propellers. The kind you couldn't get me to fly in at gunpoint.

"You fly?" I ask.

He smiles. "As a passenger only. My son is the pilot in the family. There is a small airfield just outside of town."

I nod, having seen the airport on my drive to Findlay. "I've often thought about taking flying lessons," I say truthfully. "The only problem is that I'm afraid of heights, machines, high speeds, parachutes, and dying."

"Then you're probably not a great candidate for it," he says.

I nod but don't say anything. It's his turn to make small talk, and he obliges. "You're far from home," he observes.

"I am," I say. "But I take it you're not?"

"You take it correctly. I've lived here in Center City all my life. Except for the four years I spent at Dartmouth and the three at Harvard Law."

It took him only seven sentences to get in the fact that he went to Harvard Law. That's pretty quick. I decide it wouldn't be productive to ask him if the spinning wheel made him pick Harvard over Yale. But what the hell is a Harvard Law grad doing here? "What is a Harvard Law grad doing here?" I ask, leaving out the "hell" in deference to his religion.

"Mr. Carpenter, my belief is that we are sitting on the most blessed ground on our planet. Why would I rather be somewhere else?" He says this in a tone so smug it's as if he expects me to say, "Yes, Your Eminence."

"Is there anyone in this town who is not a member of the Centurion religion?" I ask.

"No."

"Would anyone else be welcome?"

"No, they would not. Mr. Carpenter, are you writing a dissertation on my religion, or are you here to promote the interests of your client?"

"Sorry, I'm just a curious guy. Did you know the victims?"

He smiles. "Certainly. I know everyone in this town. This is a very friendly community."

"With no crime," I point out.

"Virtually none."

"How would you suggest I get all these friendly people in this friendly community to talk to me?"

"I would doubt that they would want to," he says. "Everyone loved Elizabeth and Sheryl very much."

"Many of them talked to the police," I point out.

He nods. "I'm sure it was with some reluctance. We like to keep to ourselves, but we recognize our obligations to follow the laws of the imperfect nation that contains us."

"But if you suggested that they talk to me . . . in the pursuit of justice for the victims . . ."

"I'll inform the families of your interest. That's all."

This guy is bugging me, and not because he is evasive and uncooperative. It's because he seems to consider me of no consequence. This is particularly annoying, since when I die, I want my headstone to read, "Here lies Andy Carpenter. He was of considerable consequence."

"Look, I have no interest in causing problems for you or your community," I say, "but as I'm sure they mentioned at Harvard, I must vigorously defend my client by all legal means available to me."

He barely deigns to shrug, so I continue. "And within this town there is information about the victims that is relevant, one way or the other, to this case. I can't just say, 'Well, these are religious people, so I'll leave them alone.'"

"You are getting to a point?" he asks.

"Yes. There is substantial national interest in this case. The media will descend on Findlay for this trial. If I tell them that the real truth is buried here, in Center City, your parishioners will spend all their time dodging TV cameras. There will be so many people here you'll have casinos springing up."

"Mr. Carpenter, our people have been here for one hundred seventy-one years. Our society has remained pure and untouched, despite the efforts of many outsiders to pollute it. We are capable of handling threats far greater than yours, I assure you."

"Your streets are public streets," I say.

"Inhabited by private people," he counters. "And my job is to protect that privacy, by every legal means available to me. And I will do so aggressively, every chance I get." He stands up, almost as sure a sign as taking out car keys that a meeting is over. "As I said, I will inform the families of your desire to talk to them. If they should choose to do so, they or I will contact you."

I leave, and as I exit the building, two servants of the Keeper are standing there, watching my every move. I've seen one of them before, but not the other, bringing the total to four who have monitored my movements in my two brief visits here. The new servant is the largest one yet.

I'm pissed off by my meeting, so to annoy them, and perhaps to learn something, I stop before I get to my car and look around at the street, which is mostly deserted. "Can we help you, sir?" the larger one asks.

"I'm just trying to get my bearings," I say. "I know Space Mountain is over there, so where would Pirates of the Caribbean be?"

"Sir?"

I shrug. "Never mind . . . it's probably a really long line anyway. I'll check out the Haunted House." I start to walk down the street, looking around as if I'm taking in the sights of the town.

I glance over a couple of times at the servants, who seem unsure what to do. Soon two others approach me from the other direction. I wave toward them, continuing my walk, which has reached the outskirts of the town center, which is the beginning of the residential homes. Not surprisingly, they don't wave back.

I'm getting a little nervous, but I'm comforted a little by the fact that it's broad daylight out. I see a street sign marking the street that I know to be the one on which Elizabeth Barlow lived. There are a few residents around, and I call out to one of the women. "Excuse me, can you tell me which is the Barlow home?"

The woman doesn't answer me, instead looking away, though she doesn't seem to be particularly fearful or nervous. I see a little boy, no more than seven years old, driving a toy fire truck.

"Are you going to be a fireman when you grow up?" I ask, with one eye on the approaching servants.

The boy shakes his head. "Nope, I'm going to work in the bank."

It seems a strange response, so I ask, "You're going to be a banker?"

He shrugs. "I guess."

I wonder if the wheel dictated the boy's career choice, but I keep walking, turning a corner and seeing that two more servants are waiting for me up ahead. Turning the corner was not the smartest idea, since I now find myself in front of a vacant lot with no residents around and servants closing in from the front and back. I feel a flash of panic; my annoyance at Drummond has caused me to push this too far.

Suddenly, a car pulls up and comes to a quick stop before me. It is driven by still another servant, who gets out of the car and walks slowly over to me. I recognize him instantly from the picture as Drummond's son; he has Drummond's height but is in better physical shape.

I turn and see that another man has gotten out of the passenger seat and is walking over to me. Actually, he strides over, exuding a sense of superiority that is immediately apparent. He wears a robe, almost looking like a judge, except that the robe is blue, perhaps a shade lighter than navy. He is considerably smaller than all of his servants, yet he is clearly in command.

"Mr. Carpenter," he says. It's a statement, perhaps a greeting.

"Keeper Wallace," I say.

"Yes. What exactly are you doing here?"

I smile through my nervousness. "Just checking out the town. It's quite lovely."

"I'm afraid you must leave now."

"Why is that?"

"We are a peaceful community, and your intentions seem to be disruptive. We have little tolerance for that." There is an extraordinary air about this man, which I think is a reflection of total security and confidence. He believes that nothing can hurt him, and he projects a serenity, even as he threatens me.

"My intention is to find out who killed two of your citizens."

"Do not provoke more violence in the process."

This certainly sounds like a threat, and I certainly don't want to test whether or not it is an empty one. I also don't want to appear to be a coward, even though that's pretty much what I am. All I can think to do is turn and walk the two blocks back to my car and drive off, so that's what I do, watched by my security detail every step of the way.

I head back to Findlay, which compared to Center City feels like Midtown Manhattan. The experience of being in Center City this time has left me shaken and concerned; there are things to be discovered there, but I'm at a loss how to do so.

When I get back to the house, Calvin is standing out front, petting Tara. I get out of the car and walk over to them; something about this scene worries me. "What's going on?" I ask.

"Tara's all right," Calvin says. "I wanted you to know that right away."

"What are you talking about?" I ask.

"Go inside and get a look at small-town assholedom at work," he says.

I move quickly to the front door and into the house. As soon as I enter I see it: A dummy is hanging from the ceiling fan in the living room, secured by a noose around his neck. The fan is operating slowly, and the dummy is eerily being dragged in a circular motion around the center of the room.

I turn and walk back outside, where Calvin and Tara are waiting for me. "I got here about five minutes ago and found it," he says. "Tara was in the backyard. I didn't see anybody."

Two police cars pull up, obviously having been called by

Calvin. Laurie and three officers get out and come over to us. "Where is it?" she asks.

"In the living room," I say.

"Have you checked out the house?"

I look over at Calvin, who shakes his head. "No. I just saw it and came out."

Laurie nods and signals to the other officers. They draw their handguns, and two of them walk around the side of the house. Laurie and the other one move cautiously inside the house, and Calvin and I wait for about ten minutes for them to come out. Finally, they do, and Laurie comes over to us.

"So what do you think?" I ask.

"I think you should call Marcus."

• • • • •

MARCUS CLARK answers the phone when

I call. He says, "Unhh."

That is Marcus-talk for "hello," so I say, "Marcus, this is Andy Carpenter."

"Unhh." Marcus uses "unhh" the way Willie Miller uses "schnell."

"Marcus, I'm in Wisconsin working on a case, and it's getting a little dangerous, so I really need you here, if you can make it."

"Unhh."

"I'm representing someone against a murder charge, and public sentiment is running against him. There's been some violence, a firebombing . . ."

"Unhh."

I've never had much success conversing with Marcus, and this time it's not going any better. "Listen, Marcus, Willie Miller is going to talk to you and give you all the details. Okay?"

This time he doesn't answer at all, so I hang up and call Willie, who has always been able to communicate with Marcus. I tell him the problem, and he agrees to get in touch with him right away. "You need me up there too?" Willie asks.

"No thanks, Marcus should be able to protect me."

"Hey, man, don't you think I know that? Marcus could protect you if you had the Marines after you. I'm not talking about that. Maybe I could help you out with the case, do some investigating or something. Sounds like you can use some help."

I decline, though I appreciate the offer, and Willie promises to call me back after he talks to Marcus. If Marcus is busy, perhaps if he is invading North Korea or something, then Willie vows he will make the trip himself.

Willie is a black belt in karate, and one of the toughest people I know, but compared to Marcus, he is a Barbie doll. I will feel much better if Marcus can come up here, because things seem to be getting rather dangerous.

When I get off the phone with Willie, I go back into the living room, where Calvin is working. He's been talking to a lot of kids at the school and is going over his notes. Since the kids wouldn't speak to me at all, I'm surprised that Calvin is making progress with them, and I ask him about it.

He shrugs. "It's possible that they got the idea I was once a roadie for Led Zeppelin and lost my leg when some crazed groupies knocked a huge amplifier onto me during a concert."

"Amazing how these stories get started," I say.

One of the major difficulties we will face is in making it seem possible that someone other than Jeremy committed this crime. Unfortunately, young women, and other people, are murdered all the time. It is not hard to imagine that these murders could have been random, by some passing sicko. But the fact that the bodies were then buried on Jeremy's property changes that equation dramatically. Sickos don't often find out who their victim's ex-boyfriend was, and they don't set about framing them.

We certainly must focus on Elizabeth's other ex-boyfriend, whose very existence is in question at this point. Jeremy says that Elizabeth referred to him, though never by name, and even said on that fateful night that they were running away together. Of course, I don't have a clue why that boyfriend would have killed Elizabeth just as they were planning to run away together. In any event, we must find him.

The fact is that if Jeremy is innocent, then these women were a threat to someone, or at least a cause of rage. If we can't convince the jury that such a someone is likely out there, we're finished and our client is history.

The only way we are going to pull this off is to learn all we can about the victims, a task made infinitely more difficult by the lack of access we have to their hometown. This may or may not turn out to be significant. I have to be careful not to focus too much on that town simply because its residents are so decidedly insulated and unfriendly. All evidence is that they have been that way for well over a century without having committed any murders.

Calvin and I have a ten o'clock meeting with Dave Larson, a local private investigator. Calvin had heard of him but never dealt with him directly. Laurie had given him a recommendation, though not a ringing endorsement. She said he was as good as we were likely to find in the Findlay area, while admitting that Findlay was not exactly a hotbed of private investigation.

I had pressed her with, "But he's good? He can handle himself?" And she responded with, "Have you called Marcus yet?"

Larson turns out to be in his early forties, about five foot eight, a hundred and fifty pounds. He wears glasses and carries two pencils in his shirt pocket, and keeps saying, "You got that right." He is the anti-Marcus.

"I do mostly insurance work, some divorce stuff," Larson

says in response to my question about his background. "It can get pretty hairy."

"I can imagine," I lie.

"You got that right."

"Ever do any work in Center City?" I ask.

"A couple of minor insurance cases; I think they were both motor vehicle accidents. Never did any divorce stuff, of course."

"Why 'of course'?"

He seems surprised by my lack of knowledge. "Those people don't get divorced . . . it's against their religion. They get married at twenty-one, and that's it." He laughs. "They're stuck for life."

"They get married at twenty-one?" Calvin asks, probably thinking about how many failed marriages he might have if he had started that early. "What if they don't have anyone to marry?"

Dave laughs. "That hasn't seemed to stop them so far."

"Do they *have* to get married?" I ask.

He shrugs. "You got that right."

"Why? Who makes them?" I ask.

"I don't know for sure, but I think that guy they call the Keeper wants 'em to, so they do."

"Amazing," Calvin says.

"You got that right," Dave says. "When that guy talks, those people would suck the Kool-Aid up with a straw, you know?"

I'm continuously being surprised by things I learn about that town. I've heard of religions prohibiting divorce, but dictating marriage by a certain age is outside of my experience. Of course, I've never let a spinning wheel or a guy in a dress dictate my life choices. I'd like to have the straw concession in Center City.

I roughly outline what Dave's responsibilities would be if

he takes on this job, which is basically to follow up whatever leads we give him, and report back to us. I tell him that anything he learns is confidential, since as a member of the legal team he falls under the attorney-client privilege. He looks at me as if I'm a dope for thinking he wouldn't already know that.

Dave accepts the job, asking for a salary far less than I would pay an investigator back home. I give him a retainer and tell him we'll contact him when we have a specific assignment, and he seems happy with that. I'm not sure we'll actually need him, but it's good to have him in reserve.

Calvin and I head over to the jail to see Jeremy. I like to meet with my clients fairly frequently, though it's more for their benefit than mine. They usually tell me all that they know early on, so these subsequent sessions are not often helpful to the defense. However, they do seem reassuring to the client even when the news is not particularly positive. It must be the security of knowing that somebody is on their side, working on their behalf.

Richard and Allie Davidson are at the jail visiting with their son when we arrive. It's the first time I've seen Allie since the night her house was set on fire. She thanks me profusely for helping her son, and Richard asks if they can stay while we talk. It's fine with Calvin and me, and fine with Jeremy, so I tell him that they can.

We spend some time answering Jeremy's and Richard's questions about any progress we are making. Allie is content to let her men do the talking. So far there has been very little progress, and I tell them so straight out. Jeremy is facing a very serious situation, and I'm not about to sugarcoat it.

"We need to talk to people that Elizabeth knew well," I say. "People from Center City."

"Are you having trouble doing that?" Richard asks.

"It would be easier to penetrate NORAD."

"The people in that town are crazy," Jeremy offers.

"Have you met any of them?" I ask. "I mean besides Elizabeth."

He shakes his head. "No. Sometimes when she'd go home for a holiday, I'd ask if she wanted me to come, to meet her family, but she said no. She said I didn't know what it was like, but that I wouldn't be welcome. She was embarrassed about it."

"And nobody came to visit her at school?"

He snaps his fingers. "Of course! Her sister . . . she came there for a weekend. Liz said it caused a big fight with her mother. I think her name is Madeline."

I had initially talked to a teenager when I called Jane Barlow. "How old is Madeline?"

"Probably seventeen. But she's cool. She wants to go away to school like Liz, but she's not allowed."

"Did Liz ever talk about any other friends . . . ever mention any other names?"

He shakes his head. "I don't think so. Liz used to say that inside and outside that town were like two different worlds. But it's not that she didn't like the place. She was really religious; it wasn't like anybody was twisting her arm about it."

"Did she ever mention Keeper Wallace?"

He nods. "A couple of times. She thought he was a great man. A couple of times she went all the way home for some kind of big meeting that he led."

"Did she ever describe those meetings?"

"No. Just that they were really important and that the whole town went."

I have no trouble believing that, since I was first there during one of the meetings. The streets at that time were deserted except for the ever-present servants. "Never mentioned a wheel when she was talking about her religion?"

"A wheel?" he asks, clearly having no idea what I'm talking about, so I take that as a no.

Jeremy is taken back to his cell, and his parents leave with us. Once outside, Richard asks me again about progress in the case, as if I wouldn't have been completely forthcoming in front of Jeremy, perhaps withholding something good so as not to get Jeremy's hopes up. He is disappointed when I have nothing to add, but expresses his full confidence in me. I wish I shared it.

Calvin and I go back to the house, and as we approach, he stops short, a stunned expression on his face. "You must be kidding," he mutters, almost to himself.

I look ahead, and there on the front porch is one of the scariest sights I have ever seen.

Marcus.

● ● ● ● ●

I HAVE ABSOLUTELY no idea how Marcus got here. He doesn't fly, at least not on planes, and I don't see any evidence of a car. It's possible he hitchhiked, but if any driver willingly picked up Marcus Clark, that person should be immediately committed and placed under twenty-four-hour suicide watch.

Marcus sitting on the porch of this peaceful house in this sedate little town gives new meaning to the word "incongruous." He projects pure menace and power, and Calvin says, "You'd better get him inside quick."

"Why?" I ask.

"Because in two minutes, For Sale signs are going to be popping up on this street like weeds."

"Hey, Marcus, how ya doing?" I ask. "I didn't think you'd get here so soon."

"Unhh," Marcus says. His phone and in-person personalities are remarkably similar.

"This is Calvin," I say. "Calvin, this is Marcus."

"Hello, Marcus. Andy's told me a lot about you," Calvin says gently. Everybody talks gently to Marcus when they first meet him.

"Unhh," Marcus says. He seems to have really taken to Calvin.

"Come on in," I say. "You hungry?"

"Yuh," he says. Now we're getting somewhere.

I put Marcus in the kitchen and invite him to have whatever he'd like. It turns out that what he'd like is every single edible item he sees, including pistachio nuts with the shells intact.

Marcus is about ten minutes into the carnage when the doorbell rings. I go to answer it, hoping that it's someone with a stomach pump, but it turns out it's Laurie.

"I assume Marcus is here?" she asks.

"How did you know that?"

"We got four 911 calls from people who saw him on your porch," she says.

"Was he doing anything wrong?"

"He was looking like Marcus."

No more explanation is needed, and Laurie goes into the kitchen. She gets there just in time, as Marcus is preparing to eat the dead woman's dinette set.

What follows is a transformation that I've seen a few times but still find hard to believe. The moment Marcus sees Laurie he breaks into a humanlike grin, moves to her, and hugs her. "Hey, Laurie," he says.

"Marcus, it's great to see you. How have you been?"

"Good."

They wax eloquently like this for a few minutes, and then we all sit down and discuss what Marcus's responsibilities will be here in Findlay. Laurie suggests that we make it a short list: that all he should have to do is protect my ass. I describe the situation in Center City, with the various servants ranging from burly to enormous, and he just takes it all in without responding or showing any concern. I'm not a doctor, but I don't think Marcus was born with a "concern" gene.

What Marcus does have is a significant amount of ability as an investigator and an amazing talent to get people to tell him things. I wouldn't describe it as cajoling or persuading; it's more like scaring into submission. But it works, and I'm bottom-line-oriented enough to want to use these talents.

What we decide on is that we will use Marcus as an investigator, and as a protector when I think I'm going to be in a situation that could be dangerous. Laurie thinks so highly of my physical prowess that her view is that I'm in danger every time I cross the street, so she's not thrilled with this resolution. But this time I'm calling the shots, and that's how we leave it.

"Where's Marcus going to live?" Calvin asks.

I hadn't given it much thought, and now that I do, I'm not thrilled with the possibilities. "Do you have room at your place?" I ask.

Calvin shakes his head, as if he deeply regrets that he has to say what he's going to say. "Damn . . . I wish I did. My aunt and uncle are in from Milwaukee, and they brought the twins."

"Is that right?" I ask. "You never mentioned them."

"I don't talk about them much; they're on my mother's side."

"I think Marcus should stay here," Laurie says. "You've got three spare bedrooms upstairs, and it's you he's going to protect. Staying at Calvin's house wouldn't make much sense, even if he didn't have his aunt and uncle and the twins on his mother's side in town."

I stare daggers at Laurie, but she fends them off. "What a wonderful idea," I say through clenched teeth.

While I would never let on to Laurie, I'm relieved that Marcus has arrived, even if I'm less than thrilled that we'll be rooming together. Physical courage has never been one of my defining qualities, and Marcus's presence makes me feel much more secure. Now, if Clarence Darrow would show up and help us win the case, the team would be complete.

Having been protected by Marcus before, I know how to proceed. I rent him a car, get him a cell phone, and then forget about him. I don't even have to tell him where I am going to be or when I am going to be there; he is just somehow always there when I need him. And I somehow always need him.

During the meeting, Calvin gets a phone call from one of the kids at the university who Calvin has been cultivating as possible information sources. It seems that one of Liz's friends at school overheard phone conversations she had with someone named Eddie, and it was her sense that he was her ex-boyfriend from back home. This is a potentially important development for our side, and Calvin is quite pleased with himself that he has come up with it. At the very least, it gives us a much-needed avenue to explore.

Tonight is going to be a night that Laurie sleeps over. I know this, because after Calvin leaves and Marcus goes upstairs to choose a bedroom, I say, "You want to stay over tonight?" and she says, "Absolutely." I am Andy the All-Powerful.

I'm not sure I'm doing the right thing by keeping her so close, even though she's leaving it up to me. It's feeling a little like those bad old movies where the girl says to the guy as they lie on the beach, "Is this just a summer thing, or will I see you in the city?" Well, this is just a winter thing, and I sure as hell am not going to see Laurie in the city.

On the other hand, I love her, and I love being with her, and it's counterintuitive to not want her to stay over. I just have to discipline myself to understand what it is and what it isn't, as well as where it's going and where it isn't.

I'm pretty much a master of mental self-discipline, but this is a tough one.

Laurie gives me a list, and I go to the market and buy food, since Marcus has consumed everything, and he's going to have to continue to be fed. I have my cart full when I get stuck behind two women on the cashier line. I don't know why it is, but I find that many women stand and watch their items being rung up, and only when that process is done do they open their purse and start taking out their means of payment. Do they think they are not going to be asked to pay?

When I finally get back home, Laurie starts to cook dinner. "You should ask Marcus if he wants to eat with us."

"Oh, come on," I say, though it sounds more like a whine than I intended.

"Andy, you can't not invite him to dinner. He's living here."

"He didn't sign up for the meal plan."

"Andy . . ."

I nod with resignation and go upstairs. Marcus is not at home, which is good news and bad news. I can be alone with Laurie for dinner, but it means that Marcus is loose on the streets of Findlay. So it's good for me, bad for Findlay. I can live with that.

After dinner we spend the kind of evening that I've missed even more than I realized. We open a bottle of wine and sit on the couch, with Tara between us. Golden retrievers are a master of positioning, and Tara arranges things so that I scratch her stomach while Laurie pets her head.

We watch a tape of one of our favorite movies, *A Beautiful Mind,* and I can see Laurie's eyes tear up as Jennifer Connelly says, "I need to believe that something extraordinary is possible." Well, extraordinary things can come in all shapes and sizes, and this is an extraordinary moment.

It is all so comfortable, all so wonderful, that I almost resist when Laurie asks if I'm ready to go to bed. Almost, but not quite.

Moments later we are making love, and while we are doing so, Laurie says, "Andy, I don't want this to end. We have to figure out a way that this doesn't have to end."

I don't know if she is talking about our lovemaking or about us, but either way it's got my vote.

• • • • •

MRS. BARLOW HAS agreed to talk with you" is the first thing Stephen Drummond says after he says hello.

It's a surprise to me, but I'm pleased at this first invitation to meet the good citizens of Center City. Maybe that ridiculous wheel okayed the interview. "Good," I say. "When can that happen?"

"I'm available at three this afternoon," he says.

"And why would that be significant?"

I can almost feel his smug smile through the phone. "Mrs. Barlow insists that I be there."

This is likely to cut down on the chances of my actually learning anything, but I know there is no possibility I can get this reversed. I agree to meet at three at the Barlow residence. He asks that I not get there early, probably to spare Mrs. Barlow the nightmare of being alone without her Harvard-educated lawyer for protection.

Actually, protection is a serious consideration for me. It would be paranoid of me to think I'm being led into a trap, but that town and its people make me more than a little uncomfortable.

Marcus is not home, so I call him on his cell phone and

invite him to the meeting. Based on his reaction, he's either thrilled or asleep, but I think I get him to understand that I want him at the house at two-thirty so we can drive to Center City.

The culture shock of Marcus entering Center City will be such that I almost feel I should call ahead and warn them. It's akin to when Tokyo woke up one morning and there was Godzilla strolling out of the water onto the beach. The townspeople are going to be running to the Keeper asking him what the hell is going on, because they've never experienced anything like Marcus before.

Marcus shows up promptly at two-thirty, and since he's in his car already, I get in the passenger seat and let him drive. We're about thirty seconds into the trip when I realize that classical music is coming out of the radio.

At least I think it's classical music; I'm not an expert. But there are no lyrics, and it sounds like a large orchestra, and I feel like I should be dressed up to hear it, so that fits my definition pretty well.

It's a rental car, so probably the radio was set to this when Marcus got it, and he was simply too oblivious to notice. There is as much chance that Marcus is intentionally playing classical music as there is that I'm playing center field for the New York Yankees.

"You listening to that?" I ask.

He nods. "Yuh."

"You like classical music?"

"Yuh."

"NOW PLAYING CENTER FIELD FOR THE YANKEES, NUMBER SEVEN, **ANDY CARPENTER** . . . CARPENTER . . . CARPENTER . . . Carpenter."

The twenty-minute drive feels like it takes about four hours. For the first fifteen minutes I try to make small talk, though I have no idea why. I say absolutely nothing interesting, and Marcus says nothing at all. I guess he's enraptured by the music.

I use the last five minutes to explain to Marcus what I know about Center City, its inhabitants, and its religion. He not only does not ask any questions, he doesn't nod or even blink. Yet for all his lack of inquisitiveness, Marcus has proven to be a smart guy, at least in a street sense kind of way. He's a terrific investigator, and that is a job for which morons need not apply.

We get to Center City, and I point out the few landmarks that I know. When he sees the town hall, towering above the rest of the buildings, he says, "That the church?"

"And city hall," I say. "Or both. They don't like strangers inside."

We drive on to the address we have for the Barlows, which is like pretty much every other house on every street in the town. The strange thing is that it is a farming community, yet there are no farmhouses. The farms are on the outskirts of town, while the farmers are most definitely on the "inskirts." And speaking of skirts, every woman I have seen here has been wearing one; jeans or slacks are clearly not the clothing of choice for the fashionable women of Center City.

We park in front of the Barlow house; I would know it even if I didn't see the number. That's because two of the larger servants in the town are standing on the porch, awaiting our arrival. "Those are the local tough guys," I say, but Marcus doesn't seem to look at them.

We get out of the car and walk toward the house. One of the servants says, "Good afternoon, Mr. Carpenter."

"Good afternoon," I say. "We're here to see Mrs. Barlow."

"Yes, sir. The meeting will begin shortly." He's talking to me, but he and his partner are staring straight at Marcus.

I look at my watch and see that we're five minutes early, and at that moment a car pulls up and Keeper Wallace gets out of the backseat, and the driver gets out as well. He is Drummond's son, who seems to be the servant assigned to taking the Keeper around. Drummond told me that his son is also a pilot, so maybe Wallace does more than travel around town.

Wallace has obviously taken Drummond's place as Mrs. Barlow's protector during this interview. It won't make any difference, despite the fact that they dress rather differently. Drummond is a suit-and-tie guy, while Wallace is clad in full robes and looks semi-ridiculous. I glance at Marcus to see if he has any reaction, but, of course, he does not.

Wallace walks toward the house. He greets me with a smile and a nod, and I introduce Marcus as my investigator.

He takes one look at Marcus and somehow avoids the temptation to hug him hello. Instead he turns to me. "The agreement with Mrs. Barlow was that she would speak with only you. I'm afraid Mr. Clark will have to leave."

"Nunh," says Marcus with a slight shake of the head. As an experienced and very capable bodyguard, he's not letting me out of his sight.

What happens next is almost imperceptible, but I am Andy the Great Perceiver, so I pick up all of it. The two large guys on the porch start to move toward Marcus, who, even though he's not looking at them, senses it and turns slightly toward them. He does so with an understated intensity that literally stops them in their tracks, as if somebody yelled, "Freeze."

Wallace, apparently in my class as a perceiver of subtlety, observes it too. He's smart enough to know that Marcus is not going to obey a guy standing on the street in a dress, so he decides to speak to the only people there who will listen to him.

"It is just a misunderstanding," he says to the servants.

"Please confirm with Mrs. Barlow that Mr. Clark's presence will be welcomed."

"Yes, Keeper," says one of them, and he goes inside to do just that. The other one stays behind and stares ominously at Marcus, who seems to avoid shaking in fear. When the first guy comes back with the shocking news that Mrs. Barlow is okay with Marcus, we go in.

Mrs. Barlow and her seventeen-year-old daughter, Madeline, are waiting for us in the foyer. Jeremy mentioned that he met Madeline at school. There is no Mr. Barlow around, and I know from the discovery documents that he died a few years ago.

Both greet us very politely, and each makes a practiced bow to Wallace, accompanied by a "Good afternoon, Keeper." Madeline is then sent off to her room, but I think I detect a slight rolling of her eyes, a move common to teenagers everywhere. It's the first spontaneous sign of humanity I have seen in this town.

The interior of the house is perfectly kept. Everything is meticulously maintained, and although nothing in the house seems to be of any real financial value, the feeling is that each possession is cherished and appreciated by Mrs. Barlow. On some level it makes it even more painful to think that she has lost a daughter to a horrific murder.

"Thank you for agreeing to speak with me," I say.

"The Keeper asked me to," she says, leaving no doubt that there could be no request from the Keeper that she would not rush to grant. This guy has an extraordinary hold over his parishioners.

"I'm representing Jeremy Davidson, the young man accused of the murders. Do you know him?"

She gives a half-nod. "I've spoken with him on the phone . . . I believe twice. We've never met."

"But you know he was your daughter's boyfriend? That they talked of being married?"

"I don't believe that. They were simply friends."

She's either lying or did not exactly have the kind of relationship in which her daughter shared her secrets. "So your daughter never referred to Jeremy as her boyfriend?"

She shakes her head. "No, and Liz was very open with me. If that was the case, I certainly would have known it."

"Did she tell you about Eddie?" I ask.

I see something in her eyes, only for a moment. It isn't a flash quite of fear, but maybe one of concern. She covers it up quickly, but asking her about Eddie, the name that Liz's friends at school said she had mentioned, has definitely gotten a reaction.

"I'm not familiar with anyone named . . . with anyone by that name."

She seems unwilling to even say the name, so I say it for her. "Eddie."

She nods. "Yes."

"Can you tell me the names of any boyfriends Liz ever had?"

Mrs. Barlow glances quickly at Wallace, then looks back at me. "Not really. There was never anyone serious. She was so young." Her last sentence may well be the first honest one she's said to me, and the simple truth that her daughter died so young causes her eyes to fill with tears.

Keeper Wallace sees this and intervenes. "Must you maintain such a focus on this innocent young girl's private life?"

"Did she have a *public* life?" I ask, perhaps too harshly because I'm annoyed. I'm trying to find out why this girl was hacked to death, and this guy thinks I should be asking about her favorite color.

The interview continues, but I get absolutely nowhere. At one point Madeline walks by the open door, and I request permission to speak with her, but Mrs. Barlow and Wallace rebuff me simultaneously. It's a shame, because Madeline looks like the type to say what she thinks.

I thank Mrs. Barlow, and Marcus and I leave. He hasn't said a word the entire time we were in there, but he got as much helpful information out of the session as I did. Zero.

I say good-bye to Wallace, who no doubt assumes I'm leaving his precious town for good. Instead we follow him in our car to the town hall. We all get out of our cars, me holding a manila envelope Calvin gave me, and I can feel Wallace staring at us as Marcus and I enter the building next door, in which I met Drummond.

I head to the office of the town clerk, which I saw on my previous visit. Marcus and I walk in without knocking, and the woman behind the desk seems about to have a stroke when she sees us enter.

"Good afternoon," I say.

"I'm afraid that we don't—," she says, and since it doesn't seem like the rest of the sentence is going to be terribly helpful, I interrupt her.

"We're going to need some records," I say, opening the envelope for her. "This request should speak for itself. We'll need voter rolls, school enrollments, property tax lists . . . things like that. It's all listed here."

She has no idea what to make of this, but she's frightened by it anyway. "I'll have to speak to Mr. Drummond."

I smile agreeably. "No problem. Just let me know when the information is ready, and I'll come pick it up."

Marcus and I leave, and I call Sam Willis on my cell phone. He seems happy to hear from me, and even more so when I tell him I need his help. Sam is a computer genius and can hack his way into any computer worth hacking into. It's not always legal, but very often necessary.

Sam has helped me out with computer investigations in

the past, and he enjoys doing so. He sees himself as Kojak with a keyboard. I always pay him for his efforts, but he would most definitely do it for nothing.

Sam is also a master at song-talking, and since he does it at every possible opportunity, proudly describing my "Town Without Pity" conversation with Laurie would only set him off, so I don't. Instead I tell him what I need, which is to hack into both Center City and Wisconsin state computers to get exactly the same information I just requested of the town clerk.

"No problem," he says. "When do you need it?"

"Yesterday morning," I say. "But if that's a problem, I'll take it last night."

"I'm on the case," he says.

"Can you do it without them letting you know you've been in their computers?"

"Duhhhh," he says, as a way of letting me know that he can certainly do that, and it was stupid of me to ask.

"Gotcha," I say. "Call me when you've made some progress, Sam . . ."

"Hey, wait a minute, don't get off yet. I haven't talked to you in weeks."

He's right; I've been so busy I haven't had time to even contact any of my friends. "Sorry," I say, "what's doing?"

"Things here are fine," he says. "How are things in Wisconsin? Nice women?"

"Nice women?" I repeat, to make sure I heard correctly. "Yes, very nice. Very nice women."

"That's what I figured," he says. "I mean, East Coast girls are hip, I really dig those styles they wear. And the southern girls with the way they talk, they knock me out when I'm down there."

"Bye, Sam," I say, cutting him off before he can tell me

that the Midwest farmers' daughters will really make me feel all right. He is an incorrigible song-talker.

Marcus and I no sooner arrive back at the house than we receive a faxed letter from Stephen Drummond, refusing our request for the information asked of the town clerk. He cites the town citizens' right to confidentiality, which means he must think that I, having not gone to Harvard, am a legal idiot.

I turn to Marcus. "Do I look like a legal idiot to you?"

"Unhh," says Marcus.

"I'll take that as a no."

● ● ● ● ●

CALVIN HAS ALREADY prepared the motion, called a writ of mandamus, and we file it with the court less than an hour after receiving the refusal by Stephen Drummond to provide the documents. Included in the motion is a claim that the documents are crucial to our preparation of an adequate defense for Jeremy, and we have an expectation that this claim will prompt Judge Morrison to act quickly.

He acts even more quickly than we expected and notifies the parties that he will hear arguments on Monday morning. That gives me an entire weekend to both prepare for the hearing and further familiarize myself with every aspect of the overall case. I'm also going to watch a significant amount of college and pro football. Laurie is working both days, so it will be a guys' weekend, and I'll be the only guy participating in it.

I call my bookmaker back in New Jersey to bet on the college football games. It's the first time I've spoken to him in more than a month. "Where the hell have you been?" he asks.

I can tell how concerned he is about my well-being, and it's all I can do to hold back the tears. I place a bet against Wisconsin, sort of my way of getting back at the state for my confinement here. They're playing Michigan State, but I would have bet against them if they were playing the Bonfire Girls.

Of course, Wisconsin rolls up four hundred yards on the ground and wins 38–7, leaving me thoroughly depressed. The only thing worse that could happen takes place a few minutes after the game, when Calvin comes over and tells me that he's taking me to a party. He's dressed ridiculously in gold pants and a green shirt; a sense of fashion is clearly not a requirement for admission to the party.

"A party? Are you insane?" I ask.

"Come on, you've got to get in good with the jury pool."

He's right, of course. It's important that I reduce my posture as an outsider and become more accepted by this community before the trial. But that doesn't mean I have to like it.

The party is at the home of Shelby and Tom Lassiter, and Calvin is going because Tom is a former client. Calvin informs me that it is something called hot-dish night, a traditional gathering to which everyone brings a hot dish, usually a casserole. The fact that we are bringing no such thing doesn't seem to faze Calvin, so I'm fine with it as well.

When we enter, I see that almost everyone in the house is wearing a green and gold outfit as flamboyantly ugly as Calvin's. It looks like a leprechaun convention, but it turns out that it is in honor of tomorrow's Green Bay Packers game; local residents like to dress in the team colors. As best as I can tell, no one is wearing shoulder pads or a helmet.

Three women stand together off to the side, and they seem to be staring at us. I point that out to Calvin, who says, "Those are my three ex-wives. They call themselves the merry widows."

"But you're not dead," I say.

He nods. "They live in hope."

Shelby Lassiter comes over to inquire as to whether we

want a drink, though she doesn't seem interested in what type of drink we might want. Moments later we are holding glasses of peppermint schnapps, which doesn't taste half bad. I try to picture Vince and Pete back at Charlie's drinking peppermint schnapps; they would sooner sip Drāno on the rocks.

The house we're in is not particularly large, but people keep streaming in. Three couples come in together, probably in their late thirties, and look around the room, waving and nodding hello. I turn my attention away from them, but look back a couple of minutes later when I hear loud and apparently angry talking. I can't make out most of what they are saying, but the word "murderer" comes through loud and clear.

The rest of the people in the room look as if they are watching a tennis match, glancing first at the commotion, than at Calvin and me, and back and forth, back and forth. It's making me uncomfortable, but Calvin seems unconcerned, even amused.

"I've got a feeling there are detractors in our midst," I say to Calvin.

He nods. "Story of my life." Then, "The tall guy that's the most upset is Donnie Kramer. He's got twin daughters at the university."

I understand immediately. "And we're the defenders of a guy who slashed his daughters' classmates to death."

He laughs. "Well, when you put it that way, I'm not that crazy about us either."

I find myself torn between wanting to leave because of the problems our presence is creating, and wanting to leave because the party is so insufferably boring. "I think we should go," I say.

"Leaving now in the face of this intolerance would violate every principle I hold dear," he says.

"There's a late college game on ESPN," I say. "And I've got a refrigerator full of beer."

"I'll get the coats," he says.

Thus begins twenty-four hours of almost nonstop football watching and beer drinking. Calvin is the perfect couch potato companion; I even feel comfortable allowing him to handle the remote control. Higher praise I cannot bestow on a fellow human.

But all good things must come to an end, and on Monday morning we find ourselves in the courtroom, prepared to argue our motion to get Center City to turn over the information we have requested. At the opposing counsel's table is not Lester, but Stephen Drummond.

Drummond is smarter and taller than Lester, but Lester has a better case. As a smart lawyer, Drummond must know that, but he no doubt feels that he has to go through the motions for his client. His client is Center City, and that client wants to maintain its privacy.

Morrison asks for oral arguments, and since it is our motion, I go first. For the record I list the documents we are requesting and then cite the Wisconsin Development of Public Access law. It is the state version of the Freedom of Information Act, and the writ we have filed basically insists that the government officials in Center City abide by it.

While there is virtually no question that we will prevail as a matter of law, my greater concern is to get the documents immediately. "Your Honor," I say, "Center City is basically a closed society. I have only been able to secure one interview with anyone in the town, and that was a supervised session. Yet the victims were from Center City, and it is crucial that I be able to examine various aspects of their life there. That task, difficult as it is, is made infinitely harder by our not even knowing who it is we're not reaching. Yet the unlawful withholding of these documents does just that."

Judge Morrison asks Drummond to respond, and he stands to do so. "Your Honor, Mr. Carpenter refers to our community as a closed society. Yet I drove here from there this morning, and I did not have to pass through any gates or walls or fences to do so. I am confident the same will be true on my return.

"I would submit to you that our society is not closed. It is private, and its people cherish that privacy. That has never been more true than now, when two of our children have been brutally taken from us. Now, when media people that had heretofore never heard of us shove microphones in our faces and ask us to proclaim our grief and anger.

"Mr. Carpenter has a job to do, a job we respect, but our citizens have no obligation to help him do it. We ask that you preserve our privacy by denying his request."

It's an impressive speech, but one that runs head-on into the law, which is firmly in our corner. Judge Morrison is thoroughly aware of this and rules in our favor.

The crucial moment for us comes when Drummond asks the judge for injunctive relief, which would consist of his delaying implementation of his order so as to give Center City time to appeal to a higher court. This would effectively negate our victory, since an appeals court would not act nearly as quickly.

The judge turns to me. "Mr. Carpenter?"

"We are absolutely opposed to that, Your Honor, and we believe the law could not be clearer on this. In the interests of full disclosure, I should point out that if there is a delay in our receiving these documents, we will be seeking a continuance in the Davidson case of the same length as the delay."

Game, set, and match. There is no way that Morrison wants the Davidson trial delayed, and he turns Drummond down flat. He instructs Drummond to give the documents to the court clerk within seventy-two hours. The clerk will then examine them to make sure they comply with the order. Assuming they do, he'll turn them over to us.

Drummond does not seem crushed by the news, and after Morrison adjourns the session he comes over to me and shakes my hand. "Nicely done, Mr. Carpenter, but ultimately futile."

"How so?"

"We are what we are, and no court can change that. So now you will know our names, just as we know yours. And you will know where we live, just as we know where you live."

That sounds vaguely like a threat, but I'm not at all sure. "Is that a threat?" I ask.

He laughs. "A threat? Certainly not." With that he gathers his papers and leaves.

Calvin has overheard the exchange and comes over to me. "The scumbag was threatening you. You gotta tell the judge."

"There's nothing he can do. It wasn't that overt."

Calvin is incredulous. "'We know where you live' isn't overt enough for you? He sounded like Michael Corleone."

I decide not to tell the judge, since there's essentially nothing he can do. He might help in providing police protection, but if I want that, I can go straight to Laurie. My going to the judge might also get back to Drummond, and I don't want to give him the satisfaction of knowing that he frightened me, even a little. Which he did.

Besides, I have Marcus, and I plan to ask him to watch over me even more closely from now on.

I spend the rest of the afternoon visiting Jeremy at the jail and then taking Tara for a walk. I briefly wonder if I'm being unfair to Tara by keeping her in Wisconsin so long. Maybe she misses home, the sights and smells, and the neighborhood dogs. Maybe I'm being selfish assuming she's happy just to be where I am. I make a mental note to speak to her about it.

When I get home, I call Laurie at her office and ask if she'd like to have dinner tonight. She jumps at the opportunity but balks slightly when I suggest we go out to a restaurant. She's still feeling uncomfortable with exhibiting our relationship publicly, so we compromise and decide on a restaurant in Warren, about twenty-five minutes away, out past Center City.

During the ride I bring her up-to-date on our progress, or lack of it. I have no qualms about doing so; she can be trusted implicitly. Besides, we basically have the same interest: If there's a bad guy other than Jeremy, we want to catch him.

The restaurant is called the Barn and is just that, a fairly large, spacious barn converted into a cozy restaurant, with six wood-burning fireplaces positioned throughout and sawdust on the floor. I like it as soon as I walk in, and that feeling increases when I see the TV monitors along the walls showing basketball games. Add the jukebox playing U2 in the background, and it's a fair bet that I've found my restaurant of choice in Wisconsin.

Laurie is staring at me as we walk in, watching my reaction. When I notice her doing so, she smiles. "Not bad, huh?"

There's no way I'm going to admit that Wisconsin has anything worthwhile about it, so I say, "It's not Charlie's; I can tell you that."

"That's my open-minded Andy. Wait until you taste the hamburgers and fries."

The waitress takes our drink orders and within minutes comes back with my Bloody Mary. It's got three olives and a celery stick, not too spicy, exactly the way I like it.

I order a burger and fries, and as is my policy, I ask the waitress to make sure that the fries are not only well-done, but so burned that they would have to be identified through

dental records. I do this because many places have an irrational resistance to serving their fries extra crispy, and it's
necessary to emphasize it in this way to overcome that resistance. It doesn't always work.

It does this time. The fries are perfect, the burger is thick
and juicy, the pickles crisp and delicious. Laurie continues to
watch my reaction, loving every minute of it. "Admit it, Andy,
this place is perfect."

"Perfect? You must be kidding. It's filthy . . . there's sawdust all over the floor."

But it really is perfect, and being here with Laurie makes
it even more so. I can tell that she feels the same way, because we hardly talk through the entire meal. It's a gift we've
always had together, the ability to go long periods without
saying a word yet remaining totally connected.

After dinner we drive back to my house, take Tara for a
quick walk, then settle down with a glass of wine and a DVD
of *Ray*. I didn't see it when it came out, despite the fact that
I am a huge Ray Charles fan. Jamie Foxx's performance
blows me away, as it did everyone else.

The movie ends, and Laurie takes me by the hand and
leads me to the bedroom. It's the perfect end to a perfect
evening, and in the moments after we make love and before
she falls asleep, Laurie says, "Andy, is there any chance this
trial can last forever?"

"I'll just keep asking for continuances," I say. "And even
if we win, I'll ask for a penalty phase, just for fun, to see what
would have happened."

She smiles groggily. "Good boy."

● ● ● ● ●

THE PHONE WAKES us just before midnight. I answer it, and an official-sounding voice I don't recognize asks for "Acting Chief Collins." That's quite a coincidence, since at this very moment I'm sleeping with an Acting Chief Collins. It's a requirement for Acting Chief Collins and all other officers that they leave word as to where they can be reached at all times. It must be somewhat uncomfortable for her to have to leave my number, but she has done so.

I hand the phone to Laurie, whose voice sounds wide awake and does not betray the fact that she has been sleeping. "Collins here."

She listens for a few moments, then says, "I'll be right there." She hangs up and immediately starts to get dressed. I like watching her get dressed; it's my second favorite thing to watch, with her getting undressed maintaining a comfortable lead in first place.

"What happened?" I ask.

"Some kind of traffic accident. Car on Highway 11 went off the road."

"And the chief has to go out to handle a traffic accident?"

She shrugs. "It's a small town, Andy. And it must be a bad accident."

Laurie's out of the house within ten minutes, and I'm back asleep within eleven. As I doze off, I realize that I might not be a good chief of police. If I got woken up by a call informing me of a traffic accident, I would tell them to call AAA and I'd go back to sleep.

The clock says that I've been asleep for two hours when I hear Laurie come back into the house. She hadn't said she was coming back, and I'm pleased that she chose to. I slide over to give her room to get into bed when I realize the person entering the house could be Marcus. I slide back, just in case.

I turn on the light and am relieved to see that it is Laurie entering the bedroom. That relief is short-lived when I see her face; I know this woman well, and I know that something is wrong. Horribly wrong.

"Andy, I've got something to tell you," she says.

"What is it? What's the matter?"

"It's Calvin Marshall. He's dead."

Her words hit me like a punch in the side of the head. A punch so jarring it feels like it could have been thrown by Marcus. "How?" is the longest sentence I can muster.

"Get dressed," she says. "I'll tell you on the way."

"On the way where?"

"To the scene."

Once we're in the car, Laurie says, "His car went off the road and down an embankment. His neck was apparently snapped on impact."

"I see," I say, even though I don't.

"You think that might be too easy an explanation?" she asks.

I nod. "Perhaps a tad."

"You don't believe in coincidences? You don't think it's

likely that a lawyer investigating a recent murder who is himself suddenly killed might be the victim of a tragic accident?"

"I don't," I say, "and you don't either."

"Why do you say that?" she asks.

"Because you're taking me to the scene. You think I should see it, which means you don't think it's an accident."

We're quiet the rest of the way, which is a relief. I need to clear my head, to push aside the pain as best I can, and to think.

The place where Calvin's car went off the road is twenty minutes west of Findlay, about ten minutes from the town of Carwell. As we approach, I see Laurie sag, as the sadness hits her in waves. "I've known Calvin since I was a kid," she says.

"I've only known him a few weeks," I say. "But it didn't take long to know he was funny and smart and a lunatic, and a good guy to be around. I really liked him."

The scene of Calvin's death is still a busy place. I count four state police cars, one Findlay police car besides Laurie's, an ambulance, a county coroner van, and two tow trucks.

We get out, and Laurie leads me down to where Calvin's car went off the road. It's not a particularly treacherous turn, and although it's only partially lit, I don't see skid marks. I assume Calvin hadn't been drinking—he was smarter than that—so it doesn't seem a very likely place for an accident.

Laurie notices me noticing this. "Strange, huh?" she asks, not really expecting an answer. "Come on."

She leads me down to where Calvin's car landed. The coroner's people are in the process of removing his body, which I studiously manage to look away from. I'm squeamish in general, but particularly so when it comes to criminal defense attorneys dying in the course of doing their jobs. And even more particularly when those criminal defense attorneys are close friends.

"Is your coroner competent to handle this?" I ask, even

though Dr. Peters—Clem—seemed knowledgeable when he testified at the hearing.

Laurie shakes her head. "Not really. So we ask the local veterinarian, Doc McCoy, to help out. And if he's not in, the pharmacist takes care of it." She stares at me. "Asshole."

I look around from the outskirts of the scene as Laurie goes off and confers with the state cops. It gives me more time to reflect on the tragedy of Calvin's death and how much I'm going to miss him.

It also gives me a chance to do some well-deserved self-flagellation. I called in Marcus to protect myself from the people that seemed to violently want to avenge the murders of the two girls. Probably because the break-in and the hanging figure were at my house, I assumed I was the target. It didn't enter my self-centered mind that Calvin was also Jeremy's lawyer and that he might need protection as well. And now he's dead, his neck broken, while I had a nice dinner and then snuggled up in bed with Laurie.

The more I think about it, the more I'm literally in danger of throwing up.

Laurie spends another half hour making sure that things are handled correctly. She and the state cops are treating it as a crime scene, even though that hasn't been close to being scientifically established. But it eventually will be established; I have no doubt about that.

Laurie drives me back home, and it's about five o'clock in the morning when we get there. She's going to her office to do some paperwork, so she just drops me off. As I'm getting out of the car, she takes my hand and holds it, for maybe thirty seconds, and we are completely connected, sharing the sadness that we both feel.

I enter the house, and Tara comes over and nuzzles her head against me. She has an unerring ability to know when

I need comforting; unfortunately, this time it's an assignment that even she can't handle.

I go into the kitchen to make myself a drink, and I see that the phone machine is flashing, telling me that I have a message. It could have come in at any time; I never checked it when I got home from the restaurant with Laurie.

I press play, and with the first words I get a chill down my spine. The voice belongs to Calvin.

"Hey, hotshot. You're probably out doing whatever the hell you bilegged people do to have fun. Well, don't worry, 'cause I'm on the case. I've got a lead on our boy Eddie, and I was gonna let you come watch a master in action. I'll call and update you when I get back."

Calvin never updated me because he never got back. He died following a lead, working on our case, while I was out having dinner. And he probably got his neck broken for his trouble, just about the time I was having dessert.

Sometimes I make myself sick.

• • • • •

THE FUNERAL SERVICE to honor Calvin
attracts just about everyone in Findlay, Lester Chapman being
a notable exception. Calvin's family consisted only of one
brother, who has flown in from California, and he and five of
Calvin's closest friends tell humorous and poignant anec-
dotes about his life.

Calvin's three ex-wives, the ones he referred to as the
merry widows, are here and sitting together. They're all softly
sobbing, and all in all don't look very merry.

One of the nonhumorous moments comes when one of
Calvin's friends describes how he lost his leg in combat in
Vietnam, an episode that earned him the Silver Star. Apparently, his bone cancer story was just as fake as his mountain
boulder story. I find myself hoping that his death is one of
his more elaborate lies and he'll show up and laugh at us for
buying it. Unfortunately, he doesn't make an appearance, at
least not today.

The media are back out in full force, covering the funeral
as a major news event. I'm always amazed at how quickly
media people can mobilize themselves to appear when
something happens; I have this image of them as firefighters,

waiting for a phone call to propel them down their poles and onto their vans.

The reason they are here is that they don't think Calvin's death was an accident any more than Laurie and I do. Actually, they don't have the slightest idea how or why Calvin died, but murder sells a hell of a lot more newspapers and generates far higher ratings than a simple automobile accident.

Laurie and her fellow officers are on duty at the funeral so as to ensure that there is no additional violence. I've asked her to update me on the progress of her investigation into Calvin's death, but she has properly told me I have to go through Lester or the court. At this point those reports would not be due us in discovery because it has not been established that the death is related to the Jeremy Davidson case.

Marcus surprises me by attending the funeral with me. He does so, according to Laurie, not for my protection, but to show his respect for Calvin. It's a nice gesture, and I appreciate it on Calvin's behalf.

Marcus and I walk back to the house, and I realize how dramatically the landscape of this small town has changed. It seems like every few hundred feet there is a television truck with a satellite on its roof, and newscasters are stopping townspeople and interviewing them on the street. They want their opinion as to whether Calvin's death was really accidental and their view of Jeremy's guilt or innocence. They're after local opinions, and they're in luck, because everybody has one.

As we approach the house, I am stunned to see Kevin, my associate, standing on the porch. At least I think it's Kevin; he's buried under so much clothing that he's twice his normal size, and round in shape. It's almost as if someone put an air hose up his ass. It's maybe thirty degrees, and I've

gotten used to the weather, but apparently, the hypochondriac Kevin is worried about catching a cold.

"I heard about what happened to . . . ," he starts.

"Calvin," I say.

He nods. "Calvin. And I thought you might need some
help."

Kevin has made the kind of terrific gesture that only a
good friend would make, but one that immediately triggers
my overactive guilt gland. "What about Carol and the wedding?" I ask. "And then the honeymoon?"

"I asked Carol to marry me. She said no."

"Gee, I'm sorry, Kev. Maybe she'll change her mind."

He shakes his head. "After she said no, she said 'never.' "

"She said 'never'?"

He nods. "Right before she said 'not in a million years.'
So I was thinking I should come here and pitch in . . . if you
want me."

Kevin is a terrific attorney; there's no question that I want
him, and I tell him so. But I remind him about the pitfalls,
like the need to be rather flexible with our fee structure and
the fact that the person he's replacing was killed while doing
his job. None of this deters him, so I welcome him on board.

"But, Kev, it's not winter yet. You might not need quite
so much clothing. This is Wisconsin in October . . . not the
Russian front in January."

"It's a preemptive action," he says. "If I catch a cold early
in the season, I have it all winter. Remember how much I
was sneezing last year?"

I don't remember anything about his sneezing, but I don't
want to hurt him by saying so, so I nod. "That was a nightmare," I say.

We go into the house, and Kevin begins to describe in ex-
cruciating detail his other cold-prevention measures. When
he starts listing the different forms of zinc he takes, Marcus,

who has barely said a word since Kevin arrived, shakes his head and goes upstairs.

"Marcus is staying here?" Kevin asks.

"Yes."

"Have you got room for me as well?"

This is getting worse by the day; pretty soon the house is going to need a resident adviser. "Sure. There's an extra bedroom next to his."

"I'm going to need to keep the house at a minimum of seventy-two point five degrees," he says. "For my sinuses. Are you going to be okay with that?"

"Seventy-two point five?" I ask.

He nods. "Minimum."

"Okay with me," I say. "But why don't you clear it with Marcus?"

• • • • •

THE FAX MACHINE in the kitchen is already going full blast when I wake up in the morning. As I walk toward it, I notice that Kevin is wearing an overcoat while cooking breakfast, and one of the windows is open. My guess is that Marcus didn't think much of his 72.5 temperature plan.

Marcus, meanwhile, sits shirtless at the kitchen table, drinking an entire pitcher of orange juice without seeming to pause to swallow.

I feel like I'm in a fraternity house: Phi Loony Toony.

I check the fax coming in and am not surprised that Sam has once again come through, providing us with copies of the same documents that we're scheduled to receive from Stephen Drummond. Right now they're of no value to us, but when Drummond provides us with his, we'll be ready to swing into action.

Word has come from Lester that he will not provide us with investigative reports on Calvin's death in discovery, claiming, as I anticipated, that it is not related to Jeremy's case. Judge Morrison has agreed to my request for an urgent hearing on the matter, and it's been scheduled for three o'clock this afternoon.

For breakfast Kevin and I eat the five percent of the food
that Marcus leaves behind, and then we continue the process
of familiarizing ourselves with every bit of the prosecution
evidence. More discovery documents are coming in every
day, and the new ones are the ones I read. Kevin, since he
just arrived, has started from the beginning.

Very often discovery documents contain an item that is
understated so as to seem an insignificant fact, yet it will turn
out to be a key part of the prosecution's case. It is for that
reason that I must know everything before I enter the courtroom; there must be absolutely no chance that I will be surprised.

It is while I'm reading through a new statement by one
of the people at the bar the night of the murder that I find
something that troubles me. I take Kevin and we drive out to
the bar, which I have visited twice before. It is basically midway between Center City and Findlay.

We park in the lot and get out, taking the statements with
us, so that we can re-create in our minds what took place.

"Jeremy's truck was here," I say, "and Liz's car was parked
over there."

"Right. Under the light." He adds that last fact because
Jeremy said he couldn't see who was in the car with her, yet
the prosecution will use the presence of the light to try to dis-
credit that.

"So she gets out of the car and comes over here, they talk,
then argue, and she leaves. Then, according to Jeremy, he
debates whether to go into the bar and get drunk, decides
against it, and goes home." I point. "Which is that way."

"Shit," Kevin says, realizing what I'm getting at.

I hold up one of the statements. "But Stacy Martin of Lancaster says she was leaving the parking lot at the same time
as Jeremy and that she drove off behind him, going west." I
point in the opposite direction that I pointed before.

"Which is towards Lancaster and Center City," Kevin says.

If Stacy Martin is correct, then Jeremy did not drive back to Findlay.

If Stacy Martin is correct, Jeremy Davidson lied to his lawyer.

Me.

Kevin and I go back to Jeremy's house to look around there again. I had always been vaguely troubled by the fact that the bodies had been buried out behind the house, with the only access road to that area being in the front. Yet Jeremy, who claimed to have been home, never heard a thing.

My point of view on this was that the bodies may well have been put there the next day, when Jeremy might not have been home. Jeremy's apparent lie about where he went after leaving the bar raises two more possibilities: Jeremy did not hear anything because he wasn't at home that night, or Jeremy was the one doing the burying.

Richard Davidson is home when we get there, and I ask to look around inside, while Kevin does so outside. Davidson seems surprised by the sudden request, especially since I've been there before. "Anything new?" he probes.

"Nothing much . . . just going over things again. Where is Jeremy's bedroom?"

"In the guesthouse, second floor. But you can't go in there now . . . it's not stable."

The Davidsons haven't started rebuilding the damaged guesthouse from the firebombing, so I walk outside of where Jeremy's window was. I can clearly see Kevin, perhaps seventy-five yards away, standing near the area where the bodies were buried. This makes it even less likely that Jeremy was home and didn't notice anything going on.

Kevin and I leave without sharing our concerns with Richard, and we head down to the jail to meet with Jeremy.

He is brought into the meeting room, and a guard remains posted outside.

"What's going on?" Jeremy asks, hopeful as always.

This is no time for small talk. "You didn't drive home from the bar that night. You drove to Center City." I don't know if that last part is true, but since it's a worst case, I say it as if I know for sure, to see how he will react.

I can see a flash of panic in his eyes. "What are you talking about? I told you, I—"

"This isn't a debate, Jeremy. I know where you went. What I want you to tell me is why you went there and why you lied about it."

He seems about to argue that point again and then sits back, as if defeated. I am going to hate what he has to say.

"I did go to Center City. I wanted to talk to Liz again."

"What did you do when you got there?"

"I parked about six blocks from her house, because I figured if I just drove up, her mother would call the police and throw me out. I walked the rest of the way."

"Did anybody see you?"

He shakes his head. "I don't think so. People don't stay up real late in that town. Liz used to tell me that the last show at the movie theater was at seven o'clock at night, and—"

I'm not really in the mood to hear about movie night in Center City, so I cut him off. "How did you know where her house was?" I ask, since Mrs. Barlow told me she never met him.

"Liz took me there once . . . she just wanted to show me where she lived. I actually had to crouch down in the car so her mother wouldn't be able to see me as we drove by."

"What did you do when you got to her house?"

"Her car wasn't there, so I waited. I hid behind some bushes," he says with apparent embarrassment.

"How long did you wait?" I ask.

He shrugs. "Probably a few hours. Hey, I know it sounds stupid, but the longer she wasn't there, the more upset I got. That's why I figured she was with her ex-boyfriend, and he probably wasn't 'ex' anymore."

This is a disaster. Not only will Lester be able to show that Jeremy's statement to the police contained a very significant, material lie, but the truth is very incriminating. The defendant hid in the bushes waiting for the murder victim, growing more and more upset, jealous and angry over her betraying him with another man. The only way this statement could be worse is if he said he stopped to pick up a machete on the way to her house.

I make eye contact with Kevin, and his look confirms that he thinks this is just as bad as I do. Since eye contact has never been my specialty, Jeremy notices it. "Hey, I'm sorry. I shouldn't have lied, but I was scared, and I figured it would look bad if I told the police where I really was."

I give my standard stern lecture to Jeremy about the devastating consequences of lying to one's attorney, but it's a halfhearted speech. I will never fully trust him again and will always be worried that there's another freight train coming around the next bend. His lie doesn't make him a murderer, but it certainly makes it more likely he will be convicted as one.

But what are we worried about? We're in great shape. After all, in less than two months we've already discovered that there is probably somebody in Center City named Eddie.

We're the kind of lawyers you'd mortgage the farm for.

• • • • •

IRONICALLY, THE MOST fertile

ground for our investigation might well be Calvin's death. I doubt very much that it was accidental, because I simply don't believe in those kinds of coincidences. If Calvin was murdered, it was almost certainly in the pursuit of exculpatory information for Jeremy; if that information did not exist, then Calvin would not have been a threat.

In any event, the hearing that Judge Morrison convenes is crucially important to our case, and when he calls on me to speak, I tell him so.

I basically repeat what is in the brief that Kevin wrote and submitted. I end with, "In conclusion, the defense believes that the death of Calvin Marshall might well be relevant to the matter before this court, but it is only through discovery that we can test our theory."

Judge Morrison peers down at Lester. "Mr. Chapman?"

"Your Honor, the statute could not be more clear on this matter. The defense is entitled to all investigative work done on this case relating to the murders for which the defendant is to be tried. They do not have license to receive police documents for anything else that they believe might somehow be relevant. Where would that end? Would they be entitled to examine every crime committed in this county in the hope that it would somehow tie in to their case? At this point in time, pending further investigation, I simply do not see the relevance."

Morrison turns to me, and I stand up again. "Your Honor, there has not been a murder prior to this case in Findlay in eight years. In those same eight years, only four murders have been reported in the entire county. Yet the lawyer for this defendant dies under suspicious circumstances while pursuing evidence in this very case. This is not a fishing expedition, and if Mr. Chapman cannot see the possible relevance, he is the Stevie Wonder of prosecutors."

Lester jumps to his feet. "Your Honor, I resent the personal attack in that comparison."

"Think how Stevie would feel," I say.

Morrison comes down hard on both of us, but I bear the brunt of it. When he's finished, he turns back to Lester.

"Mr. Chapman, have you reviewed the police reports in question?"

"Yes, Your Honor, in order to prepare for this hearing."

"Is the investigation into Mr. Marshall's death concluded?"

Lester shakes his head. "Certainly not, Your Honor. It's barely begun."

"So it's not definitive in its conclusions?" the judge asks.

"For the most part, no."

"I will look at the reports in camera. If I consider them relevant to this case, I will turn them over to the defense."

This is a win for us; in a major case of this kind the judge will bend over backward not to handicap the defense. He will only keep the documents from us if they are absolutely no help at all, in which case we wouldn't want them anyway.

"Thank you, Your Honor, that is quite satisfactory to our side. I would further request that if you do provide them to us, that you also see to it that we get all subsequent documents as the investigation proceeds."

He nods. "I'll make that determination when I see the materials, which you will provide forthwith, Mr. Chapman."

Lester gives a combination nod and sigh. "Certainly, Your Honor."

We've got what we wanted, but on some level it bothers me that Calvin's death has now become part of our case strategy.

I've always considered myself a semi-hermit; I have my small group of friends and no desire to expand that circle. Yet events caused me to meet and get to know Calvin, and though it may sound corny, that relationship has enriched my life. How many other millions of people are out there that could do the same, if I'd only let them? It's causing me to reevaluate how I should live my life, and I'm thinking I should make some changes. I'm sure I ultimately won't, but right now I'm thinking that I should.

I would love to stay and torture Lester some more, but the clerk tells me that the Drummond documents have been delivered to our house, so I want to hurry back to compare them to those that Sam faxed us.

As soon as we get home, we lay them in front of us and start to compare. It's a time-consuming process. I literally call out a name from Drummond's documents, and Kevin tells me if it matches the documents Sam faxed us. On the voter registration list there are two instances where Sam's copies have a name not on Drummond's, and one case where a name on Drummond's list does not appear on Sam's. None of them are named Eddie, Liz's mysterious boyfriend.

The property owner list yields two discrepancies, neither obviously significant. We're halfway through the motor vehicle records when Kevin, reading from Sam's list, says, "Edmond Carson, born 1985."

I check twice to make sure, but there is no such person on Drummond's list.

Edmond Carson, missing from Drummond's list, and the right age to be Liz's ex-boyfriend.

Eddie.

It's a sad commentary on the state of our case that we're so excited about the fact that we may have discovered the name of the victim's ex-boyfriend, who probably knows nothing about her murder. But it's all we've got right now, and we've got to pursue it as vigorously as we can.

I've had enough experience with Center City to know that it will not be terribly productive for me to go there and ask, "Can Eddie come out to play?" So Kevin and I head down to the police precinct to try to get Laurie's help.

Laurie is not in her office when we arrive, and we wait almost an hour for her to get back. When I start to tell her why we're there, she tells me to wait until she calls in Cliff Parsons. As the cop assigned to Center City, he certainly should be included, but that's not why Laurie calls him in. She's still very sensitive to how things between us will look to both local government officials and citizens alike, so if she's going to help us, she wants to do it out in the open.

I'm not a big fan of Parsons, mostly because he's good-looking, single, and around Laurie all day. I also don't like the fact that he is not particularly deferential to her, despite her higher rank. She tolerates it, explaining that sensitivities being what they are, she doesn't want to start her time as acting chief by being too heavy-handed.

To his credit, Parsons does not seem particularly annoyed that I embarrassed him on the witness stand during the preliminary hearing. He behaves professionally; if I got under his skin, he's hiding it well. I can add this to the reasons I don't like him.

I lay out what we've learned about the apparent deception by Drummond in the documents, and Parsons's first question is, "Why not take this to Judge Morrison?"

"Because there's nothing he can do that will help us. He could reprimand Drummond, he could even hold him in contempt, but it won't get us any closer to Eddie. And Drummond will just say it was a clerical error, and that will be that. But we'll have tipped him off on what we've learned."

"So what are you asking us to do?" asks Laurie.

"To locate Eddie," I say. "We can't make him talk to us, but he'll talk to you. The Centurions are very careful to pretend to cooperate with outside authorities."

"We're not your investigators," Parsons says. "You can't send us out to conduct interviews."

I know Laurie's being careful to remain independent and impartial in front of Parsons, but it's starting to annoy me that she isn't cutting him off. "We are talking about a young man who is very possibly a material witness in a murder investigation," I say. "I've got reams of paper turned over in discovery on interviews you conducted in that town. You probably talked to fifty people. Why would you refuse to talk to one more, when that person is apparently being deliberately hidden from you and from us?"

Laurie asks Kevin and me to wait outside for a few minutes, and when we're let back in, she tells us that she and Parsons have agreed to look for Eddie. Obviously, she's asserted her will but didn't want to do so in front of us. She and Parsons will drive to Center City right after lunch without calling ahead and alerting Drummond and the others as to what is going on.

"But you should know that I'll be informing the district attorney about this," Laurie says. "A report will be prepared for him when our interviews are concluded."

I'm not happy about this, but it is unavoidable. Laurie has an obligation to keep the prosecuting attorney updated on all aspects of this ongoing investigation. Not to do so would be to abdicate her responsibility, and she is too good a cop for that.

A plus is her comment that he will receive the report when the interviews are concluded. To tell him in advance would be an invitation for him to intervene and possibly find a way to derail things.

• • • • •

KEVIN AND I PLAN to hang around the
house for the rest of the afternoon, waiting for word from
Laurie about her Center City visit in search of Eddie. Marcus
is not in the house; I can tell simply by the temperature.
When Marcus is home, the windows are open and it is cold
enough to hang meat in here; when he is out, Kevin main-
tains his 72.5 degrees.

The investigative reports into Calvin's death arrive around
one o'clock; Judge Morrison has obviously decided they are
relevant to our case.

I read the summary page, which contains the conclusion
that Calvin's broken neck was the cause of death, but that it's
unlikely it was caused by the impact of the car hitting the
ground. If this is true, it's significant news for our side.

I place a call to Janet Carlson, the best medical examiner
in New Jersey and the best-looking medical examiner in the
entire world. Janet has been incredibly helpful to me since I
did her a favor a number of years ago, and now I'm calling
on her one more time. I tell her that I'd like to fax her the information contained in this report and get her professional
opinion on it.

"Wonderful," she says. "We haven't had nearly enough

deaths to keep us busy here. I was just about to call other states to see if they had any they could lend us."

"Serendipity," I say.

"Whatever," she says.

As always, Janet complains for a few minutes but then agrees to help me out. Kevin starts faxing the documents to her, even while we continue talking. I like Janet a lot, and if I decide that Rita Gordon represented the beginning of my sleeping with every woman in the justice system in New Jersey, Janet is going to be right at the top of my list.

I owe her at least that much.

At about four o'clock a squad car pulls up, and Lieutenant Parsons gets out. He comes inside and gets right to the point. "Chief Collins wanted me to report back to you on what we learned."

It takes me a moment to mentally process that Chief Collins is Laurie, so Kevin jumps in. "And what is that?"

"Well, we interviewed six people familiar with Edmond Carson. All said basically the same thing: that they had not seen him in at least six weeks."

"Did you check his house?" I ask.

He nods. "His apartment. He abandoned it at about the same time that people last saw him. He appears to have left quickly; some of his belongings are still in the apartment. He left without paying the rent that he owed, which was apparently uncharacteristic."

"So no idea where he is?"

Parsons shakes his head. "No idea at all."

"Are Stephen Drummond and Keeper Wallace aware that you are looking for Eddie?" I ask.

He looks at me for a few moments before answering, as if making sure I realize I just asked the dumbest question imaginable. Then, "I believe that is a safe assumption. There is little that goes on in that town that they are not privy to."

Parsons leaves, after claiming that the search for Eddie will remain an open investigation. I certainly respect any police department that Laurie is a member of, but his statement doesn't exactly fill me with optimism. Findlay is a small town with limited resources; we are not talking about the FBI here.

Kevin and I are about to go to the diner when Janet Carlson calls, having gone over the faxed copies of the Findlay coroner's report.

"What did you come up with?" I ask.

"The victim is definitely dead," she says.

"Wow, you big-city coroners are incredible. Anything else you can tell me?"

"The report seems mostly correct. Cause of death is a broken neck . . . the head was twisted clockwise, and death would have been instantaneous."

"Could the impact of the car have been the cause?" I ask.

"Definitely not."

"The report says 'probably not,'" I point out.

"That's because the local ME had to sign his name to it. I don't have to sign, so I say definitely not."

"Keep talking," I say.

"Okay. Falling forward into the steering wheel on impact, even at a tremendous speed and even allowing for the head to be slightly angled when contact is made, could certainly cause a broken neck. But the head would twist at a maximum ninety-degree angle. This head was virtually screwed off, at least two hundred seventy degrees."

"Linda Blair," I say, referring to the head-revolving star of *The Exorcist.*

"Linda Blair," she agrees. "Except her head turned on its own. This one had help."

"What kind of help?"

"A pair of hands. Large, powerful hands."

"Are you sure?" I ask.

"Almost positive. There are certain indentations on the skin, which the local doctor thought might be consistent with the impact of the car. I don't think so; I think they were made by large fingers pressing down very hard. But I would have had to examine the body to be sure."

"Thanks, Janet, I really appreciate it."

"Andy, I understand the victim was an attorney and he was working with you. Just be careful, okay? The person who did this is very strong. And there was no hesitation; the neck was snapped instantly, like a twig."

"How did you know it was an attorney that was killed?"

"I spoke to Laurie. We talk all the time."

It's amazing. For the last four and a half months I thought Laurie had completely cut off from her life and friends in Jersey. It turns out that I seem to be the only one she wasn't speaking to on a regular basis.

• • • • •

DINNER TONIGHT IS more than a little weird.

Laurie comes over and cooks my favorite, *pasta amatriciana*. We sit at the table, Laurie across from me and Kevin across from Marcus. Quite the little family. I half expect Kevin to say to Marcus, "And how was your day today, honey?"

Laurie and I have always tried not to talk about our work during dinner, but we rarely succeed. Tonight, since the entire team is present, we have no chance at all. Laurie is the guilty party this time, when she tells us that "I got Calvin's phone records from the night he died."

"Anything interesting?"

She nods. "And upsetting. He called me at the office."

"Any idea why?"

"Even before I called you and told you about this case, I had spoken to Calvin and expressed my doubts about Jeremy's guilt. I told him that he should call me at any time if he needed my help."

"Did anyone at the precinct speak to him that night?" Kevin asks. He is apparently going to be the designated speaker for him and Marcus, since Marcus's mouth is processing pasta at an unprecedented rate.

"Apparently not," Laurie says. "I have to assume that when he found out I wasn't in, he hung up. The call only lasted about thirty seconds."

I know Laurie is feeling guilt over not having been there for Calvin that night, and I am as well, even though our feelings are irrational. We had no way of knowing he would call that night, and obviously no reason to have waited around for that call. But the fact that Calvin died while we were enjoying a relaxing dinner is locked in our minds, so we can still feel the pain.

After dinner Laurie goes off to answer a duty call, probably a cheese overdose, and Marcus goes wherever it is that Marcus goes. It leaves Kevin and me to kick around our strategy for finding the elusive Eddie Carson.

"Why don't you call Sam Willis?" Kevin asks.

"What for?"

"Maybe he can track the kid down on the Internet. Maybe through credit card usage, or something like that."

It's a very good idea, made even better by the fact that we have no other ideas, so I call Sam.

"So how did it go?" asks Sam when he hears it's me. "Was the stuff I got helpful?"

"Very helpful," I say. "It identified our guy for us, but he's missing. Any chance you could find him online?"

Sam is uncharacteristically dubious about the prospects for doing so. "Theoretically, I could do it, but it would be like looking for a needle in a haystack. I wouldn't know where to look; I would have to stumble onto it."

It's while I'm talking to Sam that I get an idea that could work. I try to get him off the phone quickly, but he asks me about Laurie and how things are going between us.

"They're fine, Sam, but I've—"

"Watch out for yourself, Andy, I mean it. I've been there myself."

"What are you talking about?" I ask.

"Sometimes you have to be the one to end things no matter how tough it seems."

My fear is that he's going to start song-talking and maybe tell me that "breaking up is hard to do." I don't want to be rude, since Sam has been such a big help, but I really want to get off this call.

"Sam . . . ," I start, to no avail.

"I thought I told you about her," he says. "Her name was Margaret . . . we were both twenty, and I was leaving school to run away with her. She drove me crazy."

"Sam, can we talk about this some other time?"

Apparently, we can't, because he continues as if I hadn't said anything. "Things started going sour, my parents were freaking out that I wouldn't graduate, and I wanted to break it off, but I just couldn't bring myself to do it. Then one night I couldn't sleep, and about four o'clock in the morning I got up the nerve."

I give up. "What did you say?"

"I leaned over and said, 'Wake up, Maggie, I think I got something to say to you. It's late September and I really should be back at school.'"

"Bye, Sam."

"Bye, Andy."

Once I'm off the phone, I immediately dial Cindy Spodek at her house in Boston. Cindy is an FBI agent whom I got to know on a previous case. Her boss at the Bureau was directing criminal activities, and Cindy blew the whistle on him. It took considerable courage, and Cindy had to deal with strong internal resistance afterward. She has persevered, moved to the Boston office, and gotten a promotion. I've called on her for a number of favors since, and she's always come through, albeit grudgingly.

"Hello?" she answers, her voice sounding simultaneously groggy and worried. I check my watch and realize that it's eleven-fifteen in Boston.

"Cindy, Andy Carpenter. How are you? Am I calling too late? I forgot what time it is back East."

"Andy . . . yes. Much too late."

"Well, the damage is done. I need a favor."

"That's a major surprise. Can it wait until morning?"

"I suppose so, but I don't want you beating yourself up all night over not helping me when I needed you."

"I can handle the guilt," she says, at which point I hear a man's voice say, "Cindy, who is it?"

She answers him with, "It's for me, honey."

"What 'honey' are you talking to at this hour?" I ask.

"My husband, if that's okay with you. Remember, the wedding was in May? It's the one you didn't come to."

"Right. But I sent a gift."

"No, you didn't."

"Right. But I planned to, which is really what's important."

"Hey," she says, "what do you mean you forgot the time back East? Where are you?"

I tell her about being in Findlay and about taking on the case. All she really cares about is that Laurie and I are in the same town. "So what's going on with you two? Are you back together?"

"You really want to know?" I ask, sensing an opening.

"Of course," she says.

"So listen to my favor, and then I'll tell you about me and Laurie."

"You're a shithead," she says, defeated.

"You got that right," I say, victorious. "Now tell 'honey' to go back to sleep while you help your friend Andy."

I proceed to explain our need to find the elusive Eddie, and ask her whether she can utilize the FBI computers to do so. I know from past experience that if they are tracking someone, they can find out on a moment's notice whenever that person does something that enters a computer anywhere, like using a credit card.

"Are you insane?" she asks. "You think you can use the FBI as your own private investigative agency?"

"You won't believe what's going on with Laurie and me," is my response.

"You think I have nothing better to do than track down your witnesses?" she asks.

"Our life is like an episode of *The Young and the Restless*," I say.

She thinks for a moment. "It better be. What's the guy's name?"

I give her the information, and she agrees to get on it starting tomorrow. "Now tell me about you and Laurie," she says.

"Can't it wait until tomorrow?" I ask.

Suffice it to say that she doesn't feel it can wait, and I spend the next hour describing our situation, stopping every thirty seconds or so to answer questions.

Cindy, like everyone else, has always liked Laurie, and her final question is, "So where is this going to wind up?"

"I wish I knew," I say, understating the case about as much as a case can be understated.

• • • • •

THREE DAYS IS a long time to sit around and watch the temperature drop, but that's basically what we've been doing. It was absolutely freezing when I took Tara out for our walk this morning. It is as if Wisconsin spent these last days hurtling away from the sun, and based on the temperature, we must be passing Pluto about now.

Kevin started sniffling a couple of days ago, which sent him on a mission to find the best ear, nose, and throat man in the area. His task has been made more difficult by the fact that there aren't any ear, nose, and throat men in the area. Kevin has thus been reduced to seeing an internist, but his sniffling is increasing in frequency, as is his complaining about it.

I've heard nothing from Cindy about Eddie's whereabouts, though I've called her twice at her office. Each time she was too busy to come to the phone and had her assistant tell me that when she has anything, she'll let me know.

Laurie is unofficially aware of what is going on, but if I learn anything, I'm going to handle it myself. I have no legal obligation to inform the police of my investigative efforts, and I certainly don't want Lester privy to them. Nor have I told Jeremy or his parents; this has to be done with some discretion.

With nothing else productive to do, I spend my time trying to understand why any of the earliest humans could possibly have chosen this place to live. The planet was barely inhabited . . . they could have settled anywhere. It was before money was invented, so land had to be cheap in places like San Diego. Yet people said no, they'd rather live in some place so cold that frostbite occurs in about eight seconds.

And it's not like winter clothing was particularly advanced back then. Skiing also hadn't been invented yet, so there couldn't have been ski jackets, and I don't know if there was even underwear, no less long underwear. Yet for some reason someone decided that this was the place to be, and the other prehistoric losers followed.

I've always been fascinated by firsts; I like to ponder who made strange initial decisions and why they made them. Who was the first person to try a parachute? Who first looked at a slimy, disgusting raw oyster and decided to chow down on it? And who saw a tobacco plant and figured it would be a good idea to stuff some of the leaves in their mouth and set them on fire?

I probably think about these things as a way of taking my mind off the upcoming trial. It's a defense mechanism, which I need because I have not come up with an actual defense. We're two weeks away from jury selection, and unless we wind up with a jury consisting of twelve of Jeremy's relatives, we're in a lot of trouble.

It's while I'm attempting without success to convince Tara that in this weather she should take herself out for walks that Cindy Spodek calls. She doesn't even take the time to say hello.

"He just used a credit card to get forty bucks at an ATM

in a convenience store. The address is 414 Market Street, Warwick, Wisconsin."

"Thanks," I say. "I'll let you know how we make out."

"I don't know if I can stand the suspense," she says. What could be worse than an FBI wiseass?

"We've got the address," I say to Kevin as I hang up. "It's in Warwick."

He grabs the map we bought for this occasion and opens it on the table in front of us. "It's about a two-hour drive."

I'm already on the way to the door. "Let's go."

"What about Marcus?" he asks.

I can tell by the temperature in the house that Marcus is out. "I don't know where he is. Come on, this is a nineteen-year-old kid we're talking about. You can handle him."

"Me?" he asks. Kevin is about as tough as I am.

"If he gives you a problem, sneeze on him."

Once we're settled in the car and on the way, I have time to reflect on the situation we're in. We're heading to a strange town to find someone, without any idea where he's living or what he looks like. All we know is that he got some cash there; the fact is, he may have just been driving through. Another possibility is that someone else is using his credit card, as a way to throw pursuers like us off the track.

Possibly more problematic is what will happen if we find him. What we know about Eddie is that he was Liz's ex-boyfriend, that he was probably with her the night she and Sheryl were killed, and that he suddenly left Center City shortly after that night. At the very least that makes him a suspect in the murder, which in turn makes him a suspect in Calvin's murder. The first two murders were done with a knife, while Calvin's was apparently done with bare hands. Eddie may wind up being a very scary guy; I should have taken the time to find Marcus.

Halfway to Warwick we pass a lake with a posted sign

heralding this weekend's ice-fishing tournament. It gives me something to do during the drive; I can ponder if there could be anything on this planet more uncomfortable and boring than sitting on the ice with a fishing pole. Do the fish come out already frozen? I think it just might be the one sport that even I wouldn't bet on.

It starts to snow about fifteen minutes outside of Warwick, and it's falling fairly heavily by the time we reach the town. We catch a break when the convenience store where Eddie used the ATM turns out to be one of the first things we see.

We park and enter the store, which is empty except for the clerk behind the counter. He's about fifty, and wears a shirt with the word "Manager" above the pocket, though at the moment he doesn't seem to have much of a staff to manage.

"How ya doing?" I say, chummy as always.

"Fine, thanks," he says. "What can I get you guys?"

I take on the spokesman role, since Kevin seems to be eyeing the Sudafed. "We're looking for a kid, maybe eighteen, nineteen years old, who used that cash machine a little more than two hours ago."

He looks at me warily, trying to figure out what this is about. "Are you police officers?"

"No. We're lawyers, and the young man we're looking for is a potentially crucial witness in a criminal case."

"How do you know he used this cash machine?"

"We were so informed by the FBI," I say, hoping that will sound important enough to get him to tell us what he knows, which may well be nothing.

"I don't want to get in the middle of anything . . . or get anyone in trouble," he says.

"Someone is already in trouble. This young man might be able to help . . . that's all."

He nods. "There was a kid in here around that time . . . he used the machine. He was wearing a Brett Favre jersey." That won't exactly make him stand out in a crowd; here in Wisconsin everybody wears a Brett Favre jersey. The clerk continues. "No coat . . . he must have been freezing to death. That's why I noticed him."

My expectation level immediately triples; Eddie left many of his things in his apartment in Center City. His coat could easily have been one of them.

"Did you talk to him?" Kevin asks with some excitement in his voice. Either he agrees with me that we're getting close to Eddie, or he's hopeful that Warwick has an ear, nose, and throat guy.

"Yeah. I asked him if he was okay. He didn't seem right . . . and it wasn't just not having a coat. I don't know what it was . . . but he was the only customer, and I felt bad for him." This is small-town Wisconsin at its finest; back East the clerk would have reported Eddie for vagrancy.

"Do you know if he lives around here?" I ask.

He shakes his head. "He doesn't. He asked me if there was a cheap place he could stay. He was afraid the roads would get closed because of the storm."

This is rapidly approaching "too good to be true" territory. "Did you recommend a place?"

He nods. "Two of them. The Days Inn out on Route 5 and the Parker Motel."

"Where's that?" I ask.

He points. "Four blocks that way, then make your second right."

Kevin and I both thank him and head for the door. Just before I leave, I stop and ask, "By the way, how big was this kid?"

"Maybe five eight, a hundred and forty-five."

I allow myself a quick sigh of relief; between us, Kevin

and I should be able to handle someone that size. Unless, of course, he has a knife. Or a gun. Or an attitude.

The proximity of the Parker Motel makes that the likely first choice for us to try, so we drive the four blocks and park in front of the office. The two-story place is a borderline dump, and the fact that the sign advertises vacancies is not a major shock.

We enter the small office, which basically consists of a counter and a display with flyers advertising the tourist attractions in the area. There's a coffee machine, which looks like it hasn't been cleaned since the invention of decaf.

There's a girl behind the desk, maybe twenty-one years old and incongruously perky for these surroundings. "Hi, I'm Donna. Welcome to the Parker," she says. "Snowing pretty hard out there, huh?"

The office is mostly glass-enclosed, allowing her to see "out there" quite easily, so I assume the question is rhetorical. "Sure is," I say, trying to keep up the banter level.

"You need a room?"

I explain that we're looking for a guy named Eddie Carson, most recently seen wearing a Brett Favre jersey and no coat. Since the FBI mention worked so well in the convenience store, I trot it out again.

Donna's brow furrows in worry, but she's nothing if not cooperative. "I think I know who you mean . . . but we're not supposed to give out room numbers."

"I'll tell you what," I say as I write Cindy's office phone number on a piece of paper. "Call this number. It's the Boston office of the FBI. Just ask for Agent Spodek, and she'll tell you what to do."

There is as much chance that Donna will call the Boston office of the FBI as there is that she will put on a bikini and go outside and catch some rays. But the offer has its desired effect, and she looks up the room number in her register. "He's in room 207. Second floor, back towards the parking lot."

"Thank you," I say, and Kevin and I go outside. We start walking around toward where the room is when I see a car leave the parking lot at as high a speed as the snow-covered pavement will allow.

"Uh-oh. I've got a bad feeling about this."

We move more quickly toward the room, and my bad feeling is confirmed. The door is open, and no one is inside. Eddie must have been watching our arrival and put two and two together. We should have been far more careful, and by not being so, we let him off the hook. Simply put, he outsmarted us, which doesn't exactly qualify him for a Rhodes scholarship.

A few items of clothing are strewn on the floor, and a toothbrush and toothpaste are on the bathroom sink. Poor Eddie keeps having to leave places in a hurry, and his possessions are dwindling by the moment.

Kevin leans over the balcony and looks in the general direction that Eddie's car went. There is no way we are going to catch him, and the idea of trying holds little appeal for either of us.

For the most part the trip here was a fiasco, and the ride back is going to be an endless one. But one good result is that what we suspected is now a virtual certainty. Eddie either did something bad or knows something important, and it is more crucial than ever that we find him.

• • • • •

SOUNDS LIKE IT wasn't exactly a textbook operation." Laurie is talking about the unsuccessful invasion of the Parker Motel that Kevin and I executed. "If the Mexicans had tried the same approach at the Alamo," she continues, "Davy Crockett would be doing talk shows today."

We're in my house, having just finished dinner, listening to an Eagles CD. Kevin is up in his room practicing his sneezing, and as always I have no idea where Marcus is.

Laurie and I are in our favorite spot, sitting on the couch and simultaneously petting Tara. If I have to be mocked and humiliated, this is as good a place as any to have it done.

"I admit we could have handled it a little better, but I just didn't think the kid would be so paranoid. He's really scared of something."

"You think he killed the two girls?" she asks.

"It's possible, but I doubt it. Janet Carlson was pretty sure the person who killed Calvin was very strong. I'm betting it's the same person."

"But if Eddie was Liz's ex-boyfriend, and she was going to see Jeremy that night, maybe Eddie thought she was going back with Jeremy," Laurie says. "So he went crazy and killed her, and Sheryl was unlucky enough to be with her friend at the time."

I nod. "And he would have known who Jeremy was, so framing him makes sense. It all fits; I just don't believe it."

"Why not? Just because of what Janet said? She didn't even see the body."

"No, it's more something that Calvin said the first time I met him. He said that his gut doesn't trust anything that comes out of Center City."

"Eddie came out of Center City," she points out.

"And Mrs. Barlow denied that there even was an Eddie. She lied right to my face. That really pisses me off."

"You want me to tell her so tomorrow?"

"You're meeting with her tomorrow?" I ask.

Laurie nods. "A follow-up interview; I'm going out to her house. She doesn't drive, if you can believe that."

"I think you should tell her what happened. Tell her she's going to be answering questions about Eddie under oath. Maybe she'll give something up."

Laurie agrees to do it, and we both agree not to talk business any more tonight. We've got other stuff to do, stuff that a couple of months ago I thought we wouldn't be doing together anymore.

Laurie leaves at six in the morning, and I call Cindy Spodek to ask her to remain on the computer lookout for Eddie. I tell her that we missed catching him, but I make it slightly more heroic than it was in real life. In my version Eddie had a dozen bodyguards, plus a helicopter in which to make his getaway. For some reason Cindy doesn't believe me, but she does agree to keep the search going.

I need to focus less on the search for Eddie and more on the rapidly approaching trial. There is no guarantee that we are going to find Eddie, and we must be prepared to create a reasonable doubt in jurors' minds even without him.

To that end I've agreed to Kevin's request that we meet with a jury consultant this morning. I've used consultants before but lately had stopped doing so. It's not that I don't believe they can be of value, it's just that I trust my instincts more than I trust theirs.

I'm making an exception in this case because of my feeling that there's a lot that I don't know about small-town Wisconsinites. Of course, there's a great deal that the jury consultant, a woman name Susan Leidel, doesn't know about them either, because it turns out that she's come up from her office in Milwaukee.

What Ms. Leidel proposes is that we do a substantial amount of research within the greater Findlay area to get a handle on what the people think, in general, and how they view this case, in particular.

Once I learn that she has no special knowledge about the area and its people, I mentally disconnect from the meeting and let Kevin carry the ball. I sit there quietly and spend about half the meeting trying to think of a way to find Eddie and the other half recalling last night in bed with Laurie. Kevin is smart enough to make the meeting mercifully short.

While we're having lunch, Kevin says, "It's nice to see you and Laurie together like this."

"It's sort of a work in progress," I say. "I'm just not sure what we're progressing towards."

"This is not such a bad place to live, you know?" he says.

"You mean except for the part where people kill lawyers?" I ask.

"You know what I mean," he says. "There's crime everywhere, but this place sure has less than most. I'm just saying it's a nice community, and you could do worse, if you decided to stay here when this is over."

"I'd go absolutely insane, and within a year I'd kill myself," I say.

He smiles. "But that's really the only downside."

Laurie calls right after lunch to tell me that she confronted Mrs. Barlow with the latest news about Eddie but that the woman continued to deny any knowledge of him or his relationship with her daughter. I'm sure she's lying, and I continue to be amazed that she would be so resistant to finding out the truth about her daughter's death.

With jury selection rapidly approaching, I head home to start preparing for my opening statement. I jot down little notes and phrases that pop into my head, but I resist the temptation to actually write out the statement. I like to make it as extemporaneous as possible; I feel I connect better with the jury that way.

Kevin, as is his practice, gives me a lengthy memo presenting his view of what should be included in the opening statement. It is a perfect example of why Kevin and I complement each other so well.

If Kevin has a weakness as an attorney, it is that he's too detail-oriented. This fourteen-page memo brings up every imaginable nuance in the case but perhaps lacks a "big picture" approach. A fair criticism of Kevin, as evidenced by the memo, might be that he doesn't see the forest for the trees.

I, on the other hand, have a tendency to see only the forest, without even noticing that there are any trees. I pay far too little attention to detail, which is a substantial weakness. Fortunately, it is amply compensated for by Kevin's working alongside me.

Another of my weaknesses is that, while I make some effort to prepare in advance for things like this opening statement, I find it hard to get really serious about it until it is imminent. So after spending an hour or so at it tonight, my mind wanders and I wind up falling asleep on the couch while watching an NBA game on ESPN. Tara's head rests on my leg as she sleeps, and that's how we wake up in the morning.

The phone is ringing when Tara and I return from our morning walk. I rush in to pick it up, and I get it simultaneously with the answering machine.

"Hello?"

"Mr. Carpenter, this is Eddie Carson."

I'm shocked at this piece of news, but I attempt to conceal that and talk calmly. "Eddie . . . I've been looking for you."

He speaks haltingly, apparently nervous. "I know . . . I'm sorry I ran away . . . but I didn't know who you were. I thought Drummond might have sent you."

I have a thousand questions I can ask him, including why he might be afraid of Drummond, but I don't want to ask him over the phone. I know so little about what is going on that I'm afraid I could stumble upon a question that could scare him off. My sole priority now is to get Eddie in a room.

"When can we get together?" I ask. "All I want to do is talk to you."

"Okay . . . yeah . . . I'm ready to do that. I'm gettin' real scared."

"Where are you?"

"You're the only one coming?" he asks, obviously wary.

"I'll bring my associate along, if that's okay. He's a lawyer like I am."

A pause, then, "okay."

He tells me the name of another motel, on a highway about four hours from here. I'm getting a little tired of driving all over Wisconsin looking for this guy, but there's no alternative. "Just wait for me, okay? I'll be there around one o'clock."

He promises that he will, and gives me his room number. Kevin comes into the house as I'm getting off the phone, and

I tell him what just happened. As I'm doing so, I get out the map, to figure out what our route will be.

"I'll call Marcus," Kevin says, heading for the phone.

"I told him I'd just bring you," I say.

"Well, you just changed your mind," says Kevin, and I don't argue. He calls Marcus and tells him where we are going.

I speak to Kevin while he is still on the phone with Marcus. "Tell him to follow us at a distance." I want it this way so that Eddie doesn't see Marcus with us, since that could easily get him to run away again. I also don't want to have to listen to classical music for four hours.

Kevin and I are in the car within fifteen minutes. I don't see Marcus, but then again I never do. I trust that he will be there if we need him, but my hunch is that this time we won't.

This time Eddie has come looking for us.

Luckily, the weather today is fine, if one doesn't mind freezing cold, so the drive is much easier. I'm also anxious to get there before Eddie can change his mind, so my foot is a little heavier on the gas pedal than last time.

The motel that Eddie has directed us to is the Peter Pan Motor Hotel, a two-story establishment that makes the Parker Motel look like a Ritz-Carlton. As with the Parker, the parking lot wraps around the place so that guests can park in front of their rooms. My guess, based on the classiness of the place, is that many of their guests only take their rooms for an hour or so in the afternoon.

Eddie told us his room number, so there's no reason for us to stop off at the front desk. We park near the outdoor staircase, since his room is on the second floor. I look around for Marcus but can't find him . . . business as usual.

Kevin and I walk up the stairs and then around the building toward the room. I feel a flicker of nervousness at what is about to happen. It's unlikely that Eddie would be leading us into a trap, but there is always that possibility. Kevin was absolutely right to call Marcus.

We reach room 223, and I knock on the door. As I do so, I see that it is only half closed and can be pushed open. I wait for someone to answer, but no one does. I hope Eddie has gone out, maybe for a bite to eat, and will be back soon. I'll be really pissed if he's bailed out on us again.

I push open the door and call out, "Eddie?"

No answer, so Kevin and I enter the room. The bed is unmade, there are some papers on the desk, but no sign of Eddie. I go toward the open bathroom door and look in.

There is a skylight in the bathroom, with a metal latch. One end of the rope is tied to this latch, and the other end is tied to Eddie's grotesquely twisted neck as he gently swings, his feet about eighteen inches above the bathroom floor.

• • • • •

I'VE SEEN DEAD bodies before, both murder victims and otherwise, but it's not something I'm likely to get used to any time soon. For some reason the image of Eddie's shoes, slowly drifting in the air, is one I believe that I will never forget.

Kevin comes to the door to see if I've discovered anything. "Holy shit," he says, mostly to himself.

I close the door with us on the outside of it. I ask Kevin to call 911 as I look around the room, and it doesn't take long to find the note sitting on top of the desk.

It's a rambling two-page letter, in longhand but legible. I'm careful to just nudge the edges of the pages so as not to smudge any fingerprints, but there is no way I'm not going to read this. It consists of a confession of guilt to the murders of Liz Barlow and Sheryl Hendricks, as well as an apology to the victims, the victims' families, and God, for what he has done.

Included are three paragraphs in which he describes the murders as having been committed because Liz broke off their "engagement" and he just went "crazy" at the prospect of a life without her. His last paragraph is a specific apology to Jeremy for the pain he has caused him. He acknowledges burying the bodies on Jeremy's property, as well as putting specks of the victims' blood in Jeremy's truck, which he says was parked in Center City.

Kevin and I wait outside the room for the local police to arrive, since we have neither a desire to contaminate a crime scene nor hang out with a dead body. Four local patrolmen arrive in two cars, and after confirming that we are the ones who called the discovery in, they proceed to enter the room without waiting for any detectives. It is clear that their training regarding crime scenes consisted of watching two episodes of *CSI: Miami*, but that's not my problem.

The state police arrive about ten minutes later, and the officer in charge, Detective Woisheski, immediately removes the local officers from the scene, instructing them to set up a perimeter in the parking lot. My guess is, he does this just to give them something to do and get rid of them, and if a perimeter had already been set up, he might have instructed them to open a lemonade stand in the parking lot.

He tells Kevin and me to wait where we are, and it's about a half hour before he comes out of the room and over to us. "And you would be who?" he asks.

"I'm Andy Carpenter and this is Kevin Randall. We're attorneys."

He looks skyward briefly, as if for help. "Just what I need. All right, tell me what you're doing here."

"The kid hanging in the bathroom was a potential material witness in an upcoming murder trial in Findlay."

"The one where the two college girls got sliced up?"

I nod. "The very one; we're representing the accused. Eddie—that's the kid in there—has been on the run, and we've been trying to find him. He called this morning, told me where he was, and we drove right out."

"So rather than talk to two lawyers, he hung himself. Makes sense."

"Sounds like you cracked the case, Detective," I say.

"Did you read the suicide note?" he asks.

"He left a note?" I say, putting on my best shocked expression.

"Don't bullshit me, Counselor."

"I may have read part of it," I admit.

"Which part?"

"The part where there was writing."

"So if this is legit, your client walks," he says.

"I would describe it more as a horrible injustice having been averted."

"I bet you would," he says.

He questions us for another half hour, but it's clear that he sees nothing in the room or situation to make him think this is other than the suicide it seems. I'm not so sure, but I'm certainly not about to tell him that. Before we leave, I reverse the roles and get some information from him, mostly concerning what office will be the base of the investigation, and where the note will be held. That note, as Woisheski correctly noted, could well be Jeremy Davidson's get-out-of-jail card.

On the way back I call Laurie and bring her up-to-date on what has transpired. She has, of course, not been at the scene, yet she shares my immediate suspicions of it. "Why would he call to talk to you and then kill himself before he was able to?" she asks.

"Maybe he wanted to turn himself in because of his feelings of guilt, but then those feelings became so overwhelming he couldn't deal with them," I say. "Or maybe he would rather be dead than in prison."

"Maybe," she says, not believing it. "Did the scene look legit to you?"

"Pretty much," I say. "Though hangings are not in my area of expertise."

She asks if I'll give her a formal statement when I get back, and I agree, providing it's over dinner. I am a hell of a negotiator.

Kevin and I spend the drive back kicking this around from a legal standpoint. I debate whether to inform Lester of what has happened, but decide against it. I'd rather he find out from Judge Morrison, who we plan to tell tomorrow morning. We are going to tell him about it in the form of a motion to dismiss the charges against Jeremy Davidson.

Kevin and I are still discussing our legal strategy when Laurie arrives, and she volunteers to make dinner for us. We include her in the conversation, since we trust her completely. Also, whatever strategy we decide on will soon be part of our motion and therefore no secret from anyone.

During one of our breaks I turn on CNN, only to discover that Eddie's suicide is the lead story. A quick switch to the other news stations finds the same thing; it's all anyone is talking about.

I have to assume that the leak came from either the state police or the local police that arrived on the scene. I'm not happy about it; I would have preferred to spring it on Lester. But it's not all bad, since this will certainly elevate the pressure on Judge Morrison to strongly consider a dismissal of the charges against Jeremy.

There's also another benefit to the TV coverage. The cable networks have called in what seem like hundreds of former prosecutors, former judges, and current defense attorneys to comment on the developments, in the same fashion they always called on me. Since the goal is to foster disagreement among the expert guests, at least half disagree with my position. The half that agree provide their legal reasoning for doing so, and it's actually somewhat helpful in our preparation. The legal issues are fairly thorny ones, and in a way it's as if we are able to consult and pick the brains of all these people. One of them, Doug Burns on Fox News, just about provides my entire oral argument for me.

Richard Davidson calls, having just heard the news but not wanting to believe it until I have confirmed it for him. I do so and honestly say that there is a chance, but only a chance, that Jeremy will be set free. Either way, I tell him, Eddie's bad news appears to be very good news for Jeremy.

I call the court clerk first thing in the morning, asking her to inform Judge Morrison that I am requesting an urgent meeting with him and Lester. The judge is attending to personal business early this morning, but a callback tells me that I should be in his chambers at noon. The speed of the response means that it's likely the judge has also seen the news.

Kevin and I stop at the jail so that we can bring Jeremy up-to-date on what is going on. Unfortunately, his father has spoken to him already, and based on Jeremy's euphoria, Richard must have substantially overstated our prospects for success. I think if I were to hand him a cell phone, Jeremy would use it to try to get a date for Saturday night.

The only slight glimmer of worry that I see is when he says, "So this guy Eddie was her boyfriend?"

"Apparently so," I say.

"And he admitted he did it? His letter says he killed Liz?"

"Yes."

"If he lied for some reason, if he didn't do it, what'll happen then?" he asks.

I detect doubt in Jeremy's voice, so I call him on it. "Do you have reason to think he lied about it?"

"I don't know . . . I mean, I never met the guy. It's just hard to imagine that anybody who knew Liz could have killed her like that."

Jeremy's statement moves him up a major notch in my mind and increases the pressure on me to use these recent events to get a dismissal.

When Kevin and I get to the courthouse, Lester and his staff are already there, attempting unsuccessfully to look confident and unconcerned. This case was going to make Lester a star, and there's a decent chance that it is suddenly going to cease to exist.

Judge Morrison calls us into his chambers precisely at noon and basically turns the floor over to me. I relate in substantial detail the events that led to our finding Eddie in the motel bathroom yesterday, and I describe the note as I read it.

After I do so, I state my modest goal for this meeting. "At the very least, Your Honor, these are events which can have an enormous impact on this case. I would request that this court instruct the state police to turn over all relevant information and that a hearing then be held to consider it."

It's a simple request, and perfectly logical, but Lester has brought some verbal ammunition with him, and he lets fire. "Your Honor, we are dealing with an uncorroborated confession, and a hearsay one at that. This case has received substantial media coverage, and as I'm sure you are aware, confessions in such situations are frequent and notoriously unreliable."

Morrison offers me the opportunity to respond, and I say, "That would be the main purpose of the hearing, Your Honor. We could collectively examine the events of yesterday, including the veracity of the confession."

"It is for our jury to examine those facts, should they be ruled admissible at trial. I am sure that we will choose a jury quite capable of doing so," Lester says.

I let my annoyance into my voice. "If Eddie Carson killed these two young women, we shouldn't be choosing a jury. We should be setting Jeremy Davidson free, so that he can go back to college and get on with his young life."

Judge Morrison comes down on our side, which is really

the only thing he could do. He instructs Lester to deal with the state police and secure all current investigative information about Eddie's death, including independent handwriting analysis. He tentatively schedules a hearing for next week and moves jury selection back to a time to be determined.

Jeremy Davidson won't be going out on a date this Saturday night, but his future just got a whole lot brighter.

• • • • •

FINDLAY HAS NEVER seen anything like this. The national media have descended on the small community for today's hearing in numbers dwarfing those here at any time before. Eddie's suicide and confession have in a bizarre way added a cachet to the case that has made it even more appealing to those who report on the human condition.

I would imagine that the assembled reporters have mixed emotions about today's hearing. If it goes our way, Jeremy is released and the story is over. If it goes against us, they will have to spend the winter on the frozen tundra covering the trial in long underwear.

The state police have cooperated in turning over whatever they have on the case, and we have promptly received the documents in discovery. The investigation is far from complete, but a substantial amount of work has already been done. The bottom line is that the state police have found nothing inconsistent with suicide, and their handwriting expert has no doubt that it is Eddie's handwriting.

My goal is a simple one: It is to say that this evidence should be admissible if Jeremy goes to trial, and that its very admissibility should preclude Jeremy from having to go to trial at all.

The gallery is packed as Judge Morrison takes his seat at the bench. Both Lester and I have submitted briefs in support of our respective positions, but if the judge has not already formed an opinion, then it is the oral arguments that will sway him.

My only witness at the hearing is Detective Woisheski, and I take him through the entire investigation into Eddie's apparent suicide. He is an excellent, experienced witness; his answers are concise and exactly on point. My questions merely provide the road map; he's driving the car.

There is little that Lester can do with him on cross-examination, other than to repeatedly make the point that the investigation is not concluded and that it is certainly possible that information might still turn up that could lead Woisheski to believe that Eddie was murdered.

Lester then calls Laurie to the stand, in order that she can report on the Findlay side of the "Eddie investigation." His hope is that she will be able to learn that Eddie could not have committed the murders of Liz and Sheryl and that therefore his confession in the note was either fabricated or coerced.

Lester knows that Laurie is not about to do that at this point, and she does not. But she does at least slightly bolster Lester by saying that she has uncovered no independent evidence of Eddie's involvement in the murders. I cross-examine her briefly, only to get the alternative truth that she has not found anything to exonerate him either.

Once Laurie leaves the stand, the main event begins: the oral arguments. Judge Morrison decides to address the admissibility question first, and Lester states his position that the only reason Eddie's death has any bearing on our case at all is the note. And the note, continues Lester, is hearsay and therefore not admissible. Should Judge Morrison issue such a ruling, reasons Lester, then our case is unaffected. Our jury could not be influenced by a note that they are never permitted to see.

"Your Honor," I say, "the prosecution knows full well that the note represents a 'dying declaration' and is an exception to the hearsay rule." The law makes this exception in the belief that a person about to die is likely to be truthful, as well as the obvious fact that since the person is dead at the time of trial, hearsay is the only way his views can be introduced.

Lester interrupts with the expected counterargument that a dying declaration, under Wisconsin law, is only an exception to the hearsay rule to show how the declarant died. For example, a person who is in the process of dying from a gunshot can identify the shooter, and that statement would be admissible. But that's all.

I rebut, "I can only assume the prosecutor is not familiar with the law, Your Honor. He should know that the statement is in fact admissible, since it is a 'statement against interest.' Were Mr. Carson to have been unsuccessful in his suicide attempt, the statement that the note represents could have exposed him to a criminal prosecution and is therefore legally considered against his interest."

My belief is that the only area in which the law is ambiguous and not totally favoring our position is the question of whether the dying declaration can be in writing, and not spoken. There is insufficient case law on this, and it will be up to Judge Morrison to decide.

We go on to my basic premise, which is that the facts behind Eddie's demise create so much reasonable doubt about Jeremy's guilt that had it been known two months ago, Jeremy would not have even been arrested, no less brought to trial.

"There may have been probable cause at the time of the

indictment," I argue, "but it effectively has ceased to exist. And based on Detective Woisheski's testimony, it is reasonable to believe that Eddie Carson made this confession of his own free will. How, then, could a jury find Jeremy Davidson guilty beyond a reasonable doubt of the same murders that Eddie Carson credibly confessed to?"

Lester responds by repeating his argument that bogus confessions are very common in high-profile murder cases and that if the actual defendant were released every time someone else confessed to the same crime, no one would ever get convicted. It's a decent point; I just have to hope Judge Morrison doesn't feel it carries the day.

Judge Morrison promises to rule quickly on the matter and adjourns the hearing. Before the guards take Jeremy away, he asks me how I think it will turn out, and I tell him truthfully that I just can't predict.

As a defense attorney I'm single-minded of purpose: I want to get my client off. As a thinking human being I'm troubled by what I see.

Basically, I don't believe that Eddie committed suicide; nor did he kill Liz Barlow and Sheryl Hendricks. He ran away the first time we came for him, and that is not the act of a person who has lost his desire to live. Additionally, he told me on the phone that he ran because he was afraid I was sent by Drummond. If this were as straightforward as the suicide note makes it seem, why would Eddie fear Drummond?

Add to this the fact that Janet Carlson was convinced Calvin's neck was broken by a powerful man. I simply cannot see Eddie fitting that description, nor can I imagine him luring Calvin to his death. Eddie strikes me as a guy who had information, information that he realized it was dangerous to have. He may even have tried to convey that information to Calvin, then watched as Calvin was himself killed.

If I'm right, then Eddie took off and ran, until he was tired of running and saw contacting me as a possible way out. But one of the problems with this scenario is why he didn't contact the police instead.

And hovering over all this is a strong feeling of guilt that I have over Eddie's death. I believe that had I not been searching for him, he would not have been killed. I can't prove it; I just think it, and it bugs the hell out of me.

I consent to three evening interviews on the various cable news networks. They are all done from the house, and I do them in case Judge Morrison rules against us. Should he rule for us, Jeremy will be free and there will be no need to sway public opinion. But if Jeremy faces trial, I want the public, including our future jurors, to know how significant I consider Eddie's confession to be.

I wake up in the morning to two pieces of good news. First, the court clerk calls to say that Judge Morrison will issue his ruling from the bench tomorrow morning. This is amazingly fast compared to larger jurisdictions, but it fits in with what I have come to expect in this case.

Even better, Laurie calls to tell me that she has today off, and asks if I'd like to go for a drive out to the lake. It's the perfect solution for a day in which I would otherwise do nothing but obsess about the case. And if we actually walk outside near a lake in this weather, I'll freeze to death and be able to forget about the case permanently.

Laurie asks that I drive, and she sits in the passenger seat. Even though it seems that Wisconsin has more lakes than people, the one we are driving to turns out to be about two hours away. This is fine with me; I'm feeling so comfortable we could be driving to Anchorage for all I care. Besides, it's got to be warmer there.

Fortunately, the only time we spend outside is walking from the car to the restaurant we arrive at for lunch. We are brought to our table along the glass wall at the far end of the restaurant. We are overlooking Lake Netcong, which is as beautiful a place as any I have ever seen. The air is so clear that it feels like I'm wearing magnifying lenses on my eyes.

"This place is amazing," I say.

She nods. "I know. I used to come here when I was a kid. The lake hasn't changed at all."

"Was this restaurant here?"

"No . . . there was just a small stand, sold hot dogs and hamburgers. My father would take me here for picnics and rent a boat for the day so we could sail. It feels like it was yesterday, but it was a hundred years ago."

If I was harboring any hope that Laurie was longing to come back to Paterson with me, the look on her face is blowing that out of the frozen water. "I can see how much you love it here," I say.

"I do, but that's not how I would describe it. It's more like I'm connected here. It feels like where I'm supposed to be."

"Haven't we had this conversation before?" It's sounding to me like the talks we had leading up to Laurie leaving me, and I don't relish having another one.

She nods. "I'm sorry, but I'm not handling this well," she says.

"Handling what well?"

"I'm also connected to you, Andy. I love you and I'm connected to you. But you love your home and you are connected there. So I don't see a solution that gives me what I want." She points to the lake. "This and you."

"Laurie, Findlay is a nice place to live. The people are great, there's cable TV, and I find I can go outside for ten or fifteen seconds without getting frostbite. But I can't stay here forever."

"I know." Then, "Did you ever think about having a child?"

"I am a child."

She laughs, but tells me she's serious. "Do you ever think about it?" she asks again.

"Sometimes, but I always get scared by that Harry Chapin song."

"You're not going to song-talk again, are you?" she asks.

"No, there's a song called 'Cat's in the Cradle.' " She nods that she knows the song, but I continue. "It's all about this guy who can never find the time to be with his son, and then the son grows up and can't find the time to be with him."

"And you worry that you'll be like that?"

I nod. "I do."

"I think you'd be a great father," she says.

"I have my doubts," I say.

"I'm not asking you to father my child, Andy."

"Good."

She's quiet for a few moments, and I feel like I'm cowering in a foxhole, waiting for the next bomb to drop.

"Judge Morrison is going to rule in your favor tomorrow, and then you're going to leave."

"I'm not so sure. He could go either way on it."

"I still don't believe Eddie murdered those girls," she says.

I'm feeling relief and less tension now that we have seemed to change the subject. It might be a sad commentary on me that I'm more comfortable talking about vicious murders than an intimate relationship. "I don't either," I say. "But among the many things that trouble me, one in particular stands out."

"What's that?"

"Well, let's assume Eddie was murdered because of what he knew, probably who the real killer was. Then it makes perfect sense that the killer would get rid of Eddie."

She nods. "Right."

"But why force Eddie to write the note confessing to the murders? The real killer wouldn't need that for protection; the murders were already blamed on Jeremy. So why would he bother to connect Eddie to the original murders? Why wouldn't he just bury Eddie's body somewhere and let Jeremy continue to take the fall?"

She thinks for a while and then says, "Because if Jeremy goes to trial, you will still be investigating the murders, trying to find the real killer. If everyone believes Eddie did it, you go home and the book is closed."

"You're a smart cop, you know?" I ask.

"Aw, shucks," she says. "I love it when you compliment me."

"I'm glad," I say.

"And aren't you also glad I changed the subject?" she asks.

"You have no idea," I say.

· · · · ·

RICHARD DAVIDSON is standing out-

side my house at seven-thirty in the morning when I take
Tara out for our walk. It's probably ten degrees out, and I
don't know how long he's been standing here, but he looks
like a Popsicle.

"I'm just real nervous," he says, "but I didn't want to wake
you."

"You want to go in and get de-iced?" I ask. "Or you want
to walk with us?"

"I'll walk, if that's okay."

"Fine."

We walk around the block twice, which gives Richard
time to ask me a hundred and fifty times if I think Judge Morrison will let Jeremy go free without trial. I give him my standard "It's hard to tell" five or six times, but then start
shrugging, since I'm afraid my tongue might freeze if my
mouth is open too much.

The pressure he is feeling is not unlike waiting for a verdict. It should be easier, since even if this goes against his
son, they've still got the trial, but that is offset by the fact that
Richard has no experience with these kinds of things.

I invite him to have coffee with Kevin and me before

court starts, and he leaps at the opportunity. He feels that he can get some special insight into what might happen by being with us.

As I'm getting dressed, the phone rings, and the woman calling identifies herself as Catherine Gerard. She tells me that she has seen the coverage of the hearing and that it's important that she talk to me.

"What about?" I ask.

"Center City . . . that religion."

I'm running late and wishing she would get to the point. "Can you be more specific than that?"

"My husband was a Centurion," she says. "He left to marry me."

The name hits me . . . Gerard. "He wrote those articles," I say.

"Yes, that's right. That's what I wanted to talk to you about."

I tell her that I would like to talk to her very much, though in truth I'll have no need to if Judge Morrison rules in our favor. I take her number and tell her I'll be calling her back later to set up a meeting. "Is your husband willing to talk about this as well?" I ask.

"My husband is dead," she says. "They killed him."

"Who did?"

"The Centurions."

My curiosity is through the roof on this, but I have to leave. I promise her that I will be in touch, and I finish getting dressed. I meet Richard and Kevin at the diner just as Kevin is saying, "I don't know . . . it's really impossible to predict these things," when I arrive. Going by the look on his face, I doubt it's the first time he's had to say it.

I haven't had the time to think about what Laurie had to say yesterday, but right now it hits me that if Judge Morrison rules the way I am hoping, Tara and I will be out of here by tomorrow. If I am, I hope I never see another bratwurst again; the diner has reacted to the media frenzy by renaming their bratwurst sandwiches after news celebrities. Their special for today is the "Brat Lauer."

The street in front of the courthouse is the closest that Findlay can come to a mob scene. Media trucks dominate the landscape, and the townspeople are hovering in the hope that they will be admitted into the court. I see Laurie and her officers taking charge, making sure that order is maintained. It's a scene that seems completely incongruous in this town.

We have to fight through a crowd to make it into the courthouse, and we're brought into an anteroom to meet briefly with Jeremy. He seems so nervous that I'm actually concerned he is going to faint.

The entire scene feels weird to me; there is all the tension of an upcoming verdict without having had the trial. It is as if opposing football captains went out for the pregame coin toss to learn who has won the game.

Within moments the gallery is packed, and I see that Laurie has taken a position along the side wall of the room. She and I make eye contact, and I believe we are thinking the same thing: that in a few moments Judge Morrison will be the one deciding how long we are together.

The bailiff announces the judge's arrival on the bench, and the hearing begins. It will be an unusual one for me in that I will not be called on to speak. Judge Morrison will just read his decision, and that will be that.

Unfortunately, Judge Morrison decides to do more than just read his decision. He suddenly seems to relish being in the media spotlight, and he makes a long, rambling speech about the effect of this case on the community, and the need for people to come together when it is over.

"And now to the matter at hand," says the judge before citing the voluminous case law that he studied to help him reach his decision. I glance at my watch to confirm that he has spoken for twenty minutes without giving so much as a hint which way he will rule.

I actually start to lose concentration for a moment and steal a look around the courtroom to see if I can spot Laurie again. It is a change in the judge's tone that causes me to once again pay attention. ". . . this court does not have the benefit of a final determination of the investigation into the death of Edmond Carson. Yet in the interests of justice, both for this defendant and this community, further delay is unacceptable."

I sit up slightly; here it comes . . .

"It seems clear to this court that the facts as they are currently known would make it a miscarriage of justice for a jury to render a verdict of 'guilty beyond a reasonable doubt.' Therefore, until and unless these facts change, no jury should be called upon to consider doing so. I hereby dismiss the murder charges against Jeremy Davidson, without prejudice."

The room explodes, and in the moment Jeremy looks at me, hoping that I will confirm that it means what he thinks it means. I smile the confirmation, and he puts his head in his hands and starts to sob his happiness. Richard and Allie Davidson move up from their seats in the front row and hug their son, then me, and then Kevin.

Judge Morrison's ruling was an obvious victory for our side, but not necessarily a permanent one. The phrase "without prejudice" means that the charges against Jeremy could be brought again at some future time, should the facts change. Because the trial against Jeremy had not actually started, jeopardy did not attach, so double jeopardy cannot come into play.

I start to move toward the exit doors when I see that Laurie has made her way over to me. "Will you stay until tomorrow? Maybe we can have dinner tonight?"

"Sure," I say. "I'd like that."

"Congratulations on the ruling."

"Thanks."

Laurie leaves to attend to her business, and I head back to the house with Kevin. Marcus comes over to confirm that I'll no longer be needing his services.

"Unhh," he says. Saying good-bye to Marcus is always a poignant event; right now I don't think there's a dry eye in the room.

Marcus starts walking toward the door but stops and turns to me. "Kid didn't hang himself."

I nod. "I know. I think this time both the good guys and the bad guys go free."

"Unhh," says Marcus, and leaves.

I sit down on the couch, apparently looking unhappy, because Kevin says, "You down about the case or leaving Laurie?"

"I'm not down. I'm one happy camper," I say.

"Yeah . . . right." He tells me that he's on an evening flight back home and that this has been a positive experience for him. Even more positive is that Carol has left a message on his answering machine at home, saying that she wants to "talk." It's nothing definite, but I think that Kevin harbors the hope that before long he can get back on WebMD and start planning that honeymoon.

Kevin goes off to pack, and I get a phone call from Richard Davidson, once again thanking me for saving his son and asking me to send him a bill for my services. I tell him I'll get around to it, but not to mortgage the farm.

I have a genetic resistance to packing until moments before I am about to leave for somewhere, so instead I use my monthly ten-minute allowance for introspection to think about why I'm down. It's not about the case; I'm delighted that Jeremy is free, and although I believe the real murderer is still out there, that can't be my concern. Guilty people get away with things all the time; my job is to make sure that innocent people don't get put away in their stead.

I'm also not about to miss Findlay. It hasn't been an unpleasant stay, and it really is a nice town, but I can take just so much fresh air and wholesomeness. I feel more at home in a place where crime and grime are far more prevalent.

That leaves Laurie, and leaving Laurie is without doubt the reason I'm depressed. She put it very well at lunch the other day, and her words apply to me as well as her. We love each other, but there is no way we can live in the same place.

Laurie comes over at five o'clock with three bags full of groceries. She vows to make me a dinner I will never forget, but she knows better. Food has never been that important to me; give me a burger and fries and I'm happy.

Laurie makes some fantastic fried chicken and mashed potatoes, and we spend a quiet evening together, capped off by a far-from-quiet time in the bedroom. But as wonderful as this all could be under different circumstances, it suffers from a general sadness that we both feel. We are splitting up again, and this time likely for good. It would be unrealistic to expect Findlay to have more brutal murders resulting in wrongly charged defendants to lure me back.

When Laurie left last time, I at least had anger to fall back on; now I don't even have that. All I feel is the impending loss, and there's no conflicting emotion to deflect the pain. She warned me this could happen, and she let me call the shots, but here I am.

We wake up in the morning, and Laurie asks if I'll come down to her office with her. Now that Jeremy has been freed, it is incumbent on her to restart a full investigation into the deaths of Liz and Sheryl. It's likely that the investigation will be forced to conclude that Eddie was the killer, but she has to go through the process anyway. As the person who discovered Eddie's body, I'm a witness who has to be interviewed.

"Can't you interview me here?" I ask. "Or do you have to put me under hot lights and sweat it out of me?"

She smiles. "I wouldn't have to pressure you ... you'd cave quickly enough. But I do need to record it."

I agree to meet her there at ten-thirty, giving me plenty of time to take Tara for one last walk around Findlay. I run a little late, so I bring Tara with me to the police station. The sergeant at the desk doesn't look terribly kindly at that.

"You can tie her up outside while you meet with Chief Collins," he says.

"Are you familiar with the phrase 'no way, no how'?" I ask. "Please call Chief Collins and tell her that Andy Carpenter and his trusted companion are here to see her."

The sergeant does that, though he substitutes the word "dog" for "trusted companion." Laurie comes out and smiles when she sees Tara, telling the sergeant that they can bend the "no canines" rule just this one time.

Laurie brings us into the interview room, and I sit down. She closes the door behind her.

"You're going to do this alone?" I ask.

She smiles. "I believe I can handle the likes of you on my own."

She starts the recorder, gives the time and date, and then asks me to identify myself. Once I do so, she launches right into questions surrounding my involvement with Eddie and my presence in his motel room on the day he died.

I take her through my actions, leading up to the day he ran away from me at the Parker Motel. I don't include everything, since some insignificant details are subject to lawyer-client privilege, but I so inform her when I leave something out.

"So when you arrived at the Parker, what did you do?" she asks.

"Kevin and I went into the office and convinced the clerk to give us his room number. Then we went outside, up to the second floor, and around to his room. The door was open, and he was nowhere to be found. Some of his possessions were still there, as if he had left in a hurry."

"When did you hear from him next?" she asks.

"The next day. He called me and . . ." My mouth is searching for the words to finish the sentence, but my brain has intercepted them on the way and is in a state of shock.

Laurie prompts me. "He called you and . . ."

"Turn off the recorder," I say.

"What? Andy . . ."

"Turn it off, please."

She does so, probably because my tone of voice has changed so much. "What is it?" she asks.

"Laurie, when Eddie called me that day, he told me that he had run away from the Parker because he thought it might be Drummond that was chasing him. He said he hadn't known it was me."

"So?"

"So how did he find out it was me? I didn't leave a card in his room . . . I didn't give my name to the clerk. It wasn't on television or in the newspaper. Yet by the next day he had found out that it was me at the Parker. Someone had to have told him."

"Who did you tell?" she asks.

"You," I say.

"No one else?"

"No. Kevin knew, of course, because he was there, but that's it."

I can see her mind racing to answer the next question even before I ask it. "Who did *you* tell?" I ask.

"Some of my officers," she says, "but I'd vouch for them completely." She pauses as the realization hits her. "Damn."

"What is it?"

"I told Liz Barlow's mother. You said I should confront her with it."

"Was Drummond or anyone else there?"

She shakes her head. "No, I wouldn't allow it. Wait a minute, her daughter was there. She heard the whole thing. I forget her name . . ."

Madeline.

Bingo.

• • • • •

EDDIE CARSON DIED because of me. There can be no doubt about that now. I got Cindy Spodek to help find him, and then I set him up to be murdered. It doesn't matter that I didn't do it intentionally; what matters is that I did it.

I can't be sure that it was Madeline Barlow who told him I was the one looking for him. It could have been her mother, though that seems to defy logic. Or he could have found out some other way that is not yet apparent to me.

Also unknown right now is how whoever murdered him learned his new location. "Maybe they followed you," Laurie suggests.

I shake my head. "No, Marcus followed us out there. If there were someone else following us, Marcus would have seen them. Besides, Eddie had been dead for a while when we got there."

"I'll check to make sure your phone isn't tapped," Laurie says, and then makes a quick phone call to get that accomplished.

"I've got a feeling it was Madeline," I say. "There was something about that kid. She was the only one in that town who seemed like she had a mind of her own."

"She could have set Eddie up to be killed," Laurie says, "without necessarily realizing she was doing it."

The idea that I was a setup man for Eddie's murder is burning a hole in my stomach, and Laurie can see it in my face. "It's not your fault, Andy," she says. "Let it go."

"Let it go? Let it go?" She must know me well enough to know that is impossible. "Earth to Laurie, come in, please. Come in, please."

She tries to suppress a smile but can't. "What's so funny?" I ask.

"You're thinking of staying to try to solve this."

"I'm doing more than thinking about it," I admit, realizing it for the first time myself.

"Sorry. I love having you around, but I'm the police here, Andy. This is my job. Besides, you don't catch slimeballs, you defend them. Remember?"

"I won't get in your way."

"All right," she says, "let me try another approach. You'd be going after people who may well have killed four people that we know of, including a lawyer."

"I'm not going to subdue them, Laurie. I'm going to find out who they are and then turn them over to the proper authority. And if you play your cards right, that proper authority might be you."

She's not willing to accept this. "You're a lawyer, Andy. With no case, no client, and no role to play in this."

"I'm staying, Laurie."

She smiles. "Good. So how about dinner tonight?"

"You got it. Now you can turn on the recorder."

"After you tell me you're going to get Marcus back here."

I shake my head. "No, I don't need a babysitter . . . at least not now." I can see that she's not thrilled with my answer, so I continue. "I'm not going to do anything stupid or dangerous . . . honestly. Besides, with the trial canceled, the bad guys would have no reason to think of me as a threat anymore."

She frowns but turns on the recorder, and we continue the interview. I tell her the events as they happened, but my mind is elsewhere, trying to figure out how to trap what is rapidly becoming a mass murderer.

Reestablishing myself in Findlay is not a difficult matter. Basically, all I have to do is tell the real estate agent I'll be taking the place for at least another month, and dump the stuff in my suitcases back into drawers. Tara seems understanding as well, especially since I give her two biscuits to soften the blow.

I feel fairly confident that the people I'm after are in Center City; what is disconcerting is how little I know about the place. To that end I call Catherine Gerard, the woman who contacted me before the hearing. She dropped the bomb that the Centurions killed her husband, a charge that carries some weight with me in light of the recent carnage.

She answers the phone in the middle of the first ring, as if she has been waiting by the phone for my call. She is very anxious to meet with me, as I am with her. Currently, she is living in Winston, about a four-hour drive from Findlay, and expresses a nervousness about coming back to this area because of its proximity to Center City.

Winston is out in the direction of the lake where Laurie and I had lunch, so I suggest we meet at the same restaurant. It has the double advantage of being midway between Findlay and Winston and having fantastic french fries. We agree to meet tomorrow.

The tech guy that Laurie sends to my house to see if the phones are tapped, or if bugs have been placed, turns up nothing. The information about Eddie did not come from me, increasing the likelihood that it was Madeline or Mrs. Barlow. I'm still betting it's Madeline.

The obvious difficulty is how to talk to Madeline without Drummond, Wallace, and the rest of Center City finding out and either preventing or monitoring our conversation. The trick is in luring her out of that town and away from their oversight.

I come up with an idea to do just that, a plan that would require the help of Jeremy Davidson. I had planned to speak with him and his parents anyway, partially to explain an ethical dilemma that I have. Simply put, the purpose of my continuing investigation is to prove that the real killer of Liz Barlow and Sheryl Hendricks was not Eddie Carson and that his suicide note was coerced. Since that note is what prompted the dismissal of the charges against Jeremy, there is a risk that my success in this investigation could expose him to renewed jeopardy.

I call Jeremy and ask if he and his parents are available to meet with me. They are surprised that I haven't left town already, and Jeremy himself was just leaving to go back to school. Allie is not home, but Richard and Jeremy agree to wait for me, and I head right over there.

I start off by taking them through the ethical dilemma I'm facing over possibly exposing Jeremy to renewed jeopardy. I can see the concern and confusion on their faces as I do so.

"So what would have to happen for the police to come after Jeremy again?" Richard asks.

"Two things," I say. "One, I would have to prove that the note was faked and that Eddie did not murder Liz and Sheryl. Two, even though I could prove that Eddie was murdered and the note coerced, I could not show who did it."

"But Jeremy couldn't have murdered Eddie. He was in jail," Richard correctly points out.

I nod. "But someone could have done it on his behalf."

Richard is obviously troubled by this situation, as any father would be. "Let's say all this happened . . . would you be allowed to go to the police? Isn't your first obligation to Jeremy, your client?"

"Generally, but in this case it's a gray area. I would be telling the police what I learned about Eddie's death, without mentioning or referring to Jeremy. But it could have an indirect effect on Jeremy if the prosecution and police then turn their attention back to him."

"Andy, I know your intentions are good here, but it makes me a little uncomfortable," Richard says.

Jeremy, who hasn't spoken up yet, responds, "No, I'm okay with it. Please do what you have to do."

"Jeremy . . . ," Richard says.

"Dad, if Eddie didn't kill Liz and Sheryl, then whoever did shouldn't be walking around. He should be strapped to a goddamn table getting a needle in his arm."

I can tell that Richard is as surprised as I am by the intensity of Jeremy's remarks. Richard relents, and after I once again make sure that Jeremy understands the complexities of the situation, I tell him I need his help in getting to Madeline Barlow.

"I hardly know her," he says. "I only met her that one time when she came to see Liz at school."

"Did she meet any of Liz's friends?" I ask.

"Definitely. She hung out with them for a whole weekend. I was studying for a midterm I had that Monday, but Liz said she had a great time. She kept wanting to come back, but her mother wouldn't let her."

I describe my plan, which is to have Jeremy recruit a couple of Liz's friends to call Madeline and ask her if she wants to come to the school to pick up some of Liz's things, things that had been in the possession of those friends. It could be CDs or makeup or anything that might be appealing to Madeline to retrieve. They should also dangle in front of Madeline the prospect of hanging out and perhaps going to a party. When Madeline arrives, I'll be there waiting to talk to her.

Once again it is Richard who is leery and protective of his son, and once again it is Jeremy who steps up and embraces the idea. He tells me that as soon as he gets back to school, he will speak to two of Liz's friends, and he's confident they'll jump at the opportunity to help in any way they can.

I leave them, satisfied that I have a plan of attack, but all too aware that attacking is not my strong point. I'm a lawyer; my version of aggressive confrontation is to file nasty motions.

This promises to get even rougher than that.

• • • • •

HENRY WAS KILLED four and a half years

ago. About a year after he left Center City and about six
months after the articles appeared."

Catherine Gerard is wasting no time in getting to the
point; we haven't even looked at our menus yet. "How was
he killed?" I ask.

"A hunting accident. At least the police ruled it an accident, but it wasn't. They killed him."

"*They* being the Centurions?"

She nods. "Yes."

"Why would they kill him? Because of the articles?"

She nods again. "He exposed the secrets of their religion.
No one had ever done that before, and they wanted to make
sure that no one did it again."

"Why did he leave Center City in the first place?"

"Because of me," she says. "He was an accountant, and
so am I. We met at a conference; they send some of their
people out into the world to learn specialties. Mostly professional people. Henry and I hit it off right away; he didn't tell
me until later that he was married."

It's clear to me that this is a woman here to tell a story

and that probing questions by me are not necessary, at least not at this point. So I just nod and let her continue.

"He told me that it was an 'arranged' marriage and that he never loved her. He said he was planning to divorce his wife even before we met, but that I made him realize he had to do it right away."

The idea of an arranged marriage is completely consistent with what I already know about the Centurions, but divorce certainly is not. "But you would not have been welcome there," I say.

"That's for sure, but it was his wanting a divorce that made him leave. He asked the creep they call the Keeper for permission, but there was no chance. So he left, and as far as I know, he's the only one ever to do so."

"Why is that?" I ask. "What keeps people there?"

Her grin reflects the irony of what she is about to say. "Faith. They really believe in that wheel and in the Keeper. Hell, even Henry believed it. He never really forgave himself for leaving."

"Tell me about the wheel."

"Well," she says, "I've never seen it, so I can only go by what Henry told me. It's like this huge carnival wheel, the kind you try and guess what it will land on when you spin it. And it's got all kinds of strange symbols on it that supposedly only the Keeper can read."

"And that's how everything is decided?"

"That's right. There's some kind of ceremony that each person goes through when they're six years old. That's when the wheel tells them what their occupation will be, who they will marry, where they will live, everything."

She continues describing what she knows about the town and its religion, and her bitterness comes through loud and clear. "So why did Henry write those articles?"

"I suggested it; I thought it might help him deal with his

guilt by getting things out in the open." She can see me react in surprise, and she nods. "Yes, he felt guilty every day of his life for leaving, and the articles only made it worse."

"What makes them listen to the wheel, no matter what it says?" I ask. I already know the answer, I just want her to confirm it for me.

She does. "They're not listening to the wheel, and they're not listening to the Keeper. Those people have no doubt they are listening to God."

The rest of our time at lunch is more of the same, with her remembering other stories that her husband told her about life in Center City. She keeps going back to his hunting accident, and how positive she is that the Centurions murdered Henry to keep him quiet. It makes little sense to me that they would kill him after he had told all in the articles, but I don't feel like I should point that out.

As we're ready to leave, she says, "The ironic thing is that the articles had pretty much no effect. People read about the Centurions, and if they gave it a second thought, they just dismissed it as a kook writing about other kooks. It changed nothing."

Catherine Gerard wants this lunch to do what her husband and those articles did not do. She wants it to change life in Center City and to make the leaders there suffer like Henry suffered.

I'm afraid she might well be in for another disappointment.

I spend the drive back being surprised by my reaction to what Catherine had to say. In the Centurions she painted a picture of a group of people who are eccentrics at best and intolerant lunatics at worst. Yet there is a certain logic to their life.

We are a country that reveres faith, and to be a person of faith is to occupy a position of respect. The Centurions are people who take ordinary, run-of-the-mill faith and quadruple it. They turn their lives over to it.

Yet who's to say they are wrong? I certainly think they are, but what the hell do I know? They believe what they believe; and the fact that the world may disagree with them has little significance. Don't most religious people who have a particular faith believe that believers of other faiths are wrong? For example, can Christians and Buddhists both have it one hundred percent right?

Over dinner with Laurie I relate my conversation with Catherine Gerard. Laurie is less interested in the religious aspect of it than I am; she dismisses them as misguided wackos. What she focuses on is the wheel and the fact that these people can completely give up their freedom of choice to it.

I assume my normal role, that of devil's advocate. "Are they really giving up their freedom of choice if that's what they *choose* to do?"

"What do you mean?" she asks.

"I mean that, as stupid as it may sound to us, they believe in this wheel. They think that God talks to them through it. So because of that belief, they choose to follow it."

She's not buying it. "No, they're brainwashed from birth into following it. You think it's a coincidence that everybody born in that town just happens to believe in the wheel? It's pounded into their heads from the day they're born."

"Of course," I say, "but isn't that true everywhere? Don't all parents naturally instill their belief system in their offspring?"

"Not to that degree," she says. "And what kind of life is that? Everything is dictated to you. Can you imagine how horrible it would be to learn who you're going to marry, how you're going to earn a living, at six years old?"

"It certainly wouldn't be my first choice, I'll tell you that."

"It would be stifling," she says.

I shake my head. "For you and me, but apparently not for them. Name a tough decision you've had to make, one you've agonized over."

She answers immediately. "Whether or not to leave you and return to Findlay. It was torture, but it was a decision that I knew I had to make myself, and I finally made it."

"Okay, but what if you had turned it over to someone else and gave that someone full power to tell you what to do? The torture is gone, isn't it?"

She shakes her head adamantly. "Absolutely not; it would be replaced by a different kind of torture. I would feel help-less . . . childlike."

"But if you believed, if in your heart you knew, that it was God making the decision? Wouldn't that be incredibly free-ing, if you could talk to God and let him tell you what is right?"

"No one can do that. Not like that," she says. "And certainly not the Centurions."

"It doesn't matter if they can. It matters if they believe they can. That's why they'll do whatever the wheel tells them to do."

"Including murder?" she asks.

I smile my holiest smile. "That, my child, is still to be determined."

• • • • •

AS PATHETIC AS it sounds, this is my first time in a girl's dorm room. It's not for lack of trying . . . back in college there's no place I would have rather been. It was off-limits back then, even if a girl wanted to invite you in, or at least that's what the girls told me. Which is just as well, since none of them ever expressed anguish that they were so constrained.

It only took Jeremy one day to set this up. According to him, Madeline jumped at the opportunity to come here and get Liz's things when one of Liz's friends made the phone call. Even better, she said that her mother was going to be working, so she would never realize that Madeline was gone.

Liz's friend Emily checked me in at the downstairs desk as her father. She's twenty and I'm thirty-seven, so it's slightly annoying to me that the person at the desk had no trouble believing the relationship. She's left me alone in her room as we wait for Madeline to show, and I'm sitting on the bed feeling like a pervert, Peeping Tom, dirty old man, or something.

I'm not sure exactly what I'm going to say to Madeline. I'll probably act as if I know she's the one who was in contact with Eddie, even though I don't. I hope she's a typically transparent seventeen-year-old and that I'll therefore know from her reaction whether I'm right or wrong.

Madeline said she would be here by one o'clock, and at ten of one I hear people coming down the hall. The door-knob turns, and I move slightly to the side so that I won't be in her line of sight when she enters.

The door opens, and Emily says, "Come on in. There's somebody I want you to see." Madeline walks into the room and Emily backs out, closing the door behind her and leaving Madeline alone with me.

Madeline sees me, and her reactions are astonishing and completely easy to read. First there is a look of surprise, then one of recognition, and finally, a pain like I haven't seen in a very long time. I don't say a word as she starts to sob, sinking to her knees in the process.

I walk over and place my hand on her shoulder as she continues to cry. Finally, it starts to slow down, and she gets up and goes over to the bed. She sits down on it, puts her head in her hands, and gets the remaining sobs out of her system.

"They killed him," are the first words out of her mouth. "They killed Eddie. Just like they killed Liz and Sheryl."

This starts her crying again, so I wait the minute or so that this lasts before responding. "I need you to tell me all about it, Madeline."

She nods her understanding but composes herself a little more before speaking again. "I wanted to call you, to talk to you . . . but I was scared. I am so scared."

"It's okay . . . I understand. I would be scared in your position as well. But we'll make sure you're completely protected. Nothing will happen to you."

She nods again. "I don't know that much," she says.

"Why don't you just tell me what you do know?"

Another nod. "The night Liz died, she was really afraid of

something. She was with Sheryl and Eddie, and I never saw them like that. They were like frightened out of their minds."

"What scared them so much?" I ask.

"I'm not sure . . . they wouldn't tell me. They said it was better if I didn't know."

"Was this before or after Liz went to see Jeremy at the bar?" I ask.

"Before. She went there to tell him she wasn't going to see him anymore. She was running away with Sheryl and Eddie. Sheryl went with her, and Eddie stayed behind to get some things together."

That explains why Liz and Sheryl were killed and Eddie ran away. His staying behind to get some things saved his life, at least for a couple of months, until I set him up to be killed.

"Were you in touch with Eddie after he ran away?" I ask.

"Yes. He called me a few times. The last time he asked me to send him some money."

"So he told you where he was," I say.

She nods. "But I didn't have the money; I was trying to get it. Then that police lady told my mom you had been looking for Eddie, so when he called back, I told him that. I said he should call you . . . that you could help."

"Why didn't he just call the police?"

She shakes her head. "I don't know."

It's possible that Eddie was distrustful of the police because Stephen Drummond represented authority to him. Maybe he thought that contacting the police was the same as contacting Drummond. He told me that he had run that day because he thought I might have been sent by Drummond. Whatever was scaring him, Drummond was behind it.

"You've got to think, Madeline. What could have scared Liz and Sheryl and Eddie like that? Maybe they said something, some little thing, thinking you wouldn't understand."

She thinks for a moment. "All I know is it had something to do with Sheryl's boyfriend."

I was so focused on finding Eddie, Liz's boyfriend, that I spent almost no time thinking about Sheryl, and whether she might have had one as well. Yet Catherine Gerard told me that boys and girls are matched up at six years old. There's no reason to think Sheryl would have been an exception.

"What about him?" I asked. "Was it something he did? Something he said?" I'm probing for information that she unfortunately does not seem to have.

"I just don't know . . . I'm sorry," she says, getting upset at her inability to give me what I want. "They wouldn't tell me."

"Do you know her boyfriend's name?" I ask.

She nods. "Alan."

"Do you know his last name?"

She nods again. "Drummond."

Alan Drummond.

Son of Stephen.

When Eddie told me he was afraid that Drummond was coming for him, he wasn't talking about the father; he was talking about the son.

"Is it possible that Eddie was afraid of Alan?" I ask.

She says it simply, almost matter-of-factly, but it sends a chill through me. "Everybody's afraid of Alan."

I continue to question Madeline, but she has little else to offer in the way of information. Finally, she tells me that she should be going so she can get back before her mother returns home.

"If you're worried, afraid for your safety, I can get you taken into protective custody. That way no one can get near you."

"You're not going to tell anyone we talked, are you?" she asks.

"Only Laurie Collins. She's the chief of police in Findlay, and she won't repeat it. I trust her with my life."

Madeline thinks for a moment, perhaps cognizant that it's not my life we're trusting Laurie with . . . it's her own. Finally, she says, "Okay. How can I reach you if I hear anything important?"

"I don't want you to. I'll take it from here."

"But I want to help if I can," she says. This seventeen-year-old girl is easily the bravest person in this room.

I write my phone number out for her. "Call me any time of the day or night. But not from your house; call from a pay phone."

"I will," she says.

She leaves to make the drive back to Center City, and I head back to Findlay. I'm not anywhere near knowing the "why" behind the murder of three young people, but I may have just learned the "who."

● ● ● ● ●

WE WOULDN'T have anything on Al Capone if he lived in Center City." This is Laurie's way of telling me that my request to check if Alan Drummond has a criminal record is not going to be productive. I'm sure she's right; they are not about to share any details about their citizens with the outside world, and especially not negative ones. And most especially not negative ones about the son of Stephen Drummond.

We're sitting on the couch drinking wine, and Laurie is gently and absentmindedly rubbing my thigh as we talk. If she continues doing that, I'm going to forget what the hell we're talking about.

So I've got to focus. "That's a shame, because Madeline said that everyone was afraid of him," I say. "He must have done some bad things; you don't generate that kind of fear by not cleaning your plate at lunch."

"Have you ever seen him?" she asks.

I nod. "Twice. Big, powerful kid. He was wearing one of those servants of the Keeper uniforms and driving Wallace around."

"So whatever he's up to, there's a good chance Wallace and his father are behind it."

"Probably, but not definitely," I say. "You know, until now I've been thinking that this was all about the religion, about keeping everything secret. I figured these kids were going to run away, and the town leaders decided they couldn't have that happening. But this is something else . . . something bigger."

"Why do you say that?" she asks.

"Well, first of all, Henry Gerard already told the secrets, and nobody cared, remember? Why would anybody listen to these kids, when he wrote articles about it in the damn newspaper and nothing happened? But Madeline said the three kids knew something, probably about Alan Drummond, and it scared them so much they were leaving their town and their families."

"They had nobody to turn to," she says. "Alan's father is the number two guy in town, and his regular passenger is number one."

Something pops into my head. "Hey, I remember something else. The kid's a pilot; I saw a picture of the family in his father's office. They were standing in front of a plane, and Stephen told me that his son was the pilot in the family."

"So maybe he does more than drive Wallace around in a car," she says. "The question then is, where would Wallace be flying to?"

I shrug. "Maybe the wheel sends him on trips. Probably to conventions with other wackos."

"Shouldn't be too hard to find out."

"What do you mean?" I ask.

"If they're flying around, they've got to declare flight plans with the FAA. I should be able to get the records."

"It's worth a shot. When can you do it?"

"Well," she says, "I can spend a few hours on the phone now trying to find someone who can help, or we can go to bed now and I can make one phone call in the morning."

I think about this for a moment. "In which scenario are you likely to be naked faster?"

"The 'bed now, call in the morning' one."

"Then that's the one we go with."

It turns out to be a great choice, but like all good things, it comes to an end when the alarm goes off at six A.M. Laurie is showered, dressed, and out of the house in forty-five minutes, leaving me and Tara to reflect on just what the hell we think we're doing here.

I'm pleased with the progress I've made so far, and certainly not regretting deciding to stay, but I am feeling somewhat out of my element. I'm an attorney, not a detective, and I'm finding that this new role requires a different mind-set and strategic outlook.

Generally on a case I view events and information through the prism of the legal system in general and its likely effect on a jury in particular. Even though a trial is often referred to as a search for the truth, that's not my job. My job is to convince a jury to accept my truth, which is that my client is not guilty of the crime for which he or she is charged.

This detective stuff comes with a different mandate. I've got to find the real truth, actually extract it from people who don't want to give it up. By definition those people are dangerous, and by definition I am not. I have a natural inclination to avoid danger, an inclination often referred to as cowardice, which leaves me with a dilemma. It's hard to avoid danger when the truth is hiding behind it and I'm after the truth.

I'm finding that another difference between lawyering and detecting is the gaps between events. When I'm on a case, I can fill those gaps with preparation for trial. In my detecting mode, I often find that I'm sitting and waiting for something to happen, like right now, when I'm waiting for

Laurie to find out information regarding the flight plans in and out of the tiny Center City Airport.

It's almost four in the afternoon when Laurie calls me. "You got a pen?" she asks.

"I'm a lawyer . . . what do you think?"

"Take down this number," she says, and then reads me a phone number with a 202 area code, which I recognize as Washington, D.C. "It's the FAA. We got really lucky: Sandy Walsh has a cousin whose wife works there. Ask for Donna Girardi."

"Didn't you find out the information?" I ask.

"I did, but I want you to hear it from her directly. And you might have some additional questions."

We hang up and I dial the number. Within moments I'm talking to Donna Girardi. "Chief Collins said you had information about the flight plans coming out of Center City Airport."

"I do," she says. "There are no such plans."

I'm taken aback by this news, but less than fully confident that Ms. Girardi has taken the time to check through all the records. "How were you able to find this out so fast?" I ask.

"Because there is no such airport."

"It's not really an airport . . . it's more of an airfield," I say. "There's just a runway, a small hangar, and one other building. I think they just use it for their personal planes . . . it's not like United Airlines is flying in and out of there."

"Every facility that's used for takeoffs and landings, no matter how small, is required to be registered with our agency. Not to do so is a federal crime."

"It would be really great if you didn't investigate this particular federal crime for a while." One thing I don't need right now is the FAA entering the picture and tipping off the Centurions that something is going on.

"Chief Collins mentioned something about that as well.

Let's just say that a landing strip in Wisconsin is not a particularly high priority for our investigators. Especially in December."

"When might it become a priority?" I ask.

"Without some incident requiring our attention, I would say you're looking at July," she says.

I look outside at the frozen tundra that is Wisconsin and the snow that is starting to fall.

"Ms. Girardi, right now there is nothing I would like better than to look at July."

I thank her and end the call. The fact that the FAA has no record of the Center City airstrip could be crucially important. It could indicate that something illegal is happening there, and it could be the information that led to the death of Liz and Sheryl, and later Calvin and Eddie.

Or it could be of no significance whatsoever, merely a reflection of Center City's resistance to outside authority. They never reported the airstrip's existence and never filed flight plans, and no one has bothered them about it.

It does me no good to believe that this new information is unimportant. I have to focus on the airstrip, both because it's a very good lead and because I have nothing else nearly as good.

My shortage of things to focus on disappears with the ringing of my telephone.

"Hello?"

The voice is young and near panic. "Mr. Carpenter, it's Madeline. They know I talked to you. They were looking for me, but I got away."

"Where are you now?"

"I'm at a pay phone on Route 5 . . . a picnic area that people use in the summer. Near the Hampton Road exit."

"I think I know where it is. Are you alone?"

"Yes."

"Is there a place where you can go inside? To get shelter?" I'm thinking such a place would be good to hide in, but I don't mention that.

"Yes. There's a small building, they sell drinks and things in there in the summer."

"Okay, go inside. I'm coming to get you."

"Okay," she says, but her voice doesn't sound like she thinks everything's okay at all.

"It'll be fine, Madeline. I promise. No one will hurt you."

"Please hurry, Mr. Carpenter."

"I'm on my way."

I rush out to the car. It should take me about fifteen minutes to get there, providing I actually know where the hell it is. Either way, it won't be enough time to beat myself up over putting another teenager into jeopardy. My mind's eye has been flashing all week to Eddie hanging from the skylight in that bathroom, and I will simply not be able to stand it if anything happens to Madeline.

I'm five minutes away before I realize I should be calling Laurie to tell her what's happening and where I'm going. I dial her number on my cell phone, but the sergeant at the desk says that she's out of the office.

"It's Andy Carpenter. Please reach her and tell her that it's urgent she call me on my cell phone."

"She should be back in a few minutes."

"It can't wait that long. This is life-and-death." It sounds like a cliché when I say it, but I really believe it's true.

He agrees to contact her right away. I tell him where I'm going to be, and that if she can't reach my cell for any reason, she should go there immediately. I add the strong suggestion that she bring some of her fellow officers with her.

So as not to drive by it, I slow down as I reach the area where I believe Madeline called from. I spot it and pull off the road. A sign directs me to the picnic area, though the area is frozen over with snow and ice.

Off in the distance I can see picnic tables and a few sets of swings, all of which have at least another five months' vacation ahead of them. Just past them is a small building, with a car parked nearby. I assume and hope that it's Madeline's car.

I drive and park about twenty yards from the building. "Madeline?" I call out, but I get no response.

I walk toward the building, continuing to call her name and getting no response. Finally, I hear, "I'm in here."

I don't like the way this is setting up. She should have heard me the first few times I called, but she didn't answer. And if I were her, I wouldn't be calling me to come inside. I'd be coming outside, so as faster to get away to safety.

My hope is that I'm just being paranoid, but either way I have no choice. I've got to go inside. I walk up the three steps and see that the door is open. "Madeline, are you all right?"

"Yes." Her reply is shaky, worrying me even more. I reach the door. Here goes . . .

When I get inside, I don't see her at first, and then there she is, at the far corner of the room. My worst fears are realized because standing next to her is one of the servants of the Keeper. I've seen him before in the town, but he looks even larger and stronger now.

His hand rests on the back of Madeline's neck, and she's cowering from it. She's trying to control her sobs and repeating over and over how sorry she is. She and me both.

"Come in, Mr. Carpenter," says her captor. I'm already in, but there's an open door behind me, and he obviously doesn't want me running out through it. It's not the worst of ideas, but even I couldn't leave Madeline behind like that.

"Don't hurt her," I say. "She's done nothing to you." I

have no expectation that anything I say will make him any more conciliatory or compassionate, and that's not my goal. My goal is to keep him from doing anything until Laurie and her officers can get here.

"She spoke to you," he says.

"She told me nothing. She didn't know anything at all."

"You believe that?" he asks.

I start to tell him that I do, and then I realize that he's not talking to me. I half turn and see that behind me is another one just like him, only even larger. They probably represent close to five hundred pounds between them, and with a feeling of panic and dread, I realize that they are not here to warn us. They are here to kill us.

"You expected him to tell the truth?" number two asks. "You know what he is."

I can feel number two start to walk toward me, so I turn toward him, not wanting to be attacked from behind. Suddenly, he seems to turn horizontal, almost suspended in midair, as something smashes into the side of his head. That head and his shoulders fly to the left, and his feet leave the ground to the right. When he hits the ground, standing in my line of vision is Marcus Clark.

Marcus just stands there, expressionless, as his victim lies on the ground, moaning. His eyes are trained on the other servant, who no longer looks quite so confident. His hand is still on Madeline's neck, but it seems as if he's doing so to get support rather than to threaten.

"I can break her neck," he warns, and there is no doubt he is capable of just that. There is also no doubt that Marcus is undeterred by the threat as he walks slowly toward them.

I pick up motion back near the door, and I see that the guy who Marcus hit has gotten shakily to his feet. "Marcus!" I yell, and Marcus turns to see what is going on.

Apparently, Marcus didn't knock the first guy senseless,

because he's maintained enough of his faculties to know that he doesn't want any more of Marcus. He runs out the door, and as he does so, the guy holding Madeline throws her across the room. She crashes into a counter as her former captor runs out a side door.

I go to make sure that Madeline is okay, while Marcus goes out the side door to see if he can catch the two servants. I hear the sound of motors starting, and I look out the window. They are taking off in snowmobiles, which had been parked behind the building. It's why I only saw Madeline's car when I drove up.

Madeline seems shaken but all right. My cell phone rings; it's Laurie calling as directed. "We're on our way there now. What's wrong, Andy?"

"Everything's under control now, thanks to Marcus. But you should get an ambulance out here as well . . . Madeline Barlow may be injured."

I hang up and do my best to comfort Madeline, who seems to be in shock. Marcus comes back in from outside; there was no way he could go after them on the snowmobiles.

Laurie arrives within five minutes with Cliff Parsons and two other officers. The officers attend to Madeline until the ambulance arrives, while I give Laurie and Parsons a detailed accounting of what happened.

When I get to the part about the second servant coming up behind me, I say that Marcus arrived just in time. "Which is amazing, because he came here all the way from New Jersey," I say pointedly at Laurie.

"I'm sorry," she says, "I know you told me you didn't want him here, but I thought you might need him."

"*Me?* Need *him?*" I sneer. "You must be kidding."

Laurie just smiles and goes out to the ambulance, as Madeline is being loaded in. Laurie leans over, squeezes her hand, and kisses her on the head. She whispers something to her, but I can't make out what it is.

Then Laurie and Parsons go back inside to attempt to interview Marcus.

Lots of luck, guys.

• • • • •

MADELINE BARLOW has gone through more than anyone should have to. She has seen her sister and friends murdered, and she cannot get anyone in her town, including her mother, to understand the continued danger that lives among them. She has been threatened and kidnapped for simply talking to someone trying to learn the truth. Now she is away from her home, from what's left of her family, and she remains in fear for her life.

Fortunately, her physical injuries are quite minor, just a few bruises from her fall. Emotionally, she is trying to put up a good front, but she is one damaged young lady. She has adamantly refused to see her mother, though Jane Barlow has spent considerable time in the hospital lobby, hoping she will change her mind.

Stephen Drummond has called me to express outrage at my intervention in the affairs of his community and the Barlow family. He started to launch into a denial that Madeline was in any danger in Center City, claiming that we coerced her to leave. Not in the mood for any more of his bullshit, I suggested that he file a complaint with the police, and I hung up.

Laurie has assigned Cliff Parsons to investigate and try

to apprehend the two men who terrorized Madeline before themselves being terrorized by Marcus. Three days have gone by, and if any progress has been made, I haven't heard about it. Center City is a tough place to crack, and though it's part of the area Parsons has always covered, he's very much an outsider there.

Laurie has gotten Madeline placed under the control of Wisconsin Child Protective Services, even though Madeline is only five weeks from her eighteenth birthday. Legally, it makes it possible for us to find a safe place for her to stay, and I took care of that yesterday. Richard and Allie Davidson generously offered to let her share their home, and Madeline agreed, at least for now. Part of her going along with it was my promise that Marcus would help watch over her. After his performance the other day, with Marcus at her side Madeline would feel safe in Jurassic Park.

I've been visiting Madeline every day and have taken occasion to gently probe to see if she can provide any more helpful information about the case. She cannot, a fact that causes her obvious frustration.

Laurie has seen her every day as well, and she was there yesterday when I arrived. They have established a remarkably close relationship, and Laurie obviously feels very protective of her. Her motherly instincts have come to the fore, and they are impressive indeed.

The events at the picnic area have made me more anxious than ever to nail the people who killed Liz, Sheryl, Eddie, and Calvin and tried to do the same to Madeline and me. If my knowledge matched my motivation, I might even succeed.

All I really have to go on is my belief that the airstrip is central to the solution. And the only way I'm going to find out for sure is to execute a stakeout there.

I have been told by a number of cops, Pete Stanton and

Laurie among them, that there is nothing more boring than working on a stakeout. It can be endless hours of having to stay alert while absolutely nothing happens. I don't mind the endless hours or the nothing happening; you can put me in front of a TV showing sports and I'll sit there until a week from Tuesday. It's the staying alert that's the problem; I prefer drinking beer and occasional dozing.

Fortunately, I'm very rich, and it is "so not chic" for multi-millionaires to do stakeouts. I call Dave Larson and tell him that I need his help, with a stakeout of the airport as his first assignment. He's very enthusiastic about getting the work; the private eye business in Findlay has apparently experienced a bit of a slowdown these last hundred years or so.

We discuss his hours, which I suggest should be as many as he can handle. He tells me that he has an associate who will be on the scene when he can't. We also discuss his pay, and I increase what we earlier agreed upon by twenty-five percent. It's still half of what I would pay in New Jersey, but the raise makes me feel less guilty about turning him into a frozen snowman.

He asks that I inform the Findlay police about what we're doing, and I have no problem with that, especially since I've already told Laurie. Dave wants to have someone know his whereabouts in case of sudden trouble, and for some reason he doesn't consider me a significant enough emergency lifeline.

"What is it we're looking for?" he asks.

"I'm not sure . . . something bad."

"How bad?" he asks.

"Bad enough that four people got killed over it."

"Oh."

"So be careful," I say.

"You got that right."

• • • • •

I KNOW THE Bible says otherwise, but Christmas must have been invented in Wisconsin. It just looks the part. The streets remain white for days after it snows, not turning dark and dirty like what happens in the city. Virtually every house is decorated with colored lights; after dark Findlay in December becomes a frozen Vegas strip.

Laurie and I have been quite out in the open about our relationship, now that the case has been over for a while. And with Jeremy cleared of the murders, the portion of townspeople that resented my appearance on the scene seem to have gotten over it. They are making me feel welcome, though I suspect most of them are wondering exactly why I'm still here. It's a terrific question.

I've seen Madeline Barlow a handful of times, and she's doing quite well with the Davidsons. She's homesick for her mother and friends, but not yet willing to see any of them. Laurie has seen her much more often and is struck by Madeline's unwillingness to say anything negative about Keeper Wallace or the Centurion religion. Madeline considers this to be about a few bad apples, and not in any way a reflection on the lifestyle. Belief runs deep in Center City.

I'm now three weeks into the Dave Larson airport stakeout, and absolutely nothing has happened. No planes have taken off, and none have landed. The only sign of life, other than Dave, is a snowplow that arrives daily to plow the landing strip and keep it functional.

Cliff Parsons has reported no progress in finding the two guys who grabbed Madeline. No one in Center City will admit that they even exist, and there simply is no way to locate them, given the lack of cooperation within the community.

To make the futility complete, Laurie's investigations into the murders of Liz, Sheryl, and Calvin have gone nowhere as well. There has been no new evidence, no discoveries, no nothing for a while now. Short of a confession, the chances for solving these cases are looking as bleak as the terrain around here.

Yet Andy the Idiot Lawyer continues to persist, hanging around in the frozen north and waiting for something to happen. It reminds me of the old joke . . . I think I heard it as a lawyer joke, but it could have been about any group or nationality. "Did you hear about the lawyer who froze to death at a drive-in movie? He went to see *Closed for the Season.*" Well, Findlay has been closed for the season for a while now, but I'm still sitting in my car waiting for the coming attractions.

Making my mood even worse is all the holiday cheer I'm surrounded by. I tag along with Laurie to about four hundred parties, though in Findlay the word "parties" may be overstating it. They're more pleasant get-togethers with smiling people who talk about good health and toast with eggnog. It's enough to make me nauseous, with or without the eggnog, yet Laurie seems to revel in it.

Since today is Christmas, it seemed an appropriate time to give my stakeout team the day off. They've uncovered absolutely no activity of any kind at the airport, and there's no reason to think that any nefarious activity would suddenly spring up on Christmas Day.

I tell Laurie about the suspension of the stakeout, since she is the officer in charge at the precinct today. Laurie has voluntarily agreed to work on the holiday so as to give Parsons and others under her a chance to be with their families.

The net result of her generosity to her staff is that Tara and I are left alone. I turn down a bunch of invitations to spend Christmas at various friends of Laurie's, preferring to indulge my bad mood by staying home and watching a college bowl game and two NBA games.

I call in a bet on the bowl game, since why else would anyone in their right mind want to watch Toledo play Hawaii in the Aloha Bowl? I take Toledo and four points, and I realize I'm in trouble before the opening kickoff. The coaches for Toledo are wearing ridiculous flowered Hawaiian shirts, not the kind of outfits that will motivate their players to fight their hardest for dear old Toledo U.

Sure enough, Hawaii is ahead 31–3 at halftime, and unless the flower-shirted coaches are going to convince their team to blossom for the Gipper, my bet is history.

This leaves me more time to think, a pastime I haven't found to be terribly enjoyable lately. It is burning a hole in my gut that cold-blooded murderers are out there, getting away with what they've done and probably pointing and laughing at me in the process.

"You feel like going on a stakeout?" I ask Tara.

She doesn't get excited and start wagging her tail, but nor does she growl or cover her head with her paws. Tara has led a fairly sheltered life, and it's just possible she's never been on a stakeout before and therefore doesn't know what to expect.

"We sit in the car, with the heat on, and eat potato chips

and dog biscuits," I say by way of explanation. Her tail starts to wag, but I think it's the word "biscuits" that does it.

"Blah, blah, blah, blah, blah, blah, blah, biscuits," I say, and get the same wag. I think I'm detecting a pattern.

In a few minutes I've stocked the car with stakeout supplies and we're driving out toward the Center City airstrip. I'm aware it's a ridiculous, unproductive thing to do, but the possibility that something will happen on the one day we're not watching is gnawing at me.

We're at the airstrip in twenty minutes, and we take up the same position that Larson has been occupying. It only takes a quick look to see that today is no different than every other day; the place is totally quiet, with no one to be seen anywhere.

Within thirty seconds I'm bored out of my mind and Tara is asleep on the backseat. I know that it's very unlikely that anything will come of this, but just in case, I need to remain alert.

When I wake up, the clock in the car tells me that I've been asleep for almost an hour. Tara continues to sleep on the backseat; she has many wonderful qualities, but ability as a stakeout dog is not one of them.

Within moments I realize that I didn't just happen to wake up, that an increasingly loud noise did the trick. I look around, trying to find the source of the noise, which seems to be coming from up in the air. Maybe ten seconds later I see it, coming from the other side of the airstrip. It's a small cargo plane, already quite low and obviously coming in for a landing.

My heart starts pounding in my chest, and a bunch of things quickly run through my mind. One is that I have no idea what to do. Another is that I'm sorry I brought Tara; the idea of exposing her to any possible danger is simply unacceptable. Even dumber than bringing Tara was forgetting my cell phone, which leaves me with no possible way to call for help.

It's warm in the car, but I'm frozen in place, watching the scene unfold before me. The cargo plane lands and taxis toward the hangar. The large hangar door opens, revealing the presence of someone inside. I can't come close to seeing who it is from this distance, and I don't know if that person has been there the whole time, or arrived during my nap.

The plane enters the hangar, and the door comes down behind it. Once again the airport takes on that desolate, abandoned look, but this time I know better. I know that there are humans in that hangar; what I don't know is what the hell they are doing.

I briefly debate whether to leave my car and sneak across the airfield to the hangar, so as to learn what is going on. The reason the debate is brief is that the idea of it is stupid: I would be completely exposed to anyone who bothered to look outside.

So all I can do is wait, and I do so, for an hour and twenty-one minutes. That's when the door opens, but instead of the plane coming back out, a truck rolls out. It looks like any one of the trucks that carry goods out of Center City. It's hard to make out the name from this distance, but my best guess is "R&W Dairies."

The truck rolls out onto the road, heading in my direction. I'm set off from the road, and there's no way the driver will be able to see me. The unfortunate flip side of that is that there is no way I will be able to see him.

I get out of the car, leaving it running so that Tara will remain warm. I move quickly toward the road, just reaching it as the truck goes past. The side of the truck does say "R&W Dairies," and there are two people in the front seat. From my vantage point I can't see who the passenger is, but I definitely recognize the driver.

Alan Drummond.

I go back to the car and get in. I slam the door shut, which wakes up my stakeout mate in the backseat. She looks around as if to say, "What did I miss?" but I don't give her the satisfaction of telling her.

My strong desire is to go toward the airstrip and check out what might still be inside the hangar. That desire collides head-on with my self-preservation instinct, and I decide against it. I have no idea whether there are any people still in there, but if there are, I'd be a sitting duck.

I drive back to Findlay, annoyed that all this took place without me learning anything from it, but somehow rejuvenated by the process.

● ● ● ● ●

LET'S GO" are the first words out of Laurie's mouth when she hears my story. I dropped Tara off and came here to her office, and within three minutes Laurie and I are back out and in the car.

"We're going out to the airstrip?" I ask.

"That's right. We're going to check it out."

Ever the lawyer, I point out, "You don't have a search warrant."

"I've got something better than that," she says. "I've got a citizen who reported seeing a possible crime taking place."

"That would be me?"

She nods. "It would."

Laurie drives right up to the airstrip with no apparent hesitation, but makes a rather obvious concession to the possible danger by taking out her handgun as she gets out of the car.

We walk to the smaller door, the one that lets in people but not planes, and Laurie rings the bell. We hear it sounding loudly through the building, so if anyone is in there, they could not help but hear it as well. Laurie holds her gun at her side, concealed but ready.

There is no answer, so she tries twice more. Still no response.

"Can you kick it in?" she asks.

"Excuse me?" I ask, though we both know I heard her quite clearly.

She takes out a small device, which looks a little like a can opener, and calmly pops the lock. The door swings open.

I shake my head, showing my disapproval. "Illegal entry, said the defense attorney to the judge."

"I had a perfect right to do that," she says. "I believed that someone might be in distress; the citizen I was with thought he heard a scream."

"That would be me?" I ask.

"It would."

We enter the hangar and see the plane, the hold open and empty of cargo. There are no people around, no trucks, and no evidence of what might have been on that plane.

Laurie says, "So a plane comes in on Christmas Day, leaving a cargo that is taken off in a dairy truck. Doesn't sound terribly normal to me."

"Maybe somebody needed a cheese transplant, and they flew in a Gouda."

We close up the hangar and leave. Laurie drops me back off at the house, and she heads to her office. We make plans for her to come over for dinner, at which point we'll try to figure out where we go from here.

I call Sam Willis at home and ask him to get on the computer and see if he can find out anything about R&W Dairies. It only takes him about forty-five minutes to call back and tell me exactly what I expected: He can find no record of such a company.

What I believe happened today is that a cargo plane landed at the Center City airstrip, its contents were unloaded and placed on a truck, and that truck was driven away by Alan Drummond.

In legal terms I have only circumstantial evidence of this; I certainly didn't see the unloading and loading take place. Theoretically, the plane could have come in empty, and the truck could coincidentally have left empty a short while later. But as the old example goes, if you go to sleep with the streets clear, then wake up in the morning and they're covered with snow, it's a good bet it snowed that night, whether you saw it happen or not. The airstrip scenario is not quite as clear as that, but it's clear enough for me.

By the time Laurie comes over, I've formulated some theories well enough to bounce off of her. "There is no doubt in my mind," I say, "that whatever those kids were afraid of that night has to do with Alan Drummond and that airport."

She's not quite so convinced. "We're making some assumptions here," she says. "We don't know for a fact that they were afraid of Alan Drummond, only that Madeline thinks so."

"Eddie said he was afraid I was Drummond," I point out.

"He could have meant Stephen, and it could have been because Stephen is the number two man in that church. Stephen represented authority, and Eddie could have been afraid of that authority."

"You don't believe that," I say.

"That's true, but it is possible. And while we're talking about what's possible, it's also possible that there is nothing criminal going on at that airport. All we know for sure is that a plane came in and a truck left."

"A cargo plane with no flight plan came into an airstrip that according to the FAA does not exist."

She doesn't seem happy with this, so I continue. "Laurie, I agree that I am making assumptions here. But that is the only way I can move forward. If they're wrong, then they're wrong. But for now I have to assume they're right."

She nods; that makes sense to her. "Okay, make some more assumptions."

"I assume that the plane was carrying illegal merchandise of some sort, maybe drugs, maybe counterfeit money. Whatever it was had to be small enough to fit on that truck."

"Where was it coming from?" she asks.

"Canada. I spoke to Donna Girardi again today and bounced some ideas off of her. If it originated across the border, came in over Lake Superior, and flew low enough, it likely wouldn't be picked up on radar in this area. But if it flew over the U.S. most of the time, the chance of it not being detected would go way down."

"And if it weren't crossing a border, there would be no need for a plane," she says. "They could just load it on a dairy truck in the first place."

"Right . . . so here's my theory: Alan Drummond, probably acting on behalf of his father and Wallace, has been smuggling illegal goods from Canada by plane. Liz, Sheryl, and Eddie somehow found out about it. Perhaps Sheryl was the first one to discover it, since she was Alan's girlfriend, and she told her friends. Alan realized what they knew, and they were all too aware how dangerous Alan could be, so they tried to run. Liz and Sheryl didn't make it, and Eddie made the mistake of calling me."

Laurie thinks about this for a long while, weighing the possibilities. "Okay, but something else bothers me," she says. "You had someone staking out that airport for weeks, and nothing happens. The day you pull your guy out of there, in comes a plane."

"Maybe they saw Larson on his stakeout and then followed him. Maybe they were smart enough to track the guy tracking them."

"It's possible, but a stretch," she says.

"Or maybe Christmas Day was always going to be the day they did it. I'm sure the Centurions don't celebrate Christmas, but they know that nobody's out on the roads . . . everybody's home with their families . . ."

She still looks dubious as she considers the possibilities.

"Laurie, I'm a lawyer. I come up with my theory of a case, and I pursue it. This is no different; in fact, there have been plenty of times that I've had a lot less to go on. The only difference for me is that usually I have to convince a jury, but now I have to convince you."

"Why me?"

"Because I need you to take the next step."

"Which is?"

"To be there when this happens again, stop the truck, and search it."

She thinks about this for a few moments and says, "I can't spare people to watch that airport for another flight to come in. It took three weeks last time; this time they could be waiting for Memorial Day."

"You don't have to do that. I'll have Larson watch it; he'll be much less noticeable this time."

"Why is that?"

"Because he doesn't have to get close to the airport. He's just watching for a plane, and we know what direction it's coming from. He can be a long distance away."

"And where will your police officers be stationed?" she asks. It's a not-so-subtle dig at me for trying to use her department as my personal investigative staff.

I pretend not to notice. "They don't have to be stationed anywhere," I say. "From the time Larson sees the plane, we'll have at least an hour to get in position to wait for the truck. I'll call you or Parsons, and then your officers come out and stop the truck along the road."

She spends a few more minutes trying to poke holes in my plan but is unable to make a dent. Finally, she says, "Okay. I'll set it up."

"Good. I'll tell Larson."

I give her my best boyish smile of victory, with just a touch of humility thrown in. It's a specialty of mine, and to my knowledge women have no defense against it. When I use it, they are genetically compelled to kiss me.

Laurie, it turns out, must have some kind of genetic defect, because all she does is leave.

• • • • •

LARSON'S CALL takes me by surprise. It's
only been three days since we put our plan into action, much
sooner than I expected.

"I've got incoming at twelve o'clock" are his first words.
He sounds like he's talking to his tail gunner, but I resist the
impulse to say "Roger" or "Wilco." Instead I say, "Got it," and
I hang up the phone and call Laurie.

Laurie and Parsons have been alternating days being on
call, and today is her turn. She wastes no time in telling me
that she and her people will meet me at the designated area.
I drive out there, hiding my car behind nearby trees. Laurie
and three officers arrive a few minutes later in three cars and
set up for the roadblock.

Larson, as per our plan, drives toward the airport, though
he keeps a safe distance away. He is to call me when the
truck leaves and to confirm that it is again an R&W Dairies
truck.

An hour and ten minutes after the original call, Larson
calls me on my cell phone. "It's heading towards you," he
says. "R&W."

We've estimated that the truck will take five minutes to
reach us, and it makes it in four. Once it's in sight, Laurie and

her team execute a roadblock, using two of the cars. The third car circles behind the truck, blocking a possible escape to the rear. It's done with great precision, and as I watch, I feel a flash of pride and admiration.

The truck slows to a halt, and I can see Alan Drummond in the driver's seat. This time he is alone; or at least there is no one in the passenger seat. There could certainly be someone in the back with whatever merchandise was transferred from the plane.

Two of Laurie's officers have their guns drawn, though Laurie does not. "Step down from the truck, Mr. Drummond," Laurie instructs.

Alan Drummond does as he is told. He may be intimidating to the youth of Center City, but he couldn't be further from that right now. Unless I'm a very bad judge of emotions, he is close to panic-stricken at what is taking place.

"What's the matter? What's going on?" he asks.

Laurie instructs him on the proper position to assume, with his hands against the squad car and legs spread. He does so, and one of the officers frisks him, signaling with a shake of the head to Laurie that he is not armed.

"Is the back of the truck locked?" she asks.

"Hey, come on. I didn't do anything wrong" is his answer. It comes across as a bit of a whine, reflecting his fear at the way events are moving.

"Is the back of the truck locked?" Laurie repeats.

"Yes."

"Where is the key?" she asks.

His mind seems to be racing for a way out of this, so much so that he forgets to answer the question. Laurie repeats it, and he says that it's on the key ring that is still in the ignition.

One of the officers gets the key, and he gives it to Laurie. He then handcuffs Drummond and leads him back to one of the patrol cars, putting him in the backseat. Laurie and the other two officers go around to the rear of the truck. They both draw their guns while Laurie unlocks the door and opens it.

The odor of cheese slams into us the moment the door opens. Looking inside, I can see about fifteen barrels, the type that would ordinarily contain cheese, but this time they had better not. The smell is not a good sign, and Laurie makes eye contact with me that indicates she doesn't like where this is going.

It takes an hour and twenty minutes for the officers to search through the truck's cargo, though it feels like about a week. They find nothing but cheese, which I suppose on some level makes sense, since they're searching a cheese truck.

When they finish, Laurie just gives me a shake of the head to indicate what a waste of time this was. An officer takes Drummond out of the car and uncuffs him.

"What is R&W Dairies?" she asks him.

"It's a . . . it used to be a dairy company in this county," says Drummond. "They went out of business a few years ago, and we bought their stuff. We never bothered to change the name on the truck."

"What was the cargo on the plane that just landed at the Center City airstrip?"

"Nothing . . . it was empty."

Laurie asks him some more questions, but he's feeling increasingly confident, and he deflects them. She doesn't want to probe too much, so as not to reveal the little that we do know.

"You're free to go, Mr. Drummond," she says.

His face is a mask of surprise and relief. "I can go?" he says, to make sure he heard correctly.

"That's correct," Laurie says, and Drummond wastes no

time in getting back in the truck and hauling his ass, and his cheese, out of here.

Laurie walks over to me. "Well, we did it, Andy. We smashed a Parmesan cartel."

She and her officers get in their cars and leave, my humiliation complete. I have no idea what went wrong, but I'll have plenty of time to think about it. Unfortunately, thinking has not been my strong point of late.

I was wrong about what was in the truck, but no matter how many ways I look at it, I don't believe I was wrong about the big picture. Even if there had been no murders, and no one had expressed a fear of Alan Drummond, what took place today would still be absurd.

It is simply preposterous to assume that a cargo plane flew into that airstrip, set in the middle of a community whose only product is cheese, and delivered a load of cheese. Yet that is exactly what seems to have happened. What I need to figure out is why.

By the time Laurie comes over for dinner, I have it narrowed down to two possibilities. One is that our adversaries are watching Larson, and once they found out that he was still staking out the airport, they set us up to look foolish.

The other possibility, perhaps more likely, is that Laurie and I weren't careful enough and left some evidence that we searched the airstrip hangar the last time the plane came in. It signaled that we were on to them and would continue to be watching. So they set us up.

Laurie, to her credit, is not angry about what happened. She accepts the responsibility, since she went along with it willingly. But even though we both agreed on what should be done, she will suffer the most for it. Stephen Drummond will certainly file a complaint over the way his son was treated, and Laurie will at the least receive a severe reprimand.

We talk about it through dinner and afterward. It's only when we're finished and heading for bed that I think of something that I noticed on the road but hadn't thought about since. "Did you think Alan Drummond looked scared when he came down off that truck?"

She nods. "Petrified. That's one of the reasons I was so surprised when we didn't find anything."

"I felt the same thing. And I think he really was afraid. He couldn't be that good an actor, and he would have had no reason to even try."

"Which means he thought he was in trouble." Then, "Do you think it's possible he didn't know what he was carrying? That he was as surprised as we were when it turned out to be barrels of cheese?"

"Yes, I absolutely think it's possible. But if *he* didn't know what was in that truck, who did?"

• • • • •

I'M GOING TO have to adjust my goals downward. This will not be easy; downward goal adjustment has never been a specialty of mine. But it's got to be done.

I've stayed in Findlay in order to identify the one or more people who killed Liz, Sheryl, Eddie, and Calvin. I now believe that those murders were committed to cover up a criminal conspiracy, the geographical center of which is the Center City airstrip.

My recent efforts, however futile and embarrassing, have been directed toward uncovering the details behind that conspiracy. I will continue in that vein, and I may or may not succeed. But even if I do, it's a stretch to think that evidence will also be uncovered to make a charge of murder stick. So my new goal will have to be to get the bad guys put in jail for the criminal conspiracy, which will no doubt be a lesser charge than they deserve. What they deserve, as Jeremy Davidson said, is to be strapped down and have a needle inserted in their arms.

By the time Laurie leaves for work, we've come up with Plan B. I call it B even though it's very similar to Plan A. It's just that A was such a disaster it seemed logical to move on to a new letter.

We're going to continue a stakeout of the airport, though

this time Larson will not be involved. I'm going to have Marcus with me, taking him off his assignment of watching over Madeline Barlow. No one has made any kind of an effort to go after her, and Laurie will have Cliff Parsons make sure she is watched by one of their officers.

We're going to be in Marcus's car, so if anyone is watching me, my car will be parked in front of my house. Marcus will ensure that we are not followed, so there will be no reason for anyone to think the airport is being watched.

I've told Laurie I will call her, as before, if anything happens. What I've neglected to mention is that Marcus and I are going to take a more active approach. Before we call Laurie, we're going to move into the airport and try to catch the bad guys in the act, whatever that act might be.

I'm not thrilled about deceiving her in this manner, but I don't feel like there is any alternative. As civilians, Marcus and I do not have the right to do what we might wind up doing, and if Laurie had the knowledge of it, her job would compel her to prevent us from doing it.

Going into this operation, I knew there were a couple of possible downsides. For one, we could wind up getting killed. Actually, I can't picture Marcus getting killed, so I'm more worried about me. Second, we could accomplish nothing except wasting a lot of time and effort.

Sitting in the car now, about fifteen minutes into the first day, I realize I hadn't factored in another downside. I'm stuck alone in a car with Marcus.

I feel like I should make conversation, but I don't have the slightest idea how to have one with Marcus. "Sandwich?" I ask, thinking he might like one of the sandwiches I made and brought with us.

"Unhh," he says.

"I've got roast beef, turkey, and turkey pastrami."

"Unhh," he says.

"I've never actually seen a turkey pastrami, have you? I mean, do they look like regular turkeys? Or regular pastramis?"

"Unhh," he says.

"To tell you the truth, I wouldn't know what a pastrami looked like if it were sitting in the backseat."

"Unhh," he says.

"Anyway, they're in the cooler in the trunk if you want one," I say. "Just help yourself."

This time he just nods; maybe he feels like he's been chatting too much.

Suddenly, I realize that the radio is not on. I don't know if playing the radio violates stakeout etiquette, but I've got to do something to cut through the silence. "Okay if I turn on the radio?" I ask.

He shrugs his assent, and I turn it on. Classical music blares through the speakers, and in about four seconds I find myself longing for silence. "I'll tell you what," I say. "You listen to what you want for an hour, then I get the choice for an hour, then you, and so on. That work for you?"

He nods.

"Great. This your choice for now?"

Another nod.

"Okay," I say, looking at my watch. "We change over at about . . . oh . . . nine-sixteen and thirty-one seconds. Somewhere around there."

Still another nod; it looks like we have a deal. I think I'll grab myself a sandwich.

Seven hours into our stakeout, I may even be getting to like classical music. "Like" may be too strong; "tolerate" would probably be more accurate. We've just concluded the latest hour with some Beethoven, and my critical assessment would be that it's got a good beat, but you can't dance to it.

I've been using my precious hours for a combination of

news and sports, and I start this one with news. The news-caster introduces a feature piece about "the obesity epidemic in America," and I see Marcus perk up, seeming to listen intently. It surprises me, since his percentage of body fat is slightly less than absolute zero.

I lean over and turn the volume up a little, to allow him to hear better, but in a quick motion he reaches and shuts the radio off entirely. This seems to be a violation of our arrange-ment, but I don't complain because it's now obvious that Marcus wasn't listening to the newscast at all. He was listen-ing to a sound that seems to be overhead.

We are about a mile and a half east of the airstrip, and the previous planes have come in from the northeast. We chose this location to give us a vantage point from where we could see the plane without the people in the plane seeing us.

Right now the plane is coming from the same direction as the previous times, but something seems different. I soon realize that it's lower this time, perhaps in an effort to avoid radar detection.

Marcus starts the car, and we drive toward the airport. I climb in the backseat so I can watch the plane through the rear side window. Not only is it lower, but it's losing altitude in preparation for landing.

But this plane is not heading for a landing at all. It's too low, too far from the airport, and as I watch with a combi-nation of fascination and horror, its nose tilts downward and goes crashing into the otherwise peaceful countryside, about three hundred yards from us.

The resulting explosion lights up the Wisconsin sky, and even Marcus seems mesmerized by it.

Nobody could have survived this crash, and if Alan Drum-mond was on that plane, he's just answered for his crimes.

And whatever secrets he had went down with him.

• • • • •

WITHIN TEN MINUTES it seems like every fire truck and police car in Wisconsin is on the scene. The area where the plane crashed is an open field, surrounded on three sides by trees. The field might have been long enough for a successful emergency landing, but the way the plane smashed down, nose-first, it never had a chance.

Laurie arrives with three of her officers, though the state police have taken temporary control of the scene. Nevertheless, I tell her that Marcus and I witnessed the crash, and she conveys that message to the authorities. Marcus and I are then told to remain on the scene to answer questions.

The fire is put out relatively quickly, and all that remains of the plane is a charred shell. It's in pieces, but those pieces are not spread over a large amount of land, possibly because the plane was moving down vertically at the time of the crash.

A number of cars from Center City arrive as well, and I see both Keeper Wallace and Stephen Drummond. They are surrounded by at least four uniformed servants of the Keeper, though I don't recognize any of them as being the ones that kidnapped Madeline.

Both Wallace and Drummond look properly somber as

they are led in to talk to the authorities. Drummond sees me, and his face reflects his surprise that I am there, but I doubt he dwells on it very long. He's got other, bigger problems with which to deal.

I see Drummond again about twenty minutes later; he and Wallace are leaving the trailer that's been set up as command central as Marcus and I are being escorted to it. Drummond is attempting to appear composed and in control, but his face is tearstained, and the anguish is evident. Alan Drummond must have been on that plane.

Officials from both the FBI and the National Transportation Safety Board have made their way out here, and they seem to be sharing a dual command. With terrorism being the first thing that everyone thinks of when a plane crashes, the FBI will treat the location as a crime scene until they find out otherwise.

Marcus and I answer questions from FBI Special Agent Ricardo Davila. Marcus is as unresponsive as ever, which proves not to be a significant factor when he says that he didn't see the crash. He's telling the truth; I was the one in the back watching while he was driving.

I report the salient facts: that I saw the plane coming in far too low to reach the airport and that it was rapidly losing what altitude it had. The nose was pointed down, at least forty-five degrees, and if it made any effort to straighten out, I certainly didn't see it.

"What were you doing out here?" Agent Davila asks.

"We just went for a drive," I say.

He looks at me, then at Marcus. Then he looks at me again and then at Marcus again. "The two of you went for a drive?"

"That's right," I say.

He nods, though it clearly doesn't compute. "Did the plane break apart at all in the air?"

"Not that I saw. And I had a clear view."

"Nothing fell off of it? It stayed completely intact?"

"Completely intact," I say. "And there was no smoke either. Not until it hit the ground."

Davila asks a bunch of additional questions, then calls over a guy from NTSB to ask a bunch more. Satisfied that they've extracted all the information they're going to get from us, they take our names, addresses, and phone numbers and send us on our way.

Marcus and I head toward our car but stop when we see Laurie and Cliff Parsons. "Was it Alan Drummond?" I ask.

Parsons nods. "They think so, though it's difficult to identify the body in this condition. He was wearing a ring that his father says was his. They'll do DNA testing."

"Did you see anything fall off the plane?" Laurie asks.

I shake my head. "No. But the FBI asked me the same thing. Any idea why?"

"A mail carrier out on his route about four miles from here says he saw something fall out of the plane. His view was partially blocked, but he seemed certain of it."

Considering that we believe the plane was carrying illegal goods, this is a potentially significant fact. "Have they been able to determine what cargo the plane was carrying?" I ask.

"None," Parsons says. He shakes his head, as puzzled as the rest of us. "The plane was empty. Not even any goddamn cheese."

There would seem to be the possibility that the illegal cargo was thrown from the plane, which was what the witness saw falling to the ground. To believe that, one would have to accept that Alan Drummond knew the plane was going down, but rather than focus on saving himself, he saved the cargo instead. This despite the fact that his coconspirators would have no idea where he threw it, and therefore it would most likely wind up in the hands of the police.

I doubt that Alan Drummond was that brave, or that stupid.

Marcus drops me off back at the house, and I take Tara out for a long walk. I feel guilty about having left her for so long, but the truth is, she had proven to be a mediocre stake-out dog the time she went with me. By the time we get back to the house, Laurie is there, already cooking dinner. I'm glad, because there's nothing I like better after a long stake-out than a home-cooked meal.

Laurie has little more to report on the crash, except that an intensive search has not yet turned up anything that might have fallen off the plane. "If Alan Drummond knew he was going to die, why would he throw something off the plane?" she asks. "And how would someone know to look where he threw it, unless . . ."

"Unless what?" I ask.

"Could this have been planned in advance? Could he have known beforehand that the plane would go down, and he prearranged with someone where he would drop the cargo?"

"You're asking if Alan Drummond could have committed suicide? Because how else could he know the plane would go down, unless he was going to *take* it down?"

"Is it possible?" she asks. "Why would he commit suicide?"

"Just thinking out loud," I say, "but maybe he thought we were about to bring *him* down, and he was protecting his father and maybe Wallace by taking the literal fall."

"Or maybe the wheel told him to do it," she says.

It's not as far-fetched as it sounds. Be they suicide bombers or Kool-Aid drinkers, people down through the ages have sacrificed their lives in a misguided pursuit of their religion.

Why not Alan Drummond?

• • • • •

MY UNDERSTANDING of the Centurion

religion and the role of the wheel is limited. Try as I might, and I've tried pretty hard, I haven't been able to get a good feel for it. Catherine Gerard described it in some detail, and her husband's articles did as well, but the real essence of it remains somehow just beyond my comprehension.

I think this lack of understanding is more on an emotional than intellectual level. I know the mechanics of how the wheel operates; I know about the symbols that only the Keeper can decipher. I know about the ceremonies, about the decisions that are turned over to Wallace and his wheel, and how the townspeople have achieved a serenity and bizarre freedom of choice by their choosing to give up that freedom.

What I can't quite grasp, can't really believe, is the level of devotion that these people seem to have. To my knowledge, in well over a century only two people, Henry Gerard and Madeline Barlow, have in any sense turned against the town. Yet even they have not turned against the religion and have maintained their faith in its precepts.

But how far will these people go? Are there limits to what they will do in the expression of their devotion? Will they commit murder? Would they, or more specifically, would Alan Drummond, commit suicide if directed to?

Almost since the day I arrived here, things have happened that seem to defy logic. As is my style, I have been trying to make logical sense out of them, to figure out the "why" behind the actions of these people. I'm being overly kind to myself to say that I've had very little success.

But if the wheel is behind everything, then there's no way I can succeed. If actions are taken because the wheel dictates them, then the "why" questions are meaningless, and logic has no place.

I don't like to hang out in places without logic.

So I've got to get out of here.

It's time, actually way past time. I want to get back to my home and my office and my job. I want to get back to a New Jersey courtroom, where I can deal with normal thieves and murderers. I want to be with people who aren't so friendly; I can hang out with Pete and Vince for twelve years, and neither of them will tell me they hope I have a good day. It's not that they don't want me to have a good day; it's that they don't care either way.

I've packed my stuff and loaded it in the car, and I call Laurie to tell her that it's time. She comes over so we can say our good-byes, a conversation I dread with every fiber of my being. If I had twice as many "being fibers" as I actually have, I would dread it with them as well.

I don't really know how this good-bye scene will play out; I certainly misjudged the "hello" scene in my hotel room when we had sex. One thing I do know: We're not going to have sex now. Not unless she wants to.

She doesn't. From the moment she walks in, all she wants to do is hug, then sob a little, then hug some more. Hugging is not a specialty of mine, and I'm a completely mediocre sobber, so I pretty much let her take the lead.

Finally, she pulls away and says, "I'm sorry things didn't work out better for you, Andy."

"We got to spend some time together," I say.

"That was wonderful, but I'm talking about the case. I know how much you hate loose ends."

I nod. "This one is a little looser than most."

"You've got to let it go."

"That's what I'm going to be doing in a few minutes. But it will continue to bug me. You know, I don't think I've ever had a case of any kind that didn't end with me knowing who the bad guy was. I'm not saying the jury always had it right, but in my heart I knew what the truth was. Until now."

"We've been after Alan Drummond all this time, Andy. Just because he died, it doesn't make him innocent."

"Of course, I know that. Alan Drummond was certainly not innocent. But there is no way he was in it alone. Not even close."

She nods, knowing that I'm right but not wanting to say so, since she knows how aggravating I find the whole situation. She finally concedes, "There were the two guys that kidnapped Madeline . . ."

"They were just soldiers," I say. "And so was Alan Drummond. They didn't have the smarts or experience to tap Madeline Barlow's phone, or watch Larson, or anticipate our every move. That came from someone above them, with more resources and more experience. I'm betting it was Wallace, but it's just a guess."

"I'll keep working the case, Andy."

I nod. "I know." Then, "Laurie, it's time for me to go."

"Yes," she says. "You'll drive carefully?"

"I'll drive carefully."

"This is awful," she says.

"Yeah."

She gives Tara a huge hug, and Tara's tail is down, a sure

sign that she knows what's happening. She was a witness to the previous final good-bye between Laurie and me, and I think she might hate them almost as much as me.

"Good-bye, Andy. I love you," Laurie says, giving me a final hug. I don't answer her, because I seem to have grown a watermelon in my throat, and she turns and leaves.

I watch through the window as she drives off, then I take a moment to give Tara a hug of my own. "It always comes down to you and me, kid," I say, and then we head for the car and civilization.

Unfortunately, between Findlay and civilization lies Center City, and after I'm ten minutes into my drive, the sign tells me that the exit for it is coming up in five miles. My mind, possibly seizing on any opportunity not to think about Laurie, takes me on a little trip down Center City memory lane, and my various contacts with the town pass before me, starting with my first visit during the town meeting.

I think about Madeline Barlow and what she has been through. And then I think about Stephen Drummond, our first meeting, our clash in court, and his outraged phone call over what he saw as the abduction of Madeline. He vowed in our first meeting to defend the privacy of Center City citizens at every possible opportunity, and he certainly did that.

No, he didn't.

The one time he didn't rush to the defense of the town's precious privacy is when we stopped the dairy truck his son was driving, and handcuffed him while we searched it. Yet it was the one time he would have absolutely been in the right to complain, and could have profited from it. Laurie's bosses would likely have felt obligated to tell her to back off from the "harassment," and it would have significantly hampered our ability to investigate what Alan Drummond was doing.

Yet his father never said a word. Not one. I can only think of one possible explanation for that.

He didn't know it happened. His son never told him, and I can only think of one possible explanation for that.

Stephen Drummond did not know what Alan Drummond was doing. If the son was involved in a criminal conspiracy, his father was not a part of it.

As I consider all of this, I realize to my surprise that I'm not driving anymore. I'm sitting on the shoulder of the road, near the exit sign for Center City.

I no longer harbor any illusions that I'm going to make people pay for their crimes. That boat has sailed. But I would sure as hell like to learn as much as I can about what happened, and another conversation or two just might help in that regard. So I put the car in drive, get off at the exit, and head for Center City to talk to Stephen Drummond.

When I reach the center of town, I see a display near the town hall with flowers and letters posted on a bulletin board. I am struck by the irony that the first time I was here, a similar display was there for Liz Barlow and Sheryl Hendricks, and now the tribute is to Alan Drummond, who died two days ago. Again the tributes are arranged as spokes on a wheel, but this time I understand the significance of that design, whereas last time I did not.

There's a strong possibility that Stephen Drummond, in mourning for his son, will not be working today. Nevertheless, I park the car, take Tara out, and we head for his office, in the building next to the town hall.

As we approach, two uniformed servants of the Keeper come out to meet us. "Can we help you, sir?"

"I'd like to speak to Stephen Drummond," I say.

"Is he expecting you?"

"Tell him Andy Carpenter has information about his son."

One of them goes into the building to do just that, which leads me to believe that Drummond is, in fact, working today. So far, so good. Now, if he'll just see me . . .

The servant comes back out, and much to my surprise, Stephen Drummond is with him. He looks about thirty years older than the last time I saw him.

"I'm sorry for your loss," I say.

"Thank you. You had something to tell me about Alan?"

"Yes." I look at the two servants. "In private."

He nods and points across the street. "Is that your car?"

I confirm that it is, and he tells me to get in the car and follow him. He gets in his own car, and we drive four blocks, to one of the houses on the edge of town.

We get out and walk toward the house. As we near the door, Drummond realizes that Tara is with me. "I don't think we've ever had a dog in our house," he says.

"Then we can talk on the porch," I say.

He thinks about this for a moment. "No, I want you to come in."

We enter the house, and I am struck by how similar it is to the Barlows'. Simple, inexpensive furniture, only family photos on the walls. If Stephen Drummond was making big money in a criminal enterprise, he wasn't using it to pay his decorator.

He sits on a chair in the den, and I sit on the small sofa across from it, with Tara at my side. He neither offers us anything nor engages in small talk. "What did you want to say about Alan?"

"I don't believe his death was accidental. I believe he was either murdered or committed suicide, and though you don't know it, you can probably tell me which."

His face is impassive, betraying neither surprise nor anger at what I am saying about his son. "And how can I do that?"

"Is it possible that the wheel, through Keeper Wallace, instructed him to bring the plane down?"

"Not only is it impossible, it is also absurd and insulting. I neither know nor care what you think of our religion, but your lack of understanding of its values is complete. It is peaceful and beautiful, and violence of any kind has no place. What you are accusing the Keeper of is ludicrous."

I nod. "I accept that. But then it means your son was murdered."

"Explain yourself," he says. It's a two-word sentence that my keen ear notices does not contain words like "impossible," "absurd," or "ludicrous."

So I proceed to explain myself. I probably talk for about twenty-five minutes, detailing everything I know about the murders, the airport, the criminal conspiracy . . . everything.

He doesn't interrupt, doesn't say a word, and the only time he changes expression at all is when I tell him that I was there the day that Madeline Barlow was abducted and that two of the Keeper's servants were the perpetrators. I think that the expression I detect in his face at that moment is surprise; could he not know what really happened?

I conclude my soliloquy with a description of the search of Alan's dairy truck, my witnessing of the plane crash, and my belief that its illicit cargo was thrown down to the ground minutes before. When I finish, he continues to sit there, almost expressionless, for a few moments. Then he stands up and leaves the room.

I have no idea what to make of this, and Tara seems as confused as I am. It's possible he's not coming back and that Tara and I should just be on our way. I figure I'll give him five minutes and then call out to him.

At about the three-minute mark he comes back into the room, carrying a small carton, maybe a foot and a half square. He brings it over to the table next to me and sets it down. The carton has been previously opened, and he just pulls open the flaps.

He takes out a smaller box that was contained within, and

has also been opened, and hands it to me. "Do you know what this is?" he asks.

I look inside the box and take out a small bottle of pills. The legend on the label identifies the contents as OxyContin, which I know to be a painkiller that doubles as a popular recreational drug in the United States. I also see that the box has a notation that the materials were packaged in Alberta, Canada.

I explain what it is, and Drummond says, "There were three boxes just like that in Alan's room."

"They must have been smuggling them across the border from Canada. They are a fraction of the price there compared to the United States, so they can be resold here at huge profits and still be less than the legal marketplace."

He nods. "That was my fear."

"And my guess is, they weren't bringing in just the kind of drugs that can be abused. The market would be almost as good for all kinds of prescription drugs; the sale of it has even become a huge industry on the Internet."

"Perhaps he kept these aside for his own use," he says, something I was thinking but saw no need to voice.

"Alan wasn't the leader of this operation," I say. "Until today I thought that you probably were."

"And now?"

"Now my best guess would be Wallace, but it's only a guess."

"It's an incorrect one. I would vouch for the Keeper with my life."

Unfortunately, he's not able to come up with any idea who might have been directing the conspiracy, but promises to give it intense thought and effort. "I just hope I'm not too late," he says.

"Too late for what? With all the attention that the crash

brought to this area and that airfield, that operation has to shut down."

"You think it's over?" he asks, clearly doubting that it is.

"I do, only because I don't see how it can continue."

"Then you're not thinking clearly," he says. I wait for him to continue, and he does. "You believe that the crash was intentional, yet you also believe the crash ruined their chances for continuing their operation. These are smart people; why would they intentionally stop themselves?"

What he is saying is so obviously true that I'm embarrassed it eluded me. "Unless they're moving on to something else and were ready for this to end," I say.

He nods. "Exactly."

• • • • •

I'M ABOUT FIFTEEN minutes out of Center City, and I can't get the conversation with Drummond out of my mind. Since I arrived in Findlay, I've always been a couple of steps behind the people I'm chasing. If anything, that gulf is widening now.

My goal has been to figure out who they are and to stop what they're doing. I haven't given the slightest bit of thought to what they're going to do next, but Drummond is absolutely right. There is no reason to think they would have done anything to stop themselves, yet it seemed as if the plane crash did just that.

I turn toward the passenger seat to make sure that Tara is all right, something I do every few minutes. It causes me to glance at my cell phone in its case, and I see that I've received a phone call and have a voice mail message. I didn't take the phone in with me when I went into Drummond's house, so the call must have come in then.

I check caller ID and see that the call came from Laurie. I've been so focused on Drummond and Center City that I haven't thought about her at all.

I play back the message, and within moments I hear her voice, which sounds excited. "Andy, I think we got a break.

It looks like Wallace has been behind the whole thing. Cliff Parsons has gotten one of Wallace's servants to turn on him . . . Cliff says the guy is rock-solid and will testify in court. We're going to get Wallace in a few minutes and bring him in for questioning. I'll keep you posted."

I hear what she's saying, but a cold chill runs down my spine as I hear even more clearly what she *isn't* saying . . . something she doesn't know, but I suddenly know down to my very core.

Wallace is not the leader of any criminal conspiracy: he's had nothing to do with the murders, and Cliff Parsons has not gotten one of his servants to turn on him.

Because Cliff Parsons has been behind it all.

I pull the car to a screeching halt and execute as fast a U-turn as I can. At the same time, I dial Laurie's number at the station. No one answers her phone, and the call gets kicked automatically to the sergeant at the front desk.

He says that Laurie is out, so I ask to speak to Parsons, though there is little chance that he is there. When the sergeant says he's also out, I tell him that he needs to reach Laurie and have her call me. I tell him that it's again a life-and-death situation, but I don't tell him that the life on the line is hers.

I call Drummond, only to find that he has not returned to his office. No matter how much I beg, they won't give me his home number. I plead with them to reach him and have him call me, and though they say they will, I have no confidence in it. They're not accustomed to doing favors for strangers that involve any kind of invasion of privacy. Especially when the person whose privacy they'd be invading is Stephen Drummond.

The feeling of panic and dread that I have as I speed back toward Center City is overwhelming. The signs that Parsons was behind it were right there in front of me, but I never saw them. Now they are hitting me in waves.

Parsons was kept informed of our stakeouts of the airport, which explains why we were never able to catch them with anything other than a truckload of cheese. The only time he thought the airport was unwatched was when I went out there on an impulse on Christmas Day, and that is why a plane came in that day.

I never knew how the two servants who kidnapped Madeline found out she had spoken to us, but Parsons certainly knew, and directed them to do what they did. He'd been assigned to Center City for a few years and must have found a few of the servants, Alan Drummond included, that he could recruit for his scheme.

I keep turning to stare at the cell phone, as if that might get it to ring, but it refuses, leaving me alone with my thoughts and my fears.

I'd bet my life that it wasn't cargo that the postman saw fall through the clouds from the plane that day, and it wasn't a piece of the plane. It was Cliff Parsons, a former Army Airborne Ranger, who parachuted out of the plane after he killed Alan Drummond. He must have been afraid that Drummond was so scared he would talk to us, or perhaps it was time to end the scheme, and he didn't want Drummond around as a possible future witness.

The next step is all too obvious. Cliff Parsons is going to kill Laurie and make it look as though Wallace did it. Then he's going to take Laurie's job, a job he thinks he should have gotten in the first place. He must have all the money he needs; now he will get the position and respect he thinks he deserves.

He's a piece of shit, and if he does anything to Laurie, I will hunt him down until the day I die.

I make it back to Center City in less than half the time it

took me to leave, and I pull the car to a screeching halt right in front of the town hall. There are a number of people in the street, going about their business, and I'm sure they must be staring at me. For the first time, I don't see any servants in front of the place, providing security.

I leave Tara in the car, but as I run toward the building, I flick the button on my key ring, locking her in. I see a Findlay squad car parked along the side of the building, which increases an anxiety that is already threatening to explode my head.

I run up the steps, realizing as I do that I've never been in this building. It's possible no outsider ever has. But there's no one to stop me, and no one *could* stop me if they tried.

The large double doors are closed but unlocked, and I open them and rush in. I think I hear someone behind me in the street yelling, "Hey!" but I don't know who it is. I leave the doors open in the hope that they'll follow me in; I can use all the help I can get.

I enter a lobby area, though it's narrow enough to be classified a hallway. I don't see anyone, but directly in front of me are large, ornate double doors, probably fifteen feet high. I don't know where I'm going or what the hell I'm doing, so I stop to see if I can hear anything. All I hear is silence.

I get the idea that I'll call Laurie's cell phone and see if I can hear it ring in the building so I can determine her location. It's a good idea but impractical, since I left my own cell phone in the car.

I can think of two options at this point. I can stand here in the hall like a jerk, or I can rush in through those doors like a jerk. If I let my natural cowardly instincts take over, I'll stand here. Instead I listen to my head, which tells me I have to go in.

I open the doors and cautiously step inside. The scene is

stunning. I've entered through the side of what looks like a church, with rows of bench seating under a ceiling at least four stories high. There is a balcony above me which probably contains seating as well, but I can't see it from this vantage point. A large chair, almost like a throne, is to my left in the front, facing the area where the congregation would be sitting.

But it is what is behind the throne that would take my breath away, had fear not already done so. A wheel, covered with symbols that are unintelligible to me, towers over everything. It has been described to me as a large, carnival-type wheel, and while that's technically true, it's a ludicrously inadequate description. It is majestic and stunning and overpowering.

"Well, if it isn't Sherlock Holmes." The voice to my left belongs to Parsons, and as I turn, I'm not surprised to see that he is pointing a gun at me. About fifteen feet from him are Laurie, Wallace, and two servants, none of whom seem to be armed. Parsons is in control here.

"What's going on? What are you doing here?" I ask, since I can't think of anything else to say.

Parsons laughs a short laugh. "You want the official version? Your girlfriend and I came to question Wallace, but he resisted violently, and shots were fired. They were all killed; I'm the only one to make it out alive. Sorry, but you didn't make it either."

"You're a cop," I say. "You know the forensics people will take the place apart. There's no way you can pull it off."

"Sorry, Sherlock. I've got the whole thing choreographed. I'll be able to fit you in easily. Now, go over there in the corner and keep your mouth shut. It's showtime."

I make eye contact with Laurie, but there's no sign that she has any more of a solution to this than I do. I move toward the corner as told, and for a brief moment I'm close enough to make a grab for Parsons's gun. I let the opportunity, if there was one, slip away.

"Okay, Keeper-Man," says Parsons. "Spin the wheel."

"I will not," says Wallace.

"Oh, but you will. When this is over, it's not going to be in that position." He points toward the top, which seems to be the starting place. It is the one area without symbols. "You're going to spin it, and it's going to tell you to violently resist."

"I will not," Wallace repeats.

"Then your servants have ten seconds to live." He moves the gun slightly to the left, so as to point in their direction.

Wallace considers this for a moment.

"Now," says Parsons.

Wallace nods with resignation, walks over to the side of the wheel, and pulls down a large lever. The entire wheel seems to groan for a moment and then starts to turn. It is an amazing sight, though one I am not in the mood to fully appreciate.

After more than three rotations, it comes to a halt. Wallace looks up at the symbols on which it has landed, and a peaceful smile broadens across his face.

"What's so funny, Keeper-Man? What does it say?"

"It instructs us to keep calm. It tells us that we will prevail." His voice is so serene and confident that there is no doubt he believes what he is saying.

"Is that right?" Parsons asks. "Well, I got news for you. Your prevailing days are over."

Without another moment's hesitation, Parsons raises the gun, points it at Wallace, and fires.

What happens next probably takes no more than two seconds but seems to play out for me in slow motion. One of the servants, seeing Parsons about to fire, launches himself in front of the Keeper and takes the bullet in his upper chest.

As the servant falls to the floor, Parsons raises the gun again, but a tree trunk comes out of nowhere and knocks it out of his hand to the floor. It turns out that the tree trunk is a forearm, and the forearm is attached to Marcus Clark.

Parsons makes a dive for the gun, but Marcus is closer, and he kicks it across the room toward Laurie and the others. Laurie picks it up as Parsons gets to his feet, and she points it at him.

Marcus turns to her and says, "No." Somehow he is at his most eloquent in a crisis.

Parsons is now on his feet and facing Marcus. He has about six inches and thirty pounds on Marcus, plus he has his army elite training to fall back on. He comes at Marcus with a karate kick and connects with the side of Marcus's head. Marcus blinks it away, but it had to have hurt.

Parsons launches another kick, which again connects with its mark. Marcus still seems clearheaded, but I'm not sure I could tell if he weren't, and I'm getting worried.

"Laurie, shoot the son of a bitch!" I scream, my only contribution to this entire episode. But Laurie ignores me, still pointing the gun but not pulling the trigger.

Parsons comes at Marcus again with still another kick to the head, but this time Marcus just reaches his hand up and seems to pluck his ankle out of the air. Parsons screams in pain as Marcus raises his arm, his hand locked around the ankle.

Parsons's head and shoulders hit the floor with a sickening thud, but his leg is still up in the air, with Marcus's hand around it in a death vise. I can see Marcus's fingers tighten even more, and through the sounds of Parsons's screams I can hear his ankle bones cracking.

Laurie and the other servant rush to pull Marcus off him,

but I don't join in. It flashes through my mind what this man has done.

"He killed Calvin, Marcus. He broke his neck with his bare hands. And he killed those kids."

I can see this register on Marcus's face, and he increases the pressure on Parsons's ankle, which by now has the consistency of overcooked capellini. I should be embarrassed to admit that the man's agony is music to my ears, but I'm not.

Calvin, this one's for you.

Laurie is screaming in Marcus's ear: "Marcus, that's enough! That's enough!" She yells it over and over, until finally he lets go.

Wallace is leaning over the servant who was shot, and with Laurie pointing a gun at the writhing Parsons, I rush outside and scream to the people in the street that we need an ambulance.

It seems that within moments the room is filled with medical personnel, as well as Findlay and state police. Both Parsons and the wounded servant are taken off, with Parsons wearing handcuffs as he lies on the stretcher. Laurie checks and tells me that the servant took the bullet in his right shoulder and should recover.

It's maybe an hour later that the room starts to clear out, and Laurie and I walk to the door. I take a final look back at the wheel.

It was right.

We prevailed.

• • • • •

TARA IS WAITING in the car when I get there. I know that she's pissed to be treated like a dog, and she'll never buy the story that I locked her in for her own sake. I give her a couple of biscuits as a peace offering, and though she takes them, I doubt I've heard the last of this.

I drive to Laurie's house, let myself in, and wait for her to finish the myriad of interviews and paperwork that will follow today's chaos. We've both agreed that after what we've been through, we deserve at least one more night with each other.

I am emotionally exhausted and fall asleep on the couch within minutes. Laurie's entering the house wakes me, and a check of my watch indicates that I've been sleeping for three and a half hours.

Clearly exhausted herself, Laurie comes over and lies down next to me on the couch. I wouldn't describe it as a hug exactly, it's more that we just hold on to each other.

After a while we both fall asleep in that position. Laurie wakes me up at about two-thirty in the morning, takes my hand, and leads me into the bedroom. We make love, then sleep until eight in the morning. The entire time she's been home, I don't think we've said ten words between us.

It's not until we're having breakfast that we talk at all about yesterday's events. Neither of us really wants to relive it, so there isn't that much to say.

Laurie has concluded that Calvin was most likely not trying to reach her when he called the station on the night he died. She thinks he was calling Parsons, who was in the process of setting him up to be killed.

"How did you know it was Parsons that was behind it all?" she asks.

"The pieces all fit, but it wasn't until I got your message that I tried to fit them. After listening to how Drummond and everyone else in that town talked and felt about Wallace, I just didn't believe that Wallace was a crook."

"Richard Davidson was instrumental in my getting this job instead of Parsons," she says. "I wonder if that played into all this."

"It certainly could have. Who has jurisdiction over the investigation now?"

"The FBI is coming in, because the smuggling was from Canada," she says. "They're going to turn Center City upside down to find everyone involved. The people living there don't know what they're in for."

"They'll survive it, and in the long run nothing will change. They believe what they believe."

She nods. "I know. Madeline's ready to go back to live with her mother."

"Where's Marcus?" I ask.

"He just left. Had you told him to stay and watch over me?"

I shake my head. "No, and that's not what he was doing. He was still watching out for me, and when I came back, so did he." I raise my glass of orange juice in a toast. "To Marcus."

"To Marcus," she agrees, and we drink the toast.

"Actually, it's lucky he was here," I say. "If not, I might have killed Parsons with my bare hands."

She smiles. "Andy, coming back like you did was incredibly brave. And incredibly loving."

"Oh, pshaw," I say. My ability to receive compliments hasn't shown much improvement, probably because I haven't had that many opportunities to work on it.

We're silent for a few moments, since we both realize that another wrenching moment is approaching. "I think we're about to break the indoor record for painful good-byes," she says.

"I know," I say, but then I shake my head. At this particular moment my mind has no idea what's coming next; it's like my mouth is on its own. "No, I don't want to say good-bye again. Been there, done that."

"Andy . . ."

"No," I interrupt. "Hear me out. I'm going back, and you're staying here, but you can spend your vacations back East, we can meet for a hell of a lot of weekends, and I'm going to come here whenever I have time. It's not like I have a lot of clients."

"That's true," she says.

I continue, since I feel like I'm on something of a roll. "So we try it. We do more than try it . . . we make it work. And it keeps us at least somewhat together."

She nods. "And being with you part-time beats the hell out of being with you no-time."

"I'm sure it does."

"This will not be easy, Andy."

I nod and wait for her to continue.

"But it will be worth it," she says.

"Good. Now we just have to work out the details. What about seeing other people?" I ask, sounding a little like a high school freshman in the process.

She shakes her head. "No way. It's you and me, buddy boy. Rita Gordon will just have to deal with that."

Did she really just say what I thought she said? "You spoke to Rita Gordon?"

"I speak to everybody back there," Laurie says. "That's my home also. Those are my friends."

"And she told you about . . ." I end the sentence there, since I have no idea how to finish it.

"No, but I read through the lines." I know what she means: Rita's lines are really easy to read through.

"Tell me the part again about how being with me part-time beats the hell out of being with me no-time," I say.

She ignores that. "Andy, we love each other. Let's just hold on to that for now. Okay?"

I have never been as okay with anything as I am with that.

CPSIA information can be obtained at www.ICGtesting.com
Printed in the USA
LVOW08*2056080716

495659LV00004B/36/P